The Books of Nancy Moser

Contemporary Books

The Invitation (Book 1 of Mustard Seed Series)
The Quest (Book 2 of Mustard Seed Series)
The Temptation (Book 3 of Mustard Seed Series)
Crossroads
The Seat Beside Me (Book 1 of Steadfast Series)
A Steadfast Surrender (Book 2 of Steadfast Series)
The Ultimatum (Book 3 of Steadfast Series)
The Sister Circle (Book 1 of Sister Circle Series)
Round the Corner (Book 2 of Sister Circle Series)
An Undivided Heart (Book 3 of Sister Circle Series)
A Place to Belong (Book 4 of Sister Circle Series)
The Sister Circle Handbook (Book 5 of Sister Circle Series)
Time Lottery (Book 1 of Time Lottery Series)
Second Time Around (Book 2 of Time Lottery Series)
John 3:16
The Good Nearby
Solemnly Swear

Historical Novels

Where Time Will Take Me (Book 1 of the Past Times Series)
The Pattern Artist (Book 1 of the Pattern Artist Series)
The Fashion Designer (Book 2 of the Pattern Artist Series)
Love of the Summerfields (Book 1 of Manor House Series)
Bride of the Summerfields (Book 2 of Manor House Series)
Rise of the Sumemrfields (Book 3 of Manor House Series)
Mozart's Sister (biographical novel of Nannerl Mozart)
Just Jane (biographical novel of Jane Austen)
Washington's Lady (bio-novel of Martha Washington)
How Do I Love Thee? (bio-novel of Elizabeth Barrett Browning)
Masquerade (Book 1 of the Gilded Age Series)
An Unlikely Suitor (Book 2 of the Gilded Age Series)
The Journey of Josephine Cain
A Patchwork Christmas (novella collection)
A Basket Brigade Christmas (novella collection)
Regency Brides (novella collection)
Christmas Stitches (novella collection)

Children's Books

Maybe Later (Book 1 of the Doodle Art Series)
I Feel Amazing: the ABCs of Emotion (Book 2 of the Doodle Art Series)

www.nancymoser.com

Where Time

Will Take Me

Book 1 of the Past Times Series

NANCY MOSER

Overland Park, Kansas

WHERE TIME WILL TAKE ME

ISBN-13: 978-0-9986206-9-5

Published by:
Mustard Seed Press
10605 W. 165 Street
Overland Park, KS 66221

This story is a work of fiction. Any resemblances to actual people, places, or events are purely coincidental.

All Scripture quotations are taken from The Holy Bible, King James Version.

Cover design by Mustard Seed Press

Printed and bound in the United States of America

DEDICATION

To my ancestors who were instrumental in founding and developing Piermont, New Hampshire: Job Tyler, David Tyler, Jonathan and Sarah Tyler and the rest. . . Your brave spirit has given our family very, very deep roots. Thank you for coming to America. Your dream lives on.

PROLOGUE

1868
Piedmont, New Hampshire

"I'm dying."

Granny's words caused ten-year-old Justine to take a step back from the bedroom door before showing herself.

Granny couldn't die! Granny was always there. Granny was . . . Granny.

Justine heard her mother's voice and stepped forward again, peering through the crack in the doorway.

"You are not dying," Mother said. Commanded. She fingered a perfume bottle on the night stand. "Don't be so dramatic."

So Granny isn't dying?

"I'm the one who knows whether I'm dying or not, so I'd appreciate it if you'd stop arguing with a dying woman."

Granny sounded feisty. She sounded normal. Justine let herself breathe again.

"Are you going to let me speak my mind or are you going to argue with me all morning?" Granny asked.

Mother sighed. "Go on. Though I know what you're going to say, and the answer is no."

"It can't be no. You must take up our gift after I'm gone. You must continue with the Ledger. And after you, Jussie will continue our legacy."

"I am not moving back here to Piedmont."

"But this is where it begins."

Mother removed the stopper of the perfume, smelled it, crinkled her nose and put it back again. Justine loved the smell of honeysuckle. It was Granny's scent.

Then Mother said, "I left this town eleven years ago. Good-riddance was what I said then, and good-riddance is what I say now."

"Don't be rude, Mavis. Your roots are in Piedmont, it's the place where the Tyler ancestors first settled back in 1800."

"I have no interest in the past, only in the present and the future." Mother extended her arms out, as if putting herself on display. "Do you see this dress? I ordered it from Worth in Paris. It's crêpe de chine."

"It's as practical as a parasol in a downpour."

Mother huffed and sat in the chair beside the bed. "The point is, I've moved on from Piedmont. I don't belong here—if I ever did."

"You could have belonged."

Mother shook her head. "I'm weary of this. Say what you have to say and let Justine and I get back to New York."

Granny closed her eyes and a ridge formed between them. Was she hurting? Justine wanted to comfort her, but she'd been ordered to stay out.

Finally Granny's ridge eased and she opened her eyes, but her voice was raspy. "I don't know how to say it any stronger. It's imperative you do what I ask, Mavis. Past secrets must be revealed, and wrongs made right."

Mother's head shook once right then once left. "I am aware of what you went through. The condemnation, the threats. I will not put myself through all that—any of that."

"But there are truths that need to be shared," Granny said. "I regret I wasn't strong enough to follow through. But you *are* strong. You can do what I could not."

"Your neglect is not my problem," Mother said. "None of this is my responsibility. You chose your way and I chose mine."

"But the gift—"

Mother rose from the chair, forming fists at her side. "I didn't choose the gift. And as such, I refuse to—"

"'For unto whomsoever much is given, of him shall be much required: and to whom men have committed much, of him they will—'"

"'Will ask the more.'" Mother plucked a thread from her sleeve and let it fall to the floor. "I know. I *know*. Aren't you getting weary of spouting that verse at me? I'm not listening."

"But you should. You must." Granny sighed, then pointed at a dresser. "There's a letter in the top drawer for Jussie, for her to open when she's twenty. Promise me you'll give it to her."

"If it's full of this claptrap . . ."

"Mavis. You must. The Ledger and the gift can't die with me."

"Some things are better off dead."

Granny's chin quivered. "Some people you mean."

With a sigh, Mother touched Granny's hand. "Don't go getting dramatic again. I'm not rejecting you, I'm simply rejecting — "

"Our legacy. The legacy of all those who are depending on us to — "

"Enough!" Mother shuddered as if the discussion had pushed her to her limit. She went to the dresser and took up the letter, slipping it into her pocket. "There. I took the letter."

"Good. Thank you."

"We're leaving. Can I get you anything before Justine and I head back to the city?"

"I've told you what I need."

Mother turned toward the door, then shook her head. "Justine? *Tsk. Tsk.* Naughty girl. It's not polite to eavesdrop."

Justine pushed the door open. "Sorry."

"Come in here and say good-bye to your grandmother while I finalize our luggage."

Justine moved to the bed and Granny held out her hand. It felt so cold and smooth, like a pillow slip left in the night air. "Bye, Granny," Justine said.

Granny squeezed her hand and pulled her in. "You heard what I said?"

"I didn't mean to listen."

"You heard?"

Justine nodded.

"It's up to you to carry on what your Mother rejects."

"I don't understand."

"The gift will come to you when you're twenty. What you do with it then is your choice. A very important choice."

"What gift?"

"Be open to it. Then use it to carry on the Ledger. Learn from it. Add to it. Then pass it on. 'Ye shall know the truth, and the truth shall make you free.'"

Suddenly, Granny bolted forward in a fit of coughing. Justine thought it would pass, but when it didn't . . . she didn't know what to do. She put a hand on Granny's back, then poured her a glass of water.

Granny spilled it all over the covers, the glass crashing to the floor. She was having trouble catching her breath.

Justine ran into the hall. "Mother! Goosie! Come quick!"

The housekeeper got there first, took Granny's hand, and started rubbing her back, saying, "Slow. Slow now. Take a breath. Slow."

Granny gasped. Her eyes got big.

Then she fell back upon the pillows.

Her eyes closed, her mouth hung open.

There was no sound.

"Mrs. Tyler? Breathe! Mrs. Tyler!"

Justine heard feet on the stairs and ran out in the hall a second time. "Mother! Granny had a coughing fit and now she's not moving. Hurry!"

But Mother didn't hurry. She walked down the hallway at her usual pace. When she finally reached the room, she stopped in the doorway.

"Help her!" Justine yelled.

Goosie turned around, crestfallen. "She's gone! My dear Jesus, she's gone."

"No!" Justine ran to the bed and flung her arms around Granny. "You can't be dead. Come back. Come back!"

It felt strange to hug Granny and not be hugged in return. "Granny, don't go!"

Goosie stood nearby, crying. "I've been here sixty-eight years. What to do? What to do?"

Mother stepped into the room. "Oh, hush, Goosie. Stop thinking of yourself." She peered down at Granny, then sighed. "I suppose this means your father and I will miss the opera at the Pike this weekend."

Justine couldn't believe her ears. "Is that all you care about? Granny's dead!"

Mother stabbed a finger into Justine's chest. "Don't you ever talk to me like that again! Ever."

Justine knew she should be sorry for her words but wasn't sorry at all. If anything, she felt brave. "What is this gift Granny talked about? And what is the Ledger"

"None of your business."

"But it is my business. Granny said so."

"Your grandmother is dead. I'm in charge now, and I say the subject is as dead as she is. Let it die."

"Let what die?"

Mother pinched Justine's cheek until it hurt.

Justine didn't say any more. She didn't argue. But in that moment she made herself a vow.

She *would* use the gift. Somehow she would fulfill Granny's wishes.

Whatever they were.

CHAPTER ONE

1878 ~ Ten years later
New York City

Justine Braden stood before the mirror in her bedroom, admiring a dress she could never wear in public.

She stood sideways and loved how the simple lines of the Regency-era dress hung straight from the high waist. There was no pesky bustle creating an odd shelf off her backside. Nor a long, heavy fishtail train. What male dress designer—for it had to be a man—thought bustles were flattering? They made sitting awkward and created a backward tug that could be felt even when she was undressed, like the phantom feel of a familiar bracelet that lingered after it was removed.

As for the trains of the dresses Justine's wore daily. . . it took great practice to avoid stepping on them when she turned around. And finding a place for them under a dining table was perilous, for a chair leg would inevitably find a way into their folds and rip the fabric, or trip her when she stood after the meal. Justine's friends still teased her about the latter at the Halstead's dinner party.

She took hold of the slim cotton skirt and swished left and then right. It was as lightweight as a nightgown. A woman could run in such a skirt—if a woman could ever run. Which she could not. Wouldn't dare.

She took up her sketch pad and pencil and began to draw her reflection for her fashion scrapbook. The dress was a new acquisition from Mrs. Porter's Vintage Emporium. Since most of Justine's allowance was spent at this establishment, Mrs. Porter went out of her way to search out keen examples of past fashion for Justine's collection. This white cotton that was dotted with pink sprigs of rosebuds had been a bargain. Probably for the very reason that it wasn't overly embellished and draped.

Beyond sketching the dresses she owned, Justine collected illustrations from old magazines and had them pasted in the book according to their fashion decade. She was quite proud of her collection and —

The door of her bedroom opened. "Come Justine. Are you ready to —?" Mother stared at her. "What are you doing?"

"Dreaming of simpler times."

Mother took a position at her back and unbuttoned the few buttons Justine had managed without her maid's help. "Scandalous times."

"Why scandalous?"

"Seeing women's bodies as they moved . . ." She *tsked-tsked* as she finished and waited for Justine to step out of the dress.

Justine lovingly draped it across her bed. "At least women *could* move."

Mother tugged on the bell pull to summon Franny to help with the final dressing, then retrieved a citron yellow dress which was heavy with ruffles made of accordion pleats. It had bows on its backside, and was embellished with lace and fringe wherever there could be lace and fringe. It was the antithesis of comfort.

Mother pulled up short when she realized Justine wasn't wearing a bustle. "Use your brain, Justine. Now is not the time to play dress up with your so-called treasures. Morris will be here momentarily. The opera will not wait."

If only it would.

**

Justine stood at the top of the stairs, adjusted her long gloves, and eavesdropped on her mother's apologies.

"I beg your forgiveness for the delay, Morris," her mother said. "Justine was taking extra care to look her most beautiful for you."

"I don't like to be late," he said.

Since Justine knew he could be quite a bear about tardiness, she descended the stairs. She suffered an inward sigh at her mother's habit of overstating her looks. Her hair color was a drab black — if black hair could be drab — and her lips were too thin to be voluptuous. Her friend Emma had full lips and had suggested Justine bite her lesser ones to plump them. She'd tried, but found it only made her lips sore. And so, Justine accepted that she *could* be deemed handsome — which was *not* a feminine word — but never beautiful. What added to her sigh was when she realized Morris had failed to respond to her mother's "beautiful" statement, instead focusing on the logistics of the evening. It said a lot about him. Perhaps too much.

Morris looked up at her and returned his pocket watch to its home in his vest pocket. "Come, Justine. The carriage is waiting."

Nice to see you too, my love.

Morris helped the ladies with their capes. He leaned over and whispered, "You look lovely tonight."

Better late than never.

**

The line of carriages at the Academy of Music proved that Justine's sin of tardiness was shared. Everyone knew the opera often accommodated late-arrivals by delaying the curtain. For what was a performance without an audience? That so many took advantage of the fact spoke to an epidemic disdain toward the timetable of others, and a haughty confidence that *they* were worth the wait.

Morris did not abide by this attitude. He drummed his fingers against his top hat that sat on his lap. "This delay is absurd."

"Would you like to get off here?" Justine asked. "We can walk the last half-block."

"Absolutely not," Mother said. "It wouldn't be proper."

And I didn't mean it. My shoes have soft soles. They're not meant for walking on the cobblestones.

To Justine's surprise Morris tapped on the top of the carriage and within moments, the coachman had the door open and the step lowered. Morris got out first and assisted the ladies. Mother made a show of smoothing her dress as if somehow it had gotten more mussed by getting out now rather than later.

"Come now," Morris said, offering Justine his arm.

A little girl rushed toward them, offering a sprig of flowers. "A penny for a flower, miss?"

"Go on, you," Morris said, moving them past her.

But Justine held her ground. "How very pretty. I'd love to have a flower."

The girl's smile outshone the street lamps. She handed it to Justine.

"Pay her, Morris." Justine held the bloom to her nose and winked at the girl. "Two pennies, for it is an especially pretty flower."

Morris rolled his eyes but gave the girl the pennies. She bobbed a curtsy and skipped off.

As they walked toward the entrance, Morris pointed at the flower. "It's nearly dead."

"As is the girl if we don't help her."

"Two pennies will help?"

She stopped. "You're right. Let's go find her and give her two dollars."

"Don't be ridiculous."

Mother gave her a scathing look. "Behave yourself."

"I didn't think helping the needy was misbehaving."

They didn't respond, which all in all was the most telling response of all.

**

Justine didn't like opera. At least not the music — which was, of course, the point of it.

Or was it? The costumes contributed their fair share to the experience, although she knew they were horribly inaccurate. For one thing, peasant girls in the 1500s did not wear their hair in elaborate tendrils, nor wear red skirts. In the past red dye was expensive and was reserved for royalty. And those wide sleeves would get in the way of their real work: survival.

Yet opera was all about exaggeration. The costumes, the sets, the movement, the voices. Justine appreciated the story for its drama, angst, and passion. In truth, real life was often boring with its endless repetition of food, fashion, and frivolity. She knew it was wrong to complain, for with those three-Fs she didn't have to worry about three other Fs: frugality, fear, and failure. The little flower girl outside the theatre lived in a foreign world. Foreign. Another F.

The little flower girl outside the theatre was real. The ridiculous swooning and never-ending arpeggios of the singers were not.

The other purpose for the opera — perhaps *the* purpose — was to be seen. Most attendees had their proscribed places, with the upper-upper crust displayed in their family's boxes on the side. From their perch, Justine noticed that their use of opera-glasses was often diverted from the stage to the audience, peering over those beneath them with a far from benevolent eye. She was certain all of New York society had made note that her father's usual seat had been permanently procured by Morris. What a difference two years made. Where Justine *had* been an ingénue looking for a mate while sitting with her parents, she was now a young woman without a father, sitting next to her beau, with the expectation that he would propose. One of these days. She felt a twinge of guilt that her mother's status had been diminished by the loss of a man, while Justine's was about to be increased by the addition of one. There seemed something a bit wrong with that arrangement, and its dependence on men.

None too soon it was intermission. Long lines in the ladies' reception room and the ridiculous acrobatics that were involved with using the ill-smelling facilities, had caused Justine to make a habit of not drinking liquids past noon on the day of a performance.

The intermission was better spent with Morris and the other unmarrieds of their set.

Usually.

While Morris was occupied lighting a cigar with his cronies, two of Justine's friends rushed forward, their eyes bright. With gossip, no doubt. Although she knew she should abhor it, Justine enjoyed a good gossip. Wasn't it only considered gossip if it contained rumors and negativities? Surely exchanging facts wasn't a sin.

"Did you hear that Charles broke his engagement with Faye?" Mary said

She hadn't. "Why?"

"Some say he's lost interest."

"She *is* as boring as a chair."

The two giggled.

Justine spotted Faye standing forlornly with her mother on the far side of the lobby. "Faye is shy. That is hardly a crime—nor a good enough reason for Charles to leave her."

The two friends stepped closer, their eyes twinkling. "Word is that she's... she's..."

"Not enough for him." Emma's eyebrows rose suggestively and she nodded toward a group of men, where Charles was seen laughing.

Justine didn't believe their innuendo for one minute because having intimate relations before marriage was as taboo as ... as her wearing the Regency gown in public. So how could Charles make such an assessment? It wasn't fair. No girl knew how she would truly react to . . . until she got the chance to . . . which wasn't until after a couple became man and wife.

"*If* that's true, which I'm not saying it is, perhaps they shouldn't be together," Justine said.

"Perhaps," Emma said. "But with *that* and her being plain as a bucket . . . if Charles doesn't take her, who will?"

"Emma, that's rude."

"The truth isn't rude, Justine. If Charles spurned her, other men will follow suit."

"That's ridiculous."

"Perhaps. But you know it's true."

Mary sighed dramatically. "She'll never get invited to parties now."

Justine remembered why she didn't like gossip—and shouldn't like it. She could do nothing but stare at them. "If she isn't invited then the whole of society should be ashamed."

"It is what it is." Mary shook her head, letting the subject scatter to the floor to be trod upon by silk shoes. "Never mind her. Surely Morris is going to propose to *you* soon."

Justine looked across the lobby that was aglow with gas lights, opulent gowns, jewels, and flirtation. She spotted Morris with a duo of friends. He wore a tuxedo as easily as a panther wore fur.

"Does your mother already have plans for the engagement party?" Emma asked.

"It's all she talks about." Incessantly. To the point of annoyance.

"She is the most driven woman I know. What Mavis Braden wants—"

Justine finished the statement, "Mavis Braden gets." Although Justine was comfortable in any social situation, she didn't feel the need for ostentation and production as much as Mother did. And it had gotten worse since Father's death. During the first year of mourning, they'd both been held captive by society's rules of decorum. During the second year Justine was freed from "the black" while her mother carried on another year. With the two years now passed ... it was like her mother had been set free of more than the black garb. Now free of Father's checks and balances, Mavis Braden frittered and flaunted and flared with flourish. People couldn't help but notice. Whether they approved . . .

"I'm on the guest list, aren't I?"

"And me?"

"Of course," Justine said, though she wasn't at all sure they were. "If Mother has her way all of New York society will be there."

"Just think of the wedding presents. You won't have to buy a thing for years."

"Not that you won't," Emma said.

"We'll help you shop the Ladies Mile. We're very good at spending other people's money."

And your fathers'.

"We'll see," Justine said.

The two friends looked at each other and nodded. "You? Not want to shop or indulge in the latest fashion?"

"Mother and I just received a shipment from Worth."

"Did the gowns meet your high standards?" Mary asked with a smirk.

She didn't like the question. "I enjoy fashion, I study fashion, and I offered the designers some ideas."

"Did Worth implement them?"

"Most of them. I even received a note thanking me for my lovely sketches."

"You are very good at drawing. You should sketch me sometime."

The two had no idea Justine *had* sketched them — from memory. She took a second to study their eyes, which she hadn't gotten quite right.

"*Will* you sketch us?"

Justine shook her head. "I prefer fashion. I'm currently putting together a book of fashion through the ages."

Emma scoffed. "That's all well and good, but honestly, who cares what came before?"

"I have no use for history of any kind," Mary said.

Justine was weary of them. "If we ignore history we remain ignorant of its lessons."

Both women blinked. Then the pink ostrich plumes of Emma's fan stopped their dance as she reached out to touch the emerald necklace at Justine's throat. "Is this new?"

So much for a lesson about history. "It's Mother's cast-off."

"She can cast emeralds in my direction anytime. My mother only lets me wear pearls." She touched the orbs at her neck. "Boring things."

"But didn't you say the pearls were hand-strung from the Caribbean?" Mary asked.

Emma *had* said that and began to defend her pearls.

Justine barely listened, but noticed that the spurned Faye had turned away from the society around her and had a handkerchief to her eyes. Poor thing. Her mother tried to shield her, but with little success.

"If you'll excuse me."

Justine crossed the room, sidestepping the gaze of dozens of eyes. She put a hand on Faye's arm, startling her.

"Oh. I . . . I must have gotten something in my eye."

Justine slipped her arm through Faye's and said quietly. "If you ask me, you're best rid of him."

Her mother leaned in and whispered, "That's what I've told her."

"It's very brave of you to come tonight," Justine said. "Ignore the vipers. They'll bite their own tails eventually."

Faye took a deep breath and lowered her handkerchief. "Thank you, Justine. That's very kind of you."

Justine thought of another way to help. "How would you and your mother like to come to luncheon next week?"

Faye glanced at her mother, then nodded vigorously. "We'd love to."

A gong sounded, indicating it was time for the second act of "Romeo and Juliet." Justine looked in Morris' direction and saw him walking toward her. He looked confused — about what?

With barely a nod at Faye and her mother, he offered Justine his arm and led her away.

"Whatever are you doing talking to Faye? She's *persona non grata*."

"Hers is not the first broken engagement."

"She'll find another man," he said.

"How nice of you to say—"

"Her father's too rich for her to stay single."

They entered the theatre, preventing Justine from arguing with him.

Yet it was hard to argue against the truth.

**

Morris's carriage pulled in front of the Braden's Fifth Avenue mansion. "May I come inside?"

Justine peered out the window, checking the second floor. Her mother's bedroom faced the street but the room was dark. "Mother doesn't seem to be back from the opera yet. The Smiths said they would see her home."

"And they will." He nuzzled her neck. "But since she isn't here . . ."

She loved the musky smell of his hair but disliked the oiliness of the pomade. "Maybe you could come in for a short while."

The ever-ready Watson opened the mansion door for them. "Good evening, Miss Justine, Mr. Abernathy." He took her cape. "Was the opera enjoyable?"

"It was," Morris said. "Except for the usual dying-part at the end. I will never understand why Romeo killed himself."

Justine was shocked. "He couldn't live without his Juliet."

Morris put his gloves in his top hat before handing them to the butler. "I don't like weak men."

"He's not weak, he's—"

Morris flipped his hand, ending the discussion. "Watson, some sherry, if you please."

"Of course, sir." With a look to Justine, the butler left them.

Morris strolled into the drawing room and stood by the fire, warming his hands. "I will be glad when the opera season is over. I find all that shrill trilling rather tedious."

Justine had heard his complaint before—and agreed. "Then let's not go. Let's just spend time alone, you and I."

"Ah, but we have to go," he said, raising a finger. "To see and be seen is a duty."

Justine felt a headache coming on. She sat near the fire and tried to lean her head against the high back of the chair but her bustle and corset made comfort impossible. Letting Morris come inside had been a bad idea. He seemed to be in an argumentative mood, which made her long for the solitude of her bedroom where she could cuddle into her bed and close her eyes.

Watson returned with sherry and two glasses. As he began to pour, Justine said, "None for me, Watson. I'm getting a headache."

"Pour both for me then," Morris said.

"Would you like some headache powder, miss?"

"Yes, please." The lure of soft pillows and a long rest intensified. She set her head on her hand, hoping Morris would notice.

He plucked a cigar from her father's humidor and lit it.

Make yourself at home.

Soon the pungent smell of cigar smoke hovered like a fog around her. Odd how it drifted in her direction, leaving the rest of the room untainted. The aroma reminded her of Father. She didn't use to mind the smell, but now . . .

She coughed and swiped a hand in front of her face, trying to clear the air.

"Oh. Sorry, my dear." Morris took two steps away.

At least he noticed *that.*

Suddenly, there was a knock on the front door. This late? Knowing the butler was on an errand for her, Justine asked Morris, "Would you see who it is, please?"

He put his sherry down and answered it. Justine heard a man's voice, and Morris saying, "What?" and "That's awful" and "Yes, of course."

The man came into the foyer. It was a police officer. He looked in Justine's direction.

Sudden knots in her stomach made standing difficult. "Yes?" she said. "Is something wrong?"

The man removed his hat and walked to the edge of the drawing room as if it was a barrier he didn't dare cross. "Miss Braden?"

"Yes, I'm Miss Braden."

"I'm afraid I've come with bad news. There's been an accident and your mother . . . well, she's dead, miss."

No.

That's impossible.

You didn't say dead.

Did you?

Morris rushed to her side, taking her arm. "I'm so sorry, Justine."

She tried to clear her thoughts. "How? How did it happen?"

"She was crossing the street and a runaway wagon . . . I'm so sorry, miss. My deepest condolences."

The thought of her mother in pain made her chest hurt. She and Morris had briefly chatted with her at intermission. How could she be alive one minute and now dead?

Justine stared straight ahead. A part of her wanted to surrender to tears, sobbing herself into a puddle on the floor, while her pragmatic side dealt with the horrific fact that both of her parents were gone.

Watson returned with the headache medicine and a glass of water. He looked at the officer, then at Morris and Justine. "Miss?"

She raised a hand to stop the men from answering, then stepped toward this loyal servant who had been with her parents since they were first married. "Watson, my mother has died in an accident."

His brow furrowed and his lower jaw moved as if trying to voice all the thoughts his mind couldn't fathom. "She's . . . dead?"

Justine put a hand on his arm. She heard his breath catch then let go.

"I . . . I'm . . ."

"I know. Will you please tell the others?"

He opened his mouth to speak, nodded once, and left them.

The thought of all the servants hearing the news . . . Justine wished she could be the one to tell them, but knew it was best to let Watson handle it. They could react with more honesty with him doing the telling. To lose the master of the house and then their mistress a mere two years later?

My father and now my mother?

She heard the officer talking with Morris near the door. Then Morris said, "Let me get my things." He came to her, took her hands, and peered into her eyes. "Someone needs to go and . . . someone needs to go. I'll do it."

"Thank you."

"I'll come back as soon —"

She shook her head adamantly, surprised by what she needed from him. "Not tonight. I need to be by myself."

"But you should have people around. You need —"

"I need to be alone."

He studied her face and must have seen her determination, for he pulled her close, whispered, "I'm so sorry" in her ear, then left with the officer.

The sound of the closing door echoed in the cavernous foyer. When the noise finished its travels, Justine was left with the silence.

She held her breath, not daring to disturb the dreadful hush. Was this what death sounded like? Like . . . nothing?

Suddenly, the immensity of the space overwhelmed her and amplified her isolation. She lifted the skirt of her gown far higher than what was proper, and rushed upstairs and down the upper hall to her bedroom. Her spine tingled as if a monster were chasing her. She slammed the door. She couldn't breathe. She desperately needed to be free of her gown and all the layers beneath.

But she didn't want Franny here to help her undress. She didn't want anyone with her.

She kicked away her silk slippers and peeled off her long gloves, turning them inside out. She yanked the plumed headdress and threw it aside. She felt hanks of hair hanging forlornly over her ears and forehead as hairpins littered the floor. Then she frantically tried to undo the tiny buttons that ran the length of her spine, grunting and groaning with the effort.

Out! Let me out of this!

She managed to undo four or five at her waist and the small of her back. She took advantage of the opening and tugged outward again and again, reveling in the ripping sound that meant she was making headway. She tried to reach the upper buttons, but they were out of reach between her shoulder blades. But she did manage to finagle her arms out of the sleeves so she could push the top of the bodice down over her breasts. She twisted the back of the gown toward the front enough to unbutton the top three buttons.

And she was free.

Of the gown.

She untied the petticoat and bustle, stepped out of the one, and tossed the latter across the room where it toppled a vase. The tightness of her corset worked against her, and she had to pause to catch her breath. There was no way she could unlace it, but she set to work on the tiny hooks and eyes that paraded up its front. When it finally fell away she took three long breaths, feeling as if she'd been released from prison.

She caught sight of herself in the mirror and was appalled at the crazed look on her face and the wild disarray of her hair. She was down to her chemise, pantaloons, and stockings. Yet the emerald necklace still adorned her neck.

The necklace borrowed from her mother.

She won't need it now.

Justine touched the center stone and found its surface as cold as death. She undid the clasp and laid the jewelry gently on her dressing table, shaping it into a circle. With one last touch she walked away.

Her bed beckoned. She tossed the fringed pillows left then right, and yanked back the heavy brocade cover. She accepted the invitation of the glistening sheets, climbed in, and fell upon the pillows, pulling one and then another into an embrace.

Her heart pounded in her ears and she purposefully calmed her breathing. In. Out. In. Out.

God, please help me. I don't understand. I don't know what to do. I don't—

She heard muted voices out in the hall. A tap on the door. "Miss?"

"I won't need you tonight, Franny. Thank you."

A pause. Then, "Yes, miss. I'm...I'm so sorry, miss."

The voices faded.

In their absence, the silence rushed in.

And smothered her.

CHAPTER TWO

Justine closed her eyes and let the pull and tug of the hairbrush have its way with her.

"Are you all right, miss?" Franny asked as she worked on her hair. "You're so quiet."

She didn't *feel* quiet, for her mind was awash with a thousand thoughts. "With Mother gone there's so much to do. So much to think about." *I'm not used to having to think.*

"Me and the other servants are here to help in whatever way we can."

"I appreciate that. But . . ." She stopped the brush with a hand and swiveled on the bench to face her maid. "But nothing in my life has prepared me for this responsibility — or any responsibility more than choosing a dress or helping Mother pick which china service to use for a dinner party. Now *everything* is up to me."

"God will help you."

She nearly laughed. "How can He help me? He's the one who's left me here alone."

"Well . . . my . . ." Franny bit her lip. "Never mind."

Justine took her wrist. "Tell me."

Franny took a new breath. "My mother always said there's a reason for everything. A God-reason."

"A reason for my mother's death?" Tears threatened.

"Sorry. I shouldn't a said such a thing."

Justine spun back around, forbidding her tears access. "Finish up. I have an appointment at the lawyer's office regarding the will."

**

The lawyer sat behind his desk, shuffling through papers relevant to her mother's passing. "There is a lot to go over," he said.

"Can't someone else do it?" Justine smoothed her hands over her wool mourning dress. It needed pressing. "My parents never involved me in any of their affairs and I—"

He looked up over spectacles that balanced on the tip of his nose. "Do you have some relative I'm not aware of? An uncle? Aunt? Cousin?"

She suddenly felt vulnerable. "I have none of those. My parents were only children, as am I. My grandparents have passed."

He spread his hands. There was nothing he could say.

There was nothing anyone could say. She was the last of her line.

She felt a wave of panic. *I can't be the last! I'm not up to handling everything alone! I can't—*

"How old are you, Miss Braden?"

An odd question. "Twenty. Last November."

"That's very good."

"Very good?"

He took out an envelope. "This is from your grandmother, Winifred Tyler, to be given to you when you're twenty." He handed it to her.

It had her name—and the instructions—written on the envelope in a lovely cursive. "Should I open it now?"

"As you wish."

She unsealed the letter and read:

My dearest Jussie,

I feel compelled to write to you because my health is failing. At such times a person thinks deep thoughts about their life, the should-have-dones, and could-have-dones. Those questions loom large for me now . . .

One large regret is that your mother and I were often estranged. We could be civil enough, but we missed the full joy of the mother-daughter bond that would have enriched us both. Unfortunately, because of our distance, there was distance between you and I. Those missed-chances grieve me the most.

For you are our family's future, Jussie. We Tyler women share something extraordinary: the gift. It comes to us unannounced on our twentieth birthday, and if not willingly received, may go unnoticed. I used the gift briefly, but let others turn me away from it. Your mother tipped her toe in it and declared it useless. Or frivolous. Or contradictory to her own plans. I urge you to do what we could not. Go to Piedmont. Discover your gift. Discover *your* purpose, Jussie. Discover the Ledger. The responsibility is great, the task important and God-given. The Good Book says, "For unto whomsoever much is given, of him shall be much required: and to whom men have committed much, of him they will ask the more." Your mother and I failed, but you will not. You are strong where we were weak.

Go to the family home, Jussie. Then go to the cemetery and touch the names of those who have gone before. And be utterly amazed.

> Your loving grandmother,
> *Winifred Holloran Tyler*

She felt the letter drop to her lap. *The gift?* Memories flooded back to the day Granny had spoken of a special gift — on the day she died. Justine hadn't thought much about it since. And now . . . Granny said the gift was hers because she was twenty? She'd been twenty for months and wasn't aware of any gift. Was the gift a ledger? A ledger of what?

"Are you pleased?" the lawyer asked.

"Confused. "

He held out a hand. "Would you like me to take a look at it?"

Justine hesitated, then handed him the letter. She craved advice.

The lawyer read it and said, "Hmm."

"So you are as confused as I?"

"I am a man of facts and paperwork. If only family members would be concise and plain in letters they leave to those left behind. One more sentence here and there would shed much-needed light on the questions such a letter raises."

He handed it back to her. "But I do support your grandmother's direction to go to Piedmont, for that instruction melds with one from your mother."

"How so?"

"It was your mother's wishes to be buried in Piedmont, New Hampshire." He took up some papers. "I'm afraid I'm unfamiliar with the town."

"You are not alone," Justine said. "It's very small and sits on the Vermont border. My mother was born there. And Granny."

The lawyer nodded.

"But to be buried there seems strange," Justine said. "I thought Mother would want to be buried next to Father, here in New York."

The lawyer consulted the will again. "She's very clear as to her wishes. Beyond your family home on Fifth Avenue, she also left you control of the family home in Piedmont."

Justine took in the news along with the smell of leather, lemon oil, and old cigars. "I didn't know she still had it. I haven't been there for ten years, since Granny died—and neither has she." *As far as I know.*

"Apparently she kept it." He referred to a paper on his desk. "She kept in her employ a certain Goosie Anders, to watch over it."

"Goosie! She's still there?" *She's still alive?*

"I assume so."

"She was Granny's housekeeper. She was old when Granny died."

"Then she's older now."

"Why would Mother pay for the upkeep of the house all this time?"

"It must have been important to her."

I don't think so.

Suddenly, the thought of being responsible for two houses was almost too much to bear. "What am I supposed to do with it? With *them?*"

"That's something you'll have to decide. I will be here to help."

Add another decision to the list. Add another question with no answer. If only Justine and Mother had been closer. If only she'd been a better daughter. If only they hadn't argued more than they'd had meaningful discussions.

Justine returned Granny's letter to its envelope. "I still don't understand why she wants to be buried in Piedmont. She never showed interest in the place. Whenever we visited during my childhood she couldn't wait to leave."

"She obviously felt a stronger connection than she let on. I've taken the liberty of contacting a Pastor Huggins—there is only one church. He said your mother owned a plot in the cemetery near her parents and grandparents ."

"I had no idea." This made no sense.

"Pastor Huggins says everything will be made ready. Could you leave tomorrow, perhaps? It is not a thing to be delayed."

Justine didn't want to think about burying her mother. Or discovering some mysterious gift. She just wanted to spend her days as she normally did: visiting friends, working on her dress collection and sketches, and going to parties. If only someone else could handle all this and just let her be.

The lawyer continued. "I will arrange for the train transport for you . . . and her."

"And my maid." She thought of Morris. "And perhaps one other?"

"As you wish."

"I will go tomorrow morning then." Justine had a sudden thought. "I expected she would want a grand funeral with all of her friends here in New York, like Father had."

He looked over the last page of the will. "It distinctly says to have the burial *there* but says nothing of a service *here*."

It was disconcerting for her mother to be so specific about one thing, while vague about another. "I suppose I can have a formal memorial service in New York after I take care of things in Piedmont."

"That sounds logical."

Her life was suddenly all about logic. Logic and logistics. Except for that very illogical fact that Mother was gone.

It bothered Justine that she'd forgotten Morris was coming to dinner.

He swept into the drawing room upon the breeze of a March evening and kissed her on the cheek.

He stepped back. "You don't seem pleased to see me."

Be polite, Justine. "I'm sorry, I'm just having a hard time." *My mother died? Remember that, Morris?*

Obviously he didn't, for he smiled and took her hands in his. "I have a solution." He got down on one knee. "Marry me, Justine."

She blinked. *Now? You propose now?*

For nearly a year she'd waited for Morris to propose. She'd been groomed to be the wife of a rich man, to be the mistress of a grand home, and a hostess to society. Her parents had carefully chosen Morris to be "the one", and over the months, Justine had come to agree with them.

"Justine?"

Faced with the long-awaited moment she found herself giving an unexpected answer. "Not yet."

He stood, letting her hand drop. "You're rejecting me?"

"I'm rejecting your timing. Mother hasn't even been buried. Her financial advisors are handling her affairs, I'm faced with responsibilities I've never faced before, the servants are wondering what will happen to the house and their positions, and—"

"I thought *we* could move in here."

"Us?"

"It's logical. It's your house now and—"

Although he was right, his assumption annoyed her. "How do you know it's my house?"

"You're her only child. Who else would she leave it to?"

Justine didn't like that he'd thought of these things.

He walked to the mantel and moved a figurine of a cardinal a half-inch to the left. "Weren't you going to the lawyer's office today?"

"Yes."

"Was the will read?"

She needed to delay this conversation. "Let's go into dinner. Watson said it would be served at seven."

"But what did the will say?" he asked as he offered her his arm.

Although it was logical to discuss such things with the man she loved, Justine found she didn't want to. His reactions would mirror her own—which did no one any good. She knew how he would respond to her mother's odd requests, so why bother?

Distraction. She needed distraction.

**

Justine managed to speak of other things beyond her mother's will until the dessert course when Morris' questions irritated her more than the thought of telling him the details.

"Since you keep asking, I will tell you this. I have inherited this house and a house in Piedmont, New Hampshire—where Mother is to be buried."

She picked up a dessert fork to eat her tart. The sooner dinner was over, the sooner Morris would leave, the sooner she could get her thoughts in order. At least that was the plan.

"Two houses, Justine? I expected you would inherit this place. But now a second home?"

"It's nothing fancy, Morris. It's not like having a second home in Newport, if that's what you're thinking. The Piedmont house is small and nearly a century old. You wouldn't like it. It has a small kitchen in the back. A pump at the sink . . . I remember it was fun to pump the water."

He made a face. "You can sell the place."

She thought of Granny's letter. "I don't think I should. Not for a while anyway. There must have been some reason Mother held onto it."

"I never thought your mother to be a sentimental sort."

Neither did I.

A footman came in the dining room with something on a silver salver. He spoke softly to the butler.

"What is it, Watson?" Justine asked.

He brought over the tray. "Delivered on behalf of your lawyer, miss."

"Very good." She looked at three train tickets, and saw a note saying that her mother's passage was also paid for. Mother had always liked train travel . . . It was quickly becoming real.

She pushed her tart aside. "I'm sorry to cut our evening short, but I leave early in the morning and need to oversee the packing."

Morris stood and moved to pull out her chair, but Watson beat him to it.

"Which means I also have packing to do," Morris said. "What time are we leaving?"

She felt an inner nudge that surprised her and caused her to slip the three tickets beneath her napkin. The idea of having him go with her made her uneasy and full of trepidation. "We?"

"Tomorrow. What time are we leaving tomorrow?"

Her response came ahead of her cognitive decision. "You're not coming. I'm going alone."

He looked at her as if she were crazy. "Justine, be reasonable. Surely you'd like me to be there for the funeral and to help you with the house."

Surely, I should. But . . . She imagined Morris being impatient with the process, disparaging tiny Piedmont, being overly eager to get back to New York, and questioning her decisions. "I'm sorry," she said as she led him into the foyer. "I need to do this alone."

"But you've never done anything alone."

She paused to look at him. "Then perhaps it's time." *Past time.* She kissed his cheek, and he left.

There had been no embrace or tender words. Justine didn't know what she'd expected of him these past few days, but whatever need she'd experienced had remained unfulfilled.

She headed upstairs, holding the walnut railing like a life line, walking slowly as her burden sat heavily upon her shoulders. She spotted a housemaid in the upper hall, but the girl scrambled out of sight. None of the servants knew what to say to her, and she knew all of them were concerned about their own future. She felt their eyes. And their questions.

They were *her* questions.

When she entered her bedroom she found Franny in the adjoining dressing room packing a trunk. "Miss Justine. I didn't expect you up from dinner so soon. But now that you're here . . . you have your mourning dresses from your father's death. I know they are two years out of fashion but will they do? Or would you like me to order more?"

The thought of donning black each and every day added to her grief. Not only was she grieving the loss of her mother, but the loss of her youth. When would it be appropriate for her to go to social events again? How long until she and Morris could marry?

He proposed. You said 'not yet'. . .

Franny was waiting for an answer. "Pack the black taffeta for the burial service. And I'll wear the wool on the train. Between the two, that is enough for my few days in Piedmont."

"How long do you plan on staying?"

"As short a time as possible. Put in one simple day dress for good measure, perhaps the pale blue."

"Not black?" She looked appalled.

"I'm sure the people of Piedmont will forgive my breach of etiquette. And if they don't, I will suffer their opinions lightly. I'm not there to impress them, I'm there to handle family business and be gone."

"Should I pack the heavy crepe veil?"

"Absolutely not. I need to be able to breathe. And see."

And figure out what Granny's gift is all about.

"Yes, miss. I've packed a bag for myself and —"

Justine shook her head. "I'm going alone."

"What?"

Her own words shocked her. Alone? She'd just complained about being alone. But in the past hour she'd told Morris to stay home, and now Franny? It didn't make sense.

Go alone.

She shivered at the inner direction yet she had no notion to go against it. She repeated herself. "I'm going alone."

Franny looked confused. "You need a maid."

She'd thought so. Until now. "I'll get by. There's a servant in the family home. Goosie will help me."

"Goosie?" Franny made a face.

"She's been with the family for decades."

"But who's going to draw your bath?"

Justine wasn't sure the house even had a bathtub.

"And who's going to dress your hair?"

"I'll manage." Justine saw distress on her maid's face — the maid who had been with her family for twenty years. She touched her hand. "I appreciate the offer, but I need to do this by myself." *Though I'm not sure why.*

"If you say so, miss." Franny glanced at the clock. "It's early. Didn't Mr. Abernathy want to stay after dinner?"

"I asked him to go."

"Really."

Justine sank onto the tufted ottoman that centered the room, needing to let it out. "Maybe I expect too much from him. The few words of sympathy that have crossed his lips were shallow as if he was following the instructions of what to say to someone in mourning. His words haven't been heart-felt. He's only interested in how the situation affects him."

"I'm so sorry."

Justine finished her complaint. "More than anything I long for him to throw decorum aside, take me in his arms, and let me weep against his shoulder until my tears are spent."

"That doesn't sound like Mr. Abernathy."

"No, it doesn't."

"And it doesn't sound like you. Begging your pardon, miss, but I haven't seen you cry at all. Have you? A body needs to cry at times like this."

Justine hadn't cried. Not once. She'd come close a few times, but some practical matter had always interrupted her emotions, leaving the tears unreleased.

Once, when she'd come close to crying, she'd leaned against Morris for support. He'd put his arms around her. But when she'd pulled back, he'd removed his handkerchief. She was just about to tell him she didn't need it when she watched him rub his coat, brushing away the residue of her tears. He cared more for his coat than her grief.

It did no good to wallow in could-have-beens. She was going to Piedmont tomorrow morning. Within a few days she'd be back in New York City. She'd deal with Morris then.

And so much more.

CHAPTER THREE

Justine startled awake when she heard the train whistle blow.

She leaned forward as the train braked and pulled into the Piedmont depot. The station house was tiny with a ticket window taking up one side. A man came out of the building, set a cap on his head, and buttoned his coat.

The train came to a stop and the man set a step by the door, and came inside. "Anyone for Piedmont?"

"Here," Justine said.

He tipped his hat. "Are you Miss Braden?"

"I am."

"Sorry for your loss, miss. We got word you was coming." He pointed back to the baggage car. "Don't you worry about a thing. We'll get her . . .we'll get your mother to the church."

"I appreciate that, Mister . . .?

"Beemish, miss." He helped with her small valises and held her hand as she stepped down to the platform. "You know how to get to the family house?"

Justine took a moment to get her bearings. "That way?"

"Just a block. I'll have Teddy bring your luggage by."

"Thank you, sir."

He tipped his hat again then called a young man over to help.

Justine walked to the main street bordering the depot. A string of storefronts edged the road on either side – a short string. On the opposite side was a general store, a jail house, a butcher, and a smithy. On her side sat a church, the depot, and then what appeared to be a doctor's office at the far end. She turned onto the road, nodding to a woman who shook a rug out a window and to an old man who sat on the porch of the general store. They stared at her. Obviously a stranger in town was an oddity. A stranger wearing mourning. On the train her attire had afforded her attention *and* anonymity. For no one had spoken to her at all. Perhaps they didn't know what to say. What could they say to counter the fact that someone close to her had died?

Then, she saw it. There, cattycorner to the church was the house. Her house.

It's old.

She chided herself on the thought. Of course it was old. It was old when she'd been a child. Old and boxy and simple. Not at all like her family's opulent mansion in New York

As she approached, she noticed something she had forgotten. Directly across the street from the Tyler family home was a cemetery. She heard her mother's voice in her head: *Don't you step one foot over there, Justine.* It was an warning that contradicted Granny who said it was fine if she wanted to go explore. Plus there was Granny's latest mention of the cemetery in her letter, telling her to touch the names on the headstones? How odd was that? Not just odd, bizarre. Crazy even.

The sight of the narrow front porch between road and door elicited childhood memories of serving her dolls cookies and lemonade. Cookies made by —

A woman stood in the opened door, a hand to her mouth. "Goosie?"

She nodded, but her pale eyes flit this way and that, as if she wasn't all *there.* Justine walked onto the porch and held out a hand.

Goosie didn't take it.

"How nice to see you again, Goosie."

Goosie tilted her head, wrinkled up her mouth, then said, "Mavis?"

Justine took a step back. "No, it's Justine. I'm Mavis's daughter."

Suddenly Goosie's eyes cleared. "Jussie?"

"Yes, it's me. Jussie."

Goosie held out her hands. "Glad, glad. Jussie, Jussie. I —" Her eyes looked past Justine to someone coming up the walk.

The man winked and said, "She's bats, that one. Never was smart, but now her mind lives somewhere between yesterday and never."

When Justine turned around to see how the rude words effected Goosie, she was gone. She turned back to the man. "And you are?"

"Quinn Piedmont, of *the* Piedmonts." He nodded after Goosie. "As I said, don't mind that old crone. Goosie's been a servant in this house for nearly eighty years. She's a little tetched in the head, as invisible as a cobweb in the corner."

He understated. "She's been invaluable to my family, taking care of our house since Granny died."

"My house."

"What?"

"My family owns everything in this town and the surrounding area. You rent from me."

She detested his arrogance. "I thought we owned the house."

"Never have. Never will."

How incredibly rude. And odd.

He shrugged. "You must be Justine."

Although Justine wasn't one for titles, the fact he'd used her given name with such familiarity bothered her. "I'm Miss Braden, yes."

He ignored her correction and gave her a wicked smile. "I knew your mother — very well."

She suffered an involuntary shiver — and hoped he hadn't seen it. Somehow she sensed it was best not to let Mr. Piedmont know when he had the upper hand. But in truth, he *did* make her wary-bells chime.

He was well over six-feet tall, with broad shoulders, large hands, and an unruly black beard that was parted in the middle, reminding her of the forked tongue of a serpent. His dark eyes looked as though they kept a lot of secrets — none of them good.

"You here by yourself?" he asked.

She forced herself to stand a little taller. "I assure you I am quite capable —"

He laughed. "Don't go getting your bloomers in a wad. It's just that . . ." He looked at her, up, then down. "Seems Mavis did all right. You are a pleasure to the eyes, even in mourning. And all topped off with a black plume in your hat.

The ladies of Piedmont will all be wanting such a feather. I'll have to order some into the store." He pointed down the street. "The general store, right there."

It was disconcerting to have him comment about what she was wearing. "Is there something I can do for you, Mr. Piedmont?"

"I assume you'll be wanting to move out."

"I'm in no hurry."

"If you stay I *will* be increasing the rent."

What? "Why would you do that?"

"Because I've been trying to do it for ten years but could never get a hold of your mother to tell her so. And that idiot Goosie wouldn't—or couldn't—tell me where she lived. I asked her a thousand times but her intellect suits her name."

Good for you, Goosie.

Something wasn't right about this conversation. "Surely you don't have a lot of people interested in renting an old house that's in need of repair, one that sits across the street from a cemetery."

"You never know."

She was done with him. "If you'll excuse me, Mr. Piedmont. I've had a long day and will have a longer one tomorrow."

"You need someone to say a few words over Mavis' grave, I'd be happy to oblige."

No, thank you. But his mention led to a question. "I need to speak to the pastor in town. I saw the church. If you'll excuse me."

"I'll see you tomorrow, Justine."

She cringed at the thought.

**

Justine went inside to freshen up to go to the church, when she heard steps on the front porch. Then a knock. She hoped it wasn't Quinn Piedmont.

It wasn't. "Hello, Miss Braden?" said the middle-aged man.

"Yes."

40

"I'm Pastor Huggins." He gave her a bow. "I'm at your service and am very sorry for your loss."

"Thank you."

I've come to discuss your mother's service."

"I was just coming to speak with you about it." She led him into the tiny parlor where they sat. "I'm afraid I don't know the protocol for a funeral here."

"No worries, miss. Your lawyer contacted me with your mother's requests and all is arranged — including a headstone." He cleared his throat. "All is ready in the church, whenever you'd like to have the service."

"Tomorrow?"

"If you wish."

The sooner it was over, the sooner she could go home. "Tomorrow then. But here's the rub, pastor. Neither my mother or I have been here in ten years, so I'm not sure anyone will come."

"Of course they will," he said. "Many people knew Mavis and her parents. With your permission I'll spread the word that the service will begin at two, with the burial right after?"

She glanced toward the cemetery. "My lawyer said she had a spot there."

"Right next to your grandparents and great-grandparents."

Although Justine still didn't understand why her mother chose Piedmont rather than being buried next to her father in New York, she was glad she would be resting near family here, and in heaven. "I appreciate your thoughtfulness and care."

He took her hand in his. His eyes were very kind. "We're all here for you, Miss Braden."

She was thankful for it. She needed all the help she could get.

**

Justine sat with Goosie at the kitchen table. She dipped the back of her spoon in a bowl of soup, making a bit of a reddish-

41

brown something go beneath the liquid, "What's this bit here, Goosie?"

"Bacon." She nodded to the bowl.

Justine took a bite and was surprised. "It's very tasty."

"Potatoes, leeks, potatoes, leeks." Her voice deepened as if repeating something she'd been told. "Not too thick. I'll throw it out—and you with it—if it's thick, woman."

Obviously someone had treated Goosie poorly. Justine couldn't imagine her grandmother being mean. She barely remembered her grandfather, but again, she couldn't imagine him being mean enough for Goosie to remember it all these years.

After they finished their soup Goosie rose, taking her dish to the sink.

"I'll help you wash those," Justine said.

Goosie shook her head adamantly, drawing a bowl to her chest. "My dishes."

"Very well then," Justine said. "Thank you for dinner. I think I'll get to bed now."

As she headed upstairs, Justine felt very alone. She should have brought a maid along. Someone to talk to.

Because there was no speaking with Goosie.

**

Justine tried to sleep in Granny's room, but the memories of the last time she'd seen her—dying in this very bed—haunted her. So alive and then not alive. Every time she closed her eyes she heard Granny's voice: *The gift will come to you when you're twenty. Be open to it.*

She hadn't thought much about the gift in her growing up years between ten and twenty. A ledger? That didn't sound very exciting. And if the gift wasn't a material gift . . . if it was a talent? Justine had never shown any profound knack for anything but sketching so the idea she had *any* gift had faded.

Until she got Granny's letter.

Mother supposedly had the gift too, but during the few times Justine had brought it up after Granny died, she'd pooh-poohed it and told her to leave it alone. Which she had done.

But now it was all stirred up again. Granny's letter made it seem important, like it was crucial Justine understood and used it. But if Granny and Mother had ignored it, why should Justine care about using it?

Whatever *it* was.

Finally having enough of the thoughts and the sleeplessness, she sat up in bed.

A branch tapped on the window like a ghost wanting in.

Justine grabbed her wrap, tied it at the neck, and tiptoed downstairs. She entered the small parlor and gravitated to Granny's rocker near the fireplace. She sat, letting her fingers trace the curve of the well-worn arms. One arm was skinnier than the other, as if Granny had repeatedly gripped it to press herself to standing.

She closed her eyes and rocked up and back, trying to think of happier times.

She jerked when she felt something on her back. Goosie was there, putting a shawl around her shoulders. "Thank you."

Goosie nodded and scurried away.

Justine pulled the shawl close and then . . . she held the corner of it to the moonlight. It was the palest blue. Granny's shawl. She pulled it to her nose.

Honeysuckle. Granny's scent.

And then, for the first time . . .

Justine cried.

CHAPTER FOUR

Pastor Huggins was right. Her mother's service was attended by at least three dozen citizens of Piedmont. Six men volunteered as pall bearers, including Pastor Huggins and Quinn Piedmont. As they moved from the church to the cemetery across the street, a few offered their condolences and short stories about how they knew Mavis Tyler Braden.

Yet the Mavis they spoke of was foreign to Justine. They remembered a young Mavis before she moved to New York City, married, and became a mother. None of the attendees knew the woman Justine knew. It was as if she was attending the funeral of two different women.

Justine tried to remember what was said and the names of those who'd spoken to her, but the day was a blur as her grief hit her with full force.

She stood next to the grave and watched her mother being lowered into the ground.

"In the name of the Father, the Son, and the Holy Spirit..." Pastor Huggins said.

Suddenly, Justine's legs gave out. She felt hands catching her. "Let me fall . . ." she sobbed.

But the man did no such thing. Instead, he swept her into his arms. "I'll take her back to the house."

Justine was appalled that she'd made a scene yet clung to the neck of the man as he carried her across the street and into the house.

He laid her on the settee, plumping a pillow beneath her head.

"I'll get you some water."

She tried to sit up. "I'm fine."

He gently pushed her down. "Give yourself a few minutes." He pulled a chair close and took her wrist.

She pulled it away. "What are you doing?"

"I'm a doctor. I'm taking your pulse. Checking your heartbeat. May I?"

She nodded. While he held her wrist she had a chance to fully see him. He was twenty-something, with light brown hair swept straight back to reveal a widow's peak above blue eyes. His facial features were small, but when he finished his counting and smiled...

She couldn't help but smile back. "How am I?"

He sat back. "How do you think you are?"

"Better." She sat up, rearranging her black skirt to cover her ankles. "I don't know what came over me. I am not one of those women who faints. I have never collapsed before."

"You have never had to bury your mother before."

Touché.

She glanced toward the cemetery. "Should I go back?"

"No need." The doctor moved to the window and parted the lace curtain. "Everyone has dispersed."

She felt like a fool. "So much for making a good impression."

"Was that your goal?"

"No, but..." She sighed. "Are you always so frank?"

His smile turned into a grin, and he held out his hand. "I'm not Frank. The name is Harland. Harland Jennings."

"Dr. Jennings."

"Just so. I work with Dr. Bevin. He's been the doctor in town for over fifty years. I recently finished my studies in Boston."

"I'm from New York City." She shook his hand. "Justine Braden. Nice to officially meet you."

He moved his chair back to its proper place facing the fireplace. "We *have* met before."

"When? I haven't been here since I was ten, since my grandmother —" She suddenly remembered a boy of eleven or twelve who'd let her roll his hoop down the middle of the street. "I remember now. Hoop rolling."

"You weren't very good at it."

"It was my first time."

"Then I suppose you're forgiven."

She shook her head, studying him. "I commend you on two accounts, Dr. Jennings."

"Only two?"

"Do you wish to hear my commendations or not?"

He waved a hand.

"I commend you on carrying me the distance in my time of need."

He raised a finger. "Without dropping you."

"Without dropping me."

"And two?"

He was a cheeky one. "I commend you for making me laugh on a day where laughter seemed very far away."

"You're welcome."

She sighed and looked around the room. "If only I knew what to do next."

"Are you staying in Piedmont?"

"Heavens no. I'm a New Yorker through and through."

"Sorry to hear that."

He did not let her get away with anything. "Have you been there?"

"I have not, so I supposed my opinion is biased."

"You obviously like it here in Piedmont."

"It is home—a distinction that increases each attribute and overshadows all insufficiencies."

Her thoughts sped back to *her* home. "My parents and I live in a large . . ." She was going to say "mansion" but it sounded pompous. "A large home. But now there is only me."

"Your father is no longer with you?"

"He died two years ago. A heart attack."

"I'm so sorry. To be an orphan . . ."

She didn't like the label. "An orphan makes it sound as though I'm a child."

He shook his head. "Being an orphan has no age limitations." He looked around the room. "What are you going to do with *this* house?"

"Probably move out."

"But your family has lived here for generations. If I remember town history correctly, your great-grandparents built it at the turn of the century."

Built it? "I thought the Piedmonts owned all the land."

"They do, but they allow people to improve on it—with their permission."

"And then make them pay rent too?"

He shrugged. "The whole town is set up that way."

"Isn't that rather . . . strange?"

"There were a lot of strange arrangements made during Colonial times. A new country meant new challenges. They made things up as they went along."

Justine nodded at the portrait above the fireplace. "That's my great-grandmother when she was my age. I never met her."

"She's very pretty. You take after her."

"Flattery, Dr. Jennings?"

"Truth, Miss Braden."

They heard steps on the porch and Goosie opened the door. Pastor Huggins pushed past her, going to Justine immediately. "Are you all right?"

"I am quite recovered. Dr. Jennings took good care of me."

"I am recovered too," Dr. Jennings said with a wink.

"I hope the service was as you hoped?" the pastor asked.

"It was lovely. Thank you for making it so."

Dr. Jennings stood. "We should let you rest. Just know we are here for you."

"In any capacity," Pastor Huggins said.

Dr. Jennings grinned. "In any capacity."

They left her alone with Goosie. "Other than me making a fool of myself, I think the day went well, don't you?"

Her head bobbed. "Good, good men. Good."

"Yes, they are."

**

After lunch, Justine sat on the front porch in a rocker. Up and back. Up and back. She remembered sitting on Granny's lap and feeling the resonance of her soft humming. She'd always felt safe. Loved.

Granny's love had been very different from the love of her parents. Her father, for all his charm and business acumen, seemed nervous in Justine's presence. As though he wasn't sure if he was doing things right. Although he'd been a believer in the "children should be seen and not heard" philosophy, he had occasionally let Justine into his study, where she'd play quietly on the floor, paging through books as she enjoyed the spicy smell of his cigars. She'd loved to watch him work, his spectacles balanced on the tip of his nose, on the verge of falling off—though they never did. Not once. As he leaned forward over important papers she enjoyed the rhythm of his pen, dipping into the ink, then writing, then dipping again. Occasionally he had looked up as if only then remembering she was still there. His smile would seal the memory.

Her mother was never affectionate. A pat on the head had to suffice, with a "good night then" when it was time to retire for the night. Franny and a governess had been in charge of the details of her day to day living.

But unlike Father, Mother had been very vocal with Justine, always offering her two-cents in any situation. Every situation. Mavis Braden had been bossy and hard to please. Justine desperately longed for affirmation, but always fell just-that-much short. Her mother's maternal mantra had been, "Use your brain, Justine."

Justine was surprised to hear herself say the words aloud, as though her mother spoke from the grave. She closed her eyes, wrapped her arms around herself, and whispered, "I'm trying to use my brain, Mother. I truly am."

"I'm sure you are."

She opened her eyes to see Quinn Piedmont walking in front of the house. He strode to the edge of the porch and winked at her.

She hated that he'd overheard. "It's not polite to sneak up on people."

"You're sitting outside in full view. As was my approach."

She stood and smoothed her black dress. "May I help you?"

"I came to see if I could help *you*."

"Pardon?"

"You collapsed at your mother's grave."

Oh yes. That. "I am quite recovered. Thank you." She moved to the door. "If you'll excuse me."

He lingered. "What *are* you going to do with this house?"

How she wished she'd stayed inside. "You'll get your rent. Other than that, I don't see that my plans have anything to do with you, Mr. Piedmont."

He leaned against a post of the porch and stroked his beard. "You may think that, but in truth your plans have much to do with me."

She hated to ask . . . "How so?"

"Because I'm the mayor."

Who would elect you? "I didn't know that."

"You're forgiven for being ignorant. That's why I'm here. To educate you as to how things work in Piedmont."

She suffered a shiver. "That doesn't sound very welcoming."

"Not my intent to be welcoming or not welcoming." He stood upright and pointed up the street. "See all that? Up there?"

"The businesses?"

"Them, and the land beyond." He pointed in the other direction. "And most of the land that-away too. As I told you yesterday, it belongs to my family."

"As you said."

He took out a pocket knife and began to clean his fingernails. "We own this town. The land and the rights were deeded to us by George Washington himself in gratitude for my grandfather's service during the War of Independence."

"How generous of him."

"My grandfather, Isaac, was a brave man of sacrifice."

"I commend him for his service."

Quinn jumped in with more braggadocio. "My father and I own *the* general store. The only such store in town."

"By design?"

His glare made Justine wish she could take back the words. While banter had been appreciated — and easily reciprocated — when talking with Dr. Jennings, it was obviously less predictable and pleasant when speaking with Quinn Piedmont.

He put the knife away and set himself squarely at the bottom step. "The point is, Miss Braden, you'll be wanting to get back to whatever life you had in the city, meaning you'll be wanting to move out of this house."

She had a thought. "Mother kept paying rent for ten years after Granny died. Did you ask her to move out too?"

For the first time he seemed unsure of himself—but only for a moment. "Like I told you. I couldn't get a hold of her."

For whatever reason—known or unknown—her mother had kept the house. She'd even kept Goosie on to look after things. There must have been a good reason.

And so Justine set herself squarely at the top of the steps and—with butterflies in her stomach—said, "I am not willing to move."

He blinked. Twice. "There's no reason for you to stay."

She found the courage to sigh and even smile. "There's no reason for you to want me out. Your rent will be paid."

His mouth opened. Then closed.

"Good day, Mr. Piedmont."

With that, she went inside, closing the door behind her. She leaned against it, her heart beating crazily in her chest. When she looked up she saw Goosie smiling at her.

"You heard?"

Goosie drew Justine into a hug.

"I'm glad you approve."

Justine heard movement outside and felt a twinge of nerves. Surely Quinn hadn't come back?

Women's voices. Footfalls on the porch. A knock.

Goosie nodded to the parlor, where Justine retreated. Then Goosie opened the door.

"Afternoon, Goosie. We've come to see Miss Braden."

Goosie stepped aside and a gaggle of four women swept in, each carrying a dish or basket. They saw Justine. "We've brought food."

"How kind of you." She nodded to Goosie who pointed to a small table where they set their offerings. "Please, come in."

As Goosie began to take the food to the kitchen, Justine motioned toward the chairs. There were just enough.

"Thank you for coming by," she said. "That is very kind of you."

The oldest woman spoke first. "You left so suddenly…"

"Are you all right?" the youngest one asked.

"I am fine. I was just overcome." She offered a smile. "You have the advantage. May I know your names, please?"

The oldest woman reddened and put a hand to her mouth. "Oh my. How thoughtless of us. I am Mrs. Huggins, the pastor's wife, and this is Mrs. Beemish, whose husband is the—"

"Station master," Justine said. "I have met both of your husbands. They have been very kind."

The women seemed pleased. "We have many good men in Piedmont."

"And a few not so good," said the third woman under her breath.

"Rachel!" Mrs. Huggins said.

The thirty-something woman rolled her eyes. "They get after me for being blunt, but with four children I don't have time for subtlety. I'm Rachel Moore, my husband is the butcher."

"Nice to meet you, Mrs. Moore." Justine appreciated her honest manner.

"Rachel."

Justine nodded and looked at the youngest woman, a petite girl of her own age or younger with white blond hair and rosy cheeks. "And you are?"

"Mabel Collier." She eyed Justine's black dress. "Seeings how you are from the city I'd hoped to see some fashion."

"Mabel, behave yourself," Mrs. Huggins said. "Miss Braden is in mourning."

"A girl can like pretty things at all times." She looked at Justine. "Isn't that right, Miss Braden?"

"I believe that might be true."

"Fashion is near impossible to get in Piedmont. Quinn never orders any decent yard goods."

"As if he would," Rachel said.

"I ask him to," Mabel said with a plaintiveness that implied she usually got what she asked for. "I ask him real nice."

Mrs. Beemish looked squeamish. "Don't go asking Quinn for favors, Mabel. You know better than that."

Rachel agreed with a nod and looked at Justine. "Remember me mentioning some men who weren't so good?"

"That's enough," Mrs. Huggins said. "We shouldn't burden Miss Braden with gossip."

"It isn't gossip if it's true." Rachel said. "I asked him to order in some special sewing scissors once—which he did—but the price was exorbitant. When I complained he said I could work off the cost by trimming his beard and hair." She raised and lowered her eyebrows suggestively. "I told him to keep his dumb scissors and not to talk to me like that again, or I would trim off something else."

"You didn't!" Mrs. Beemish said.

"I didn't, but I wanted to."

Mabel nodded whole-heartedly. "My Harland told me that he and Dr. Bevin had to put Mr. Wainwright's arm in a sling over the price of a plow. Quinn was to blame and—"

"Enough!"

The air tingled with Mrs. Huggins' admonition. She smiled apologetically at Justine. "You have enough to deal with, without our petty dramas."

But I want to hear all about him. I knew Quinn was trouble from the first moment I met him.

Yet she was also interested in something else Mabel had said. "I met Dr. Jennings," she said. "He was my hero, getting me home from the funeral." *He's your Harland?*

"That's my Harland," she said.

There it was again. "You're betrothed?"

The blush in Mabel's cheeks intensified. "Not as yet."

"But she's hopeful," Rachel said.

Mabel nodded, but looked away.

Although Justine knew Mabel hardly at all, and Dr. Jennings only a little, her instincts said they were not a good match. Either way, it was none of her business. She decided to change the subject to one that seemed appropriate. "Did any of you ladies know my mother?"

"Slightly," Rachel said. "But she left Piedmont when I was ten or so."

"Not at all," Mabel said.

"My husband and I didn't move here until 1860," Mrs. Huggins' said. "I believe she moved away a few years earlier."

"I knew her," Mrs. Beemish said. "And your grandparents. Your grandmother was a dear friend."

"We all knew *her*," Mrs. Huggins said.

"She is sorely missed," Mrs. Beemish said.

Implying my mother is not?

Mrs. Beemish plucked a piece of lint from her navy skirt. "Your grandparents were very upset when your mother ran off like she did."

"She ran off?" Mabel asked. "I didn't know that. To where?"

"New York City."

The city was named with distaste. Had any of them even been there?

Justine defended it. "My parents were married in New York. I was born there. I live there. It's a city full of excitement, entertainment, and opportunities." *Top that.*

"Mmm," Mrs. Huggins said.

Justine felt badly for letting them get her ire up. There was no need to alienate them. "There are advantages and disadvantages to all locales."

"Indeed." Mrs. Huggins stood.

"It wasn't just Mavis who went to New York." Mrs. Beemish had a mischievous glint in her eyes.

"Sarah! Gossip wasn't appropriate then and it isn't now."

"We all know the stories."

"I don't," Mabel said.

Mrs. Beemish sat forward in her chair and lowered her voice. "Story is . . . she went with Quinn, and his brother Thomas went after them."

Mrs. Huggins raised her chin. "The truth is, the Piedmonts often travel to the city for buying trips."

"Monkey business," Mrs. Beemish said under her breath.

"Again, Sarah," Mrs. Huggins said. "I warn you to mind yourself."

Their words spurred Justine's interest. "Quinn has a brother?"

"Had. Thomas. He died years ago. He was the pastor in Piedmont. Delbert and I moved here to fill the position after he passed."

Mrs. Beemish seemed ready to burst with information so Justine gave her a nudge. "Please tell me what you can, Mrs. Beemish. I would like to know my mother's history."

The woman looked toward Mrs. Huggins, and she gave a reluctant nod. "I suppose, since it *is* her family's business. But simplify, please."

With a nod Sarah shared. "Your mother and Quinn ran off to New York City without telling a soul—make of it as you will. Thomas went after them. But then Quinn returned soon after. And later Thomas."

"What about my mother?"

All four women shook their heads. "She never came back, except to visit. With you."

"What happened between her and Quinn?" The idea of them together made Justine cringe.

" *That,* we don't know," Mrs. Beemish said. "We can only guess."

"Sarah . . ."

Mrs. Beemish shrugged. "A few months later we received word she had gotten married. Your grandparents were very upset about it, for they weren't invited and knew nothing about it."

"That would make the year 1857. My father was Noel Braden."

Mrs. Huggins spread her arms. "See there now? Everything worked out. Mavis found a good man to love and had herself a fine family." She smiled at Justine. "For here you are, their lovely daughter." She reached over and poked Rachel's arm. "Come now, ladies. We should go. We just wanted to stop by and offer our condolences."

The other ladies also stood. "But I'd like to . . ." Rachel looked at the others, then continued with what she was going to say. "We're meeting tomorrow morning at my house for quilting. We would love to have you come."

"She's in mourning, Rachel," Mrs. Beemish said.

The idea of being in a setting where her curiosity about her mother, Granny, and Quinn Piedmont might be satisfied was tempting. "I'd love to come," she said.

Rachel beamed. "Second house on the left, past the livery. Ten o'clock?"

"I will be there."

As she let them out, Mabel paused to ask, "Do you know how to quilt?"

"You can teach me."

The girl didn't seem pleased with the answer.

After they left, Goosie came out from the kitchen. "Eat?"

Justine nodded and headed to the kitchen. "Is Dr. Jennings engaged to Mabel Collier?"

"Pfft," Goosie said, rolling her eyes.

Which was exactly what Justine thought about it.

**

Justine couldn't sleep. The dance of the night breeze ruffled the curtains and lured her to the window seat. She sat, drawing her knees close, covering them with her nightgown. She pulled one of the curtains aside.

Her view across the road was the cemetery, which made Justine question her ancestors' choice. Why would anyone build a house in such a location? Piedmont wasn't a crowded metropolis where space was rare. In fact, there were no other residences close by, as if all other citizens chose their parcel at the other end of town. To give themselves distance?

The site wasn't marked with a sign, but had three large maples on the corner, with a large boulder between them. She'd seen the year 1800 etched into it.

The moon was round and bright and Justine could fully see the headstones. She could even see her mother's new grave.

So close and yet so far.

The reality of the day fell upon her with new weight. Mother was gone. She was alone.

Yet not alone.

Father, help me...

CHAPTER FIVE

While Goosie made oatmeal on the stove, Justine sat nearby with her sketchpad, drawing the woman as she worked. Her pencil flew over the page, once again making herself marvel at the process. How did she see something and her hands know what to do with it? Not everyone could draw. She did not take it for granted. It was a gift.

Her pencil paused as she finalized the bow tying Goosie's apron. *Is my art the gift Granny talked about?*

As if sensing her question, Goosie turned around and nodded at the paper. Justine held it up for her to see. "It's not finished."

Goosie smiled and put her hands on her wide hips. "Big."

"Beautiful."

She went back to her stirring.

"Goosie . . . could Granny sketch like this?"

She shook her head adamantly.

"After Mother died, the lawyer gave me a letter from Granny. It talked about a gift. I just wondered if it had something to do with drawing."

She looked at Justine over her shoulder, shook her head again, then pointed toward the front of the house.

"I don't understand."

Goosie set the spoon aside and led Justine through the dining room and out onto the porch. She pointed at the cemetery. "Gift."

"A cemetery?"

She made a whooshing motion with her hands, up and out.

"Their spirits went to heaven. Yes, I believe that too."

A crease formed between Goosie's eyes as she shook her head. She pointed toward heaven and shook her head.

"They most certainly *did* go to heaven."

More shakes of the head. Goosie made the whooshing motion again, adding a sound effect, but then made both hands go in the same direction, behind her. "Back."

If only she could fully talk. "I'm sorry, I — " Justine smelled something burning. "The oatmeal!"

They both ran to the kitchen and found the breakfast ruined. "Sorry, sorry. Burn, burn."

Justine put a hand on her back. "No worries." She pointed to the basket of rolls one of the ladies had brought over. "A roll is plenty."

Goosie held up the pot of coffee.

"Yes. Please."

Goosie nodded toward the dining room. Although Justine had eaten her first meal in the kitchen with Goosie, since then the woman had insisted she eat in the dining room. Old habits died hard.

Justine sat in her usual place, the place of her childhood as Goosie brought a roll on a china plate, along with a Mason jar of boysenberry preserves. She poured the coffee.

"Plans?" Goosie asked.

"The quilting bee at ten, at Rachel Moore's."

"Who?"

"Rachel Moore, the wife of the — "

Goosie shook her head. "Who?"

"Who's going to be there?"

She nodded.

"Mrs. Huggins, Mrs. Beemish, Mabel Col — "

Goosie touched Justine's arm and shook her head. "Mabel."

"You don't like Mabel?"

"Trust."

"You don't trust her?"

She made a face.

"Why not?"

She made pinching motions with her hands, near her face. "Talk, talk, talk, talk…"

Justine laughed. "If you're implying she's a gossip, I think they all are."

Goosie shrugged.

"Don't worry about me. I'm used to gossip. Small town or big city, it's ever-present. Unfortunately, I've indulged in it a bit myself now and then."

Goosie made more "talking" motions with her hands as she went back to the kitchen.

Her warning made Justine second-guess the outing. Why nurture a relationship with four women she might never see again? Yes, she might be able to get information about her mother and the whole running away incident, but since her mother's life had turned out fine, what did it matter?

Mother was buried. Justine's time here could be at an end — if she chose it to be. She could return to New York and instruct her lawyer to break the lease.

She looked around the simple dining room and let herself remember childhood meals here. Nice memories, but also memories of frustration as she was forced to sit still far past when she was done eating while the adults talked about... whatever adults talked about. *I wish I would have paid attention.*

Her gaze fell upon the yellow wallpaper dotted with bouquets of pink roses. One particular floral grouping caught her attention and she stepped close. There, amid the stems, leaves, and petals, she spotted her name written in pencil in a tiny childish hand: Justine Braden. Granny had caught her in the act, and she'd tensed, knowing she would get in trouble. But instead, Granny had taken the pencil from her, and had chosen her own space to write *her* name: Winifred Tyler. "There," Granny had said. "We've claimed the house for all time."

Justine touched her name and then Granny's. Her throat tightened. *This is our house, Granny. I won't let the likes of Quinn Piedmont have it. Ever.*

After linking the past to the present she knew she would go to the quilting bee. She would take a few days to reestablish her family's place in Piedmont. Granny had been gone ten years. The Tyler name and presence had lapsed.

Until now.

"I'm here, Granny. I'll try to make the family proud."

With her head bowed, she caught sight of her black skirt. Her mourning garb. And suddenly the duty of dousing herself in black seemed absurd and the antithesis of the hope and determination she'd just felt upon seeing the names upon the wall.

"I'm done with black." She called toward the kitchen. "Goosie, help me change please."

She might as well give the ladies something to talk about.

**

It was time to go to Rachel's. Justine didn't want to go empty handed, so she asked Goosie to give her Granny's sewing kit: a small basket with needles, pins, thread, and a scissors inside.

Walking down the main street while *not* wearing mourning drew the expected attention. Justine nodded, said good morning, and braced herself for the ladies' reaction.

She was not disappointed.

"Come in," Rachel said, with a full scan of Justine's silver-blue day dress. "Where is your black?"

"What? No black?" she heard Mrs. Huggins say.

Two school-age children rushed in to see the stranger, one with a baby on her hip. "I like your dress," the oldest girl said.

"Me too," said a younger girl. A little boy of two or three hid behind her skirt.

"Hello there," Justine said to him.

He grinned, then hid his face.

Rachel shooed them away. "To the back, all of you. You know your job on quilt days." She turned back to Justine. "I apologize for them."

"No need. They're lovely. You're very blessed."

"Only on every third Thursday." Rachel led her into a neatly appointed parlor, where the other three ladies sat around a large quilting frame. To intercept more comments about her choice of attire, she held up Granny's sewing basket.

"I came prepared."

"You know how to sew?"

"I've done my share of embroidery. I have a never-finished pillow top at home. But as I said before, I'm willing to learn." She moved to the one free chair next to Mrs. Beemish. "For me?"

"Of course," the woman said.

Mabel eyed her as she moved to her place on the far side of the frame. "Bustles are higher in New York than here."

Justine glanced over her shoulder toward the drapery of her bustle. "It's quite ridiculous, don't you think?"

Mrs. Beemish reached over and touched the pleats that formed a ruffle on the three-quarter sleeves, then fingered the lace ruffle beneath it. "So fine."

"The lace matches the lace at your neckline," Mabel said.

What could she say? "Yes, it does."

"I appreciate the covered buttons," Rachel said. "That's a lot of work."

Not for me, for the dressmaker.

"I adore fashion." Mabel glanced down at her own dress. "But we're not wealthy like you. People around here don't have money to keep up with the latest styles."

Justine was wearing one of her simpler dresses. What would they think of her more elaborate clothes? "I didn't mean to offend. To show off. I assure you—"

"But where is your mourning, Justine?" Mrs. Huggins asked. "Fashion is one thing, but decorum is another."

She was ready with her answer and put a hand to her heart. "My mourning lies ever-present in here."

After a moment's hesitation, they nodded, acceding the point.

She settled onto the spare chair, adjusting her bustle to get comfortable. "Besides, I simply couldn't wear black a moment longer. It was such a beautiful spring day, and I was reminiscing about happy times with my grandparents and looking forward to an enjoyable visit with you fine ladies." She smiled and looked at each one in turn. "I know Granny would approve of me setting the black aside."

"And your mother?" Mrs. Beemish asked. "Would she approve?"

"She'd be appalled."

There was a moment of silence, then laughter.

Justine felt the weight of her decision scatter to the floor beneath the quilting frame.

"Actually," Mrs. Huggins said, "in her day, Mavis would have done the same thing."

Mrs. Beemish nodded. "She was quite the rebel, your mother."

"So I've heard. But that's not the mother I knew," Justine said. "She was always very focused on what was socially proper."

"New York society is not Piedmont society," Rachel said.

"If only it was," Mabel added, wistfully.

They all looked at her. "Are you dissatisfied with our company, Mabel Collier?"

"Oh no." Her cheeks reddened. "It's just that I think it would be grand to live in a big city like Miss Braden."

"Justine. Please call me Justine."

Mabel nodded. "I've never been much of anywhere."

"You've been to Haverhill for your grandmother's birthday," Rachel said.

"Haverhill's not that much bigger than here." She threaded a needle with white thread and handed it to Justine.

"Thank you."

Mabel continued. "Harland talks fondly of Boston and all the people and hub-bub."

"He told me he went to school there," Justine said.

Mabel sucked in a breath. "He told you that?"

She didn't understand. "It wasn't a secret, was it?"

"Well, no, but . . . he barely knows you."

Justine took note of her defensive tone. "He *was* the one who carried me back to the house when I collapsed. We talked briefly. He is very kind."

"Yes, he is," Mabel said.

"Don't pounce on the girl, Mabel," Rachel said. "Jealousy is never flattering."

"I'm not—"

"Harland was acting as a doctor, as a chivalrous man," Mrs. Huggins said. "We can always use more of those."

The ladies nodded.

Mrs. Beemish added more advice. "If you get jealous every time he gives aid to a female, you will have a very—"

"I am not jealous!"

Which only proved she was.

Justine held the needle over the quilt. "Tell me how to begin."

**

Two hours later, the three ladies thanked Rachel for her hospitality. Mrs. Beemish continued south to her home, leaving the other three to walk together through town.

"I'm sorry my stitches weren't small enough," Justine said.

"Quilting takes practice," Mrs. Huggins said. "And you were a great help threading a supply of needles for us. These old eyes find that task difficult."

"I'm glad I could help."

The doctor's office was on their left, marked by a shingle hung over the farthest doorway. The nearest door seemed to be for living quarters.

Mabel must have seen the direction of her gaze. "Dr. Bevin is *really* old," she said. "Soon Harland will take over completely, and—"

"Hush now," Mrs. Huggins said. "Just because someone has years on them, doesn't make them useless."

She ignored the admonition. "I'm going to stop and see Harland. It's such a lovely day, maybe he'll take me for a walk."

As if hearing his name, Harland appeared in the doorway of the office, using a rock to prop open the door. He stood up and said, "Well, looky here. Three of Piedmont's most esteemed, most delightful, most beautiful—"

"Most flattered women," Mrs. Huggins said with a blush to her wrinkled cheeks. "Good day to you, Harland."

He offered a little bow. "And to you. What has brought you out?"

"Quilting." Mabel went to his side and slipped her arm through his. Claiming him. "We tried to teach Miss Braden, but she wasn't very good at it."

"Mabel!" Mrs. Huggins said. "Where are your manners?"

"It's true," Justine said. "I will stick to sketching."

"You're an artist?" he asked.

"I draw. There is a distinction."

"I'd like to see some of your—"

"Harland, take me for a walk," Mabel said. Whined.

He glanced back in the office. "I'm afraid I can't right now. Doc wants me to do a good clean of the office."

"I'll help."

He looked as though he wanted none of it, but was gracious. "Come in then. Ladies, enjoy your day."

Justine and Mrs. Huggins continued their trek. Justine wanted to comment on Mabel's possessiveness, but it wasn't her place.

She didn't have to.

"Harland will get no work done now. If Mabel wants to take a walk, they will take a walk."

Justine tried to think of something nice to say. "She's very pretty."

"Of which she is well aware."

Justine held in a smile.

They passed the general store on the right. There was an old man sitting outside with a blanket over his legs. Justine raised a hand in greeting. "It's a beautiful morning, isn't it, sir?"

He looked surprised, then looked down at his lap.

Mrs. Huggins took her arm. "I wouldn't do that if I were you."

"Greet an old man?"

"Quinn's made it known that his father is not to be bothered. We're to leave him to himself."

"Why?"

She postponed her words by propelling Justine past the store. "During this last year, Arnold started talking crazy."

"How?"

"Like saying 'we lied' and 'we are the hills.'"

"What does that mean?"

"Who knows? More than once my husband tried to speak with him and get to the bottom of his comments, but Arnold got agitated, and then Quinn forbade such discussions in the future. Says his father has gone simple and it's best to leave him to himself."

"That sounds lonely."

"Indeed. One time I went to the porch to be neighborly, making small talk about the fine weather we were having. Quinn stormed out and took his father inside. Since then, I walk on by so Arnold can stay in the fresh air."

"That doesn't sound right. In any way."

Mrs. Huggins shrugged. "I bring him bread once in a while. He likes my rolls. But Quinn always commandeers them."

"Does he share them with his father?"

"I assume so." She sighed. "I doubt it."

"I know God doesn't like gossip, but from what I've heard — the facts I've heard — it sounds like Quinn Piedmont is an awful man."

"A man with power. He's the mayor."

"So he informed me. Why don't you vote him out?"

"Fred Simmons ran against him once, but when his barn burned down he had to withdraw to have the time to rebuild it."

One plus one equaled . . . "Was Quinn responsible?"

She shrugged. "Delbert says there *is* evil in the world."

"That doesn't mean we let it have its way."

Mrs. Huggins stopped walking and faced her. "Begging your pardon, Justine, but I don't think you have the right to come into Piedmont and tell us how to do things."

"I'm sorry. You're right. It's just that I've always had a strong sense of justice. When there are wrongs, I want them made right."

"An admirable trait." She smiled and took Justine's arm again. "Are you living up to your name? Justice . . . Justine?"

"I was told Granny gave me the name."

"Your grandmother was a very just woman."

As they neared the corner of the church and the Tyler house, cattycorner, Justine saw Goosie hanging clothes on a line in the back. "You say that Arnold Piedmont started speaking strangely, and . . . Goosie does that too."

"She didn't use to be that way."

"Really?"

"She used to be a part of our quilt group, always active in church. She was quite sociable."

"Goosie?"

"After your grandmother died and she was left alone to care for the house, she withdrew, stopped coming around. Delbert and I went to talk to her, to find out if something was wrong, but she only spoke in short sentences and occasional babble."

"Something must have happened."

"That's what I think too, but if it did, she's not telling." Mrs. Huggins let go of her arm. "I'm heading to the church. Delbert should be done writing his sermon and will want to try it out on me."

"So you have to hear—get to hear it twice?"

Her smile was bittersweet. "Such is love's duty."

Justine turned to go help Goosie, but saw she was already inside. The mention of the Huggins's love spurred her to want to write a note to Morris.

Once in the house she set aside her bonnet and shawl and sat at the desk in the parlor. In a small drawer she found a piece of paper and a fountain pen: *Dear Morris.*

Her mind went blank. What could she tell him? That the house was run by a woman who'd stopped using complete sentences? That the mayor was a bully—or worse? That he'd ostracized his own father? That one woman of the town claimed as her own the kind doctor who'd saved Justine from a fainting spell—though he seemed decidedly less interested in said woman? That the gift Granny had written about was still a mystery—one Justine *had* to solve?

Justine set the pen in its holder and spoke to the room. "He won't care about any of this. He only cares about whether I've rid myself of the house and when I'll be back."

She stared at the paper. She *could* write some meaningless twaddle about how she was doing fine, Piedmont was fine, the house was fine. And even add a line, "I miss you. Wish you were here." Yet she couldn't say any of it.

Because none of it was true.

She set the realization and the letter aside as she heard Goosie humming in the kitchen. Goosie, who used to socialize and talk, but who now remained alone and quiet. What had happened to change her so dramatically? Was the old Goosie still in there?

Justine went into the kitchen and saw Goosie had set up an ironing board and had an iron heating on the stove. She sprinkled a blouse on the table with a palm-full of water.

The old woman shook her head. "Wrinkles."

"I've never ironed before and wouldn't want to risk burning anything, but I can sprinkle."

Goosie shrugged and showed her how much water to use, and then how to carefully fold and roll up the blouse to keep it damp. She handed Justine an apron from a pile and began to iron a skirt.

Justine wasn't sure how to broach the subject of Goosie's "change" until she realized the work they were doing offered an opening. "I'm so sorry you've had the burden of this house these last ten years. Mother and I should have come to help."

She shrugged.

"I'm here now."

Goosie gave her a glance. "New York."

Oh. Yes. Justine would be returning to New York. "You could come with me."

Goosie let out a laugh, shaking her head.

Maybe she was right. Goosie had lived in this house most of her life. To make her change now . . . would it be a pleasant opportunity? Or would it cause Goosie undue stress and anxiety? It was a decision for another day.

"I had a nice morning with the quilting ladies."

"Good."

"Mrs. Huggins said you used to quilt with them. She said you used to be quite active in town."

Goosie's forehead furrowed. "Past."

"Yes, it's the past. But . . ." Justine took the iron out of the old woman's hand and set it on the stove. Then she put her hands on Goosie's upper arms and looked at her. "What happened after Granny died? "

For a brief moment Justine saw a glimmer in Goosie's eyes, as though a veil had been lifted, revealing the bright sheen of the truth.

But then the woman shook her head and touched Justine's cheek. "Good."

"Thank you. You're good too. Very good. And obviously very loyal. Things don't have to stay like this. You don't have to shoulder this responsibility alone. I'm here now."

She nodded.

"Do you want me to keep paying the rent on the house?"

Goosie nodded adamantly. "Yes. Yes. Yes…"

"All right. Calm down. I'll keep the house. You're staying."

Goosie took a fresh breath, then took up the iron.

At least *that* decision was taken care of.

Morris would not be pleased.

Chapter Six

Justine got out of bed. It was a new day — a day when she'd tentatively planned to go home. Her previous plans had involved spending a day traveling to Piedmont, a day burying her mother, and a day wrapping up any house business before returning to New York.

Which — with her decision not to give up the house — *was* wrapped up, just not in the way Justine had expected. There was no reason she had to stay, yet surprisingly, no reason she wanted to leave.

It was quite confusing. Before Mother died, before coming to Piedmont, Justine's life had been finely ordered according to Mother's social calendar — which she kept meticulously up-to-date in an elegant cursive. Woe to the appointment that was changed, causing a despised cross-out. Although that too was done with great care, with a single line noting the deletion.

"I have no calendar here." Hearing her words made Justine laugh. She had no one to visit, accost, meet, or entertain. If she wanted to, she could sit in the house all day — or better yet, go out on the porch and read a book. Or take up her sketch pad and venture out to find inspiration.

She smoothed the covers on the bed — another foreign act. There was something satisfying about making all the bedclothes right and proper, just so.

She looked across at the cemetery. Perhaps she should visit her mother's grave and sketch the beautiful trees and setting. It wouldn't be the usual subject matter for a young woman's pencil, but Justine had never been confined by the usual.

She moved to get dressed yet found the idea of putting on the black deplorable and putting on the blue too ostentatious. She was in a foreign land here, the land of small-town New England where the only sounds from her window were the songs of birds and the occasional clop-clop of a lone horse.

Justine needed to wear something . . . local. She opened the armoire and saw a sage green dress on a hook. She had a faint memory of Granny wearing it. She held it to her face and drank in Granny's scent. The honeysuckle was prominent, but the scent went deeper than that, to the very essence of her grandmother. Not good, not bad, it just *was*. Did everyone have their own scent like this?

She held the dress at arm's length. The sleeves were long and finished with a cuff. The neckline was simple and high with a white collar and buttons down the front. The skirt was full, as befitted the style of Civil War America. There was not a single bit of drapery to cover a bustle.

"It's perfect." She removed her nightgown, put on her chemise, corset, and petticoat, then slipped the simple cotton dress over her head, buttoning it up the front. The fact it fit created an additional sense of closeness. The last time she'd seen Granny, she'd been ten. Now, Justine was grown. Now, she could relate to Granny, woman to woman. She moved to a mirror and saw the full of it, smoothing the dress against her hips. "What do you think, Granny?"

"Pretty."

Goosie stood in the doorway, ironed linens in hand.

"Is it all right for me to wear it?"

She nodded and looked teary.

"I feel like I'm getting to know Granny more now than I ever knew her as a child."

Goosie went to a porcelain box on the bureau. She took out a lovely cameo brooch and handed it to Justine.

"It's lovely. Thank you."

She pointed at the pin again and said, "Abigail."

It took Justine a moment. "My great-grandmother, Abigail Holloran?"

"Yes."

"This was hers?"

Goosie shook her head and pointed at it one more time. "Her."

"This *is* her?"

"Yes."

Justine studied the face. The profile in the cameo was beautiful, with wavy hair pinned up, and flowers on her shoulder and at the hairline.

"You," Goosie said with a nod.

"You think I look like her?"

Goosie grinned. Then she touched the dress and said, "Granny," then touched the brooch and said, "Great-granny."

Justine squeezed her hand. "I never felt very connected to the extended Tyler family, but now. . . "

Goosie beamed.

Justine kissed her cheek, then took up her sketchbook. "Speaking of family, I'm going to the cemetery to visit a few."

Suddenly, Goosie's eyes grew large. She put her hands on Justine's shoulders. "Careful."

What an odd thing to say. And yet, Granny had spoken about the cemetery, instructing her to go there. "It will be fine." She wrapped Granny's shawl around her shoulders and moved to leave. "I won't be gone long."

Goosie looked worried.

**

After gathering a small bouquet of daffodils from the flower beds by the porch, Justine walked across the street to the cemetery. There was a certain freedom in the simple action. In New York she never ventured out alone. Most of the time she rode in a carriage, with the coachman helping her in and out. Butlers opened doors for her, maids drew her bath, dressed her, and cleaned her room, while a bevy of kitchen help created delicious meals. If she was in need of the slightest, most frivolous thing, she could tug on a bell pull and a servant would carry out her wishes. She remembered — with shame — once calling a footman to sharpen her pencils. How embarrassing.

As she walked, she realized her hair still hung in a single nighttime braid on her shoulder. So be it. Except for the cameo she was as unadorned as a woman could be. Once she passed the first trio of trees that adorned the corner, she celebrated her freedom by setting down her art supplies and flowers in order to take a full swirl, her arms outstretched. She giggled at the joy of it.

Then she caught herself. She was in a cemetery, a place where giggling was unseemly. But even that thought couldn't stop her smile.

Walking among the headstones, her curiosity was piqued. Who were these people? How did they die? How did they live? She felt like a stranger which made her sad that she had never met any of them, for obviously most had known her mother and grandmother—and even great-grandmother. It felt like a hole in her personal history.

A forty-ish man approached her from a small shed. He was quite handsome with reddish hair and a full beard. She remembered seeing him in the background during her mother's funeral. "Come to pay a visit, Miss Braden?"

"I am, Mister . . .?"

"Just call me Simeon. I'm the caretaker here. Have been for nigh on forever."

"It's nice to meet you."

He nodded, then gave her a double-take. "You look mighty pretty in green. Then he took his leave. "Let me know if you need anything."

What could she need in a cemetery?

She walked to her mother's grave and was pleased to see the headstone already in place.

Mavis Tyler Braden
b. 1837 d. 1878
Beloved wife and mother

She placed the flowers then remembered that Granny's grave was nearby. She took half of the flowers and moved to her headstone.

Winifred Holloran Tyler
b. 1806 d. 1868
God's gifts can't be returned

What a curious epitaph. Justine knelt in front of the stone, arranged the flowers, and then traced her fingers over her grandmother's name. *I'm living in your house, Granny, wearing your dress. I hope you don't—*

Suddenly, Justine felt a wind whip around her as though she was in a tube. She held the shawl close and closed her eyes against its fury. She sucked in a breath, and was about to cry out, when the wind calmed as quickly as it had stirred. She let out the breath she had been saving and put a hand to her chest where her heart beat double time. "What was that?"

She opened her eyes and found herself not in the cemetery at all, but standing in front of Granny's house. Yet the porch was gone. Had the wind blown it away? She scanned the area and saw no debris.

And how had she gotten here? Had the wind lifted her into the air and dropped her? Only a few seconds had passed. She touched her hair, which should have been a wind-blown mess, but found the braid smooth against her shoulder.

This doesn't make sense.

The sound of a horse and wagon pulled her away from her questions and she looked to the right, toward the business part of town. The church was there. The steeple was being repaired. If the wind had caused damage how could they be fixing it so soon?

And oddly, the road's surface was rough and muddy. And the buildings of main street . . . there were some missing. The structures that were present seemed recently built. The entire street had a new, yet rustic feel to it.

Two women walked toward the general store, but their clothes were odd and out of place . There were no bustles of any kind *or* wide skirts, and their waistline was up near the bosom. The skirts were narrow and the sleeves were puffed at the top and tight to the wrist—with no drapery or embellishment of any kind.

Like the Regency dress I recently bought from Mrs. Porter's Emporium.

The men wore breeches and high boots. Brown coats. Flat-brimmed hats.

Everything looked as if it were from another . . .

Time?

No. That's not possible.

Justine's observations were cut short when a young woman ran toward the house from the cemetery. Two beefy men ran after her.

"Winifred! You come back here!"

Winifred? Her grandmother's name was Winifred. But the girl was very young, as young as Justine.

The girl rushed past Justine, into the house, with the two men close behind.

"Woman, didn't I tell you to stop spending time in that graveyard?" He stopped when he saw Justine. "Who are you?"

"Justine."

"My wife hire you?"

Wife? Justine thought quickly. "Yes, sir."

"Then stop standing here like a nit and get inside and help Goosie get dinner."

Justine slipped by the men and went into the house, afraid of being hit. She quickly moved past her grandmother who was standing in the front room, and headed toward the back of the house, toward the kitchen — which oddly was in a separate building, its door open.

Justine found herself face to face with Goosie — a far-younger Goosie, a woman in her thirties. She was seeing Goosie and her grandmother, fifty years in the past? It was impossible to fathom.

"Who are those men?" she asked Goosie. "They're going to hurt — "

Goosie shushed her and moved closer to the back door of the house, to eavesdrop.

Her grandmother was arguing with the man who had called her wife, yet he didn't look anything like the Grandpa Ross Justine knew when she was little. Grandpa Ross had brown hair and was average height. This man's hair was raven black and he was huge. He reminded her of Quinn Piedmont.

They heard a slap and Granny — Winifred — cried out. Justine stood upright, ready to rush to her aid, but Goosie held her back. "We don't dare. You don't want to know what happens if you interfere."

It was a relief to hear her speak in full sentences.

The man's voice was hard and insistent. "I won't have no wife of mine talking to dead people. I don't care what you and yours did in the old country, you're here now and I'll have none of it. People think you're a witch, and if you say anything about the past or our family, I'll let them think what they want and try you as one. Kill you as one. Right, Arnold?"

The other man was Arnold Piedmont, the old man who sat in front of the store? But he was young too.

For the first time, Arnold spoke. "He's right. Behave or you'll get yours — and worse. You can count on it."

Poor, dear Granny. It was two against one.

Yet instead of acquiescing to her bully husband, Winifred confronted him. "You leave me be, Ned. Since we're married and I'm a Piedmont now, it's my right to learn about our family, so I went back to visit your father, Isaac, and I . . ."

"You what?"

"I went back into his life." She paused. "But your father wasn't called Isaac Piedmont. He had another name. What do you have to say about that?"

Justine pressed a hand to her head. *Back into his life like I've traveled back into yours?* Was this the gift that Granny embraced but Mother ignored?

Suddenly they heard Winifred being slapped, punched, and thrown to the floor. Justine rushed into the room. "You leave her alone!" She ran to Granny's side. There was blood on her cheek.

Ned turned toward *her*, and Justine saw a flash of evil in his eyes.

"Stay out of it, girl, or I'll give you some of the same." He turned to his wife, "Where's that book I see you and Goosie huddled over? I want it. I won't have you writing your nonsense down."

"I don't know what you're talking about." Winifred took Justine's arm. "Help me up. I have things to do."

As soon as she was standing, Ned shoved Justine aside and was in Winifred's face. The two of them screamed at each other, their voices overlapping. When he took hold of Winifred's shoulders and Justine and Goosie tried to pry his hands away. But then Arnold pulled Goosie back.

As Ned squeezed Winifred's upper arms, she screamed in pain. Justine tried to pry them loose, but his grip was like iron.

Somehow, Winifred got hold of his lower arms and pushed him back with all her might. Ned looked surprised at her effort and even smiled. But then Winifred managed to get her foot in his gut and shoved with all her might.

He lost his balance and fell backward.

His head hit the fireplace mantel with a horrible crunching sound. Then he dropped with a thud, his scull hitting the andiron.

He was motionless. As was everyone in the room.

"Is he . . . is he dead?" Winifred finally asked.

Arnold knelt beside his brother and barked an order at Goosie. "Get Doc Bevin!"

Justine put her arm around Winifred, who stared at her husband. "I didn't mean to..."

"He's bleeding," Arnold said after touching his head. "Get a towel!"

Winifred dashed to the kitchen and came back with one. It quickly turned crimson.

"Arnold, I didn't mean for him to fall. I was just trying to get away."

"They'll be no getting away from this, Winifred. I'll make sure of that."

A doctor arrived with Goosie, along with three other men. Justine prayed Ned would be all right, for Granny's sake. If he died there would be hell to pay.

The doctor listened to his chest and felt his neck for a pulse. Then he said, "He's gone."

"Winifred did this!" Arnold pointed at her. "Take her. Hang her for murder!"

Two of the men took Winifred's arms.

She yanked her arms free. "It was an accident. *He* was attacking *me.*"

Justine grabbed onto her courage. "She's telling the truth. Look at her! He did that to her and would have done worse."

The doctor looked at the cut on Winifred's cheek, and saw that her face was red and puffy, her arms bruised.

"Back down, men," he said, standing. "Evidence corroborates what they say."

Arnold towered over him by a good six inches. "What about what I say, Doc? That's me brother."

"And we all know what a kind and gentle man he was." He turned to the other men. "Go get a wagon boys. Let's get Ned out of here."

Arnold huffed out the door, muttering under his breath.

Once the room was free of the influence of the Piedmont brothers, the air settled. The doctor told Winifred to sit as he opened his bag. "Goosie, get me a wet cloth, please?"

He pulled a chair close and examined the cut. "It'll heal." Goosie brought the cloth and he proceeded to clean the wound and bandage it.

"I really didn't mean for him to die," Winifred said quietly.

"I know you didn't. And we all know how difficult and downright mean Ned Piedmont could be." He gently wrapped a bandage over the cut and around her head. Then he held Winifred's face in his hands. "Why'd you marry him, Winifred?"

She shrugged. "With Ma and Pa gone from the fever, it was lonely here with just me and Goosie."

Justine felt a wave of empathy — and surprise. To think that her grandmother had lost both her parents at a young age just as *she* had.

"Ned *could* be nice," Winifred said with a sigh. "At first anyway."

The doctor shut his medical bag with a click. "How old are you, Winifred?"

"Twenty."

I'm twenty.

The doctor continued. "There are other young men around. You can find some *nice* man to marry."

"Not many men at all here in Piedmont."

"People are traveling through every day, and many are staying. I'll say a prayer that God brings you a good one next time."

"I'd appreciate that, Doc."

He peered at the place where Ned had died, a puddle of blood marking the spot. "It's not that I'm glad Ned is gone—rest his soul—but it's not a bad thing to cut the influence of the Piedmont brothers in half. Ned was the mean one. Arnold . . . he's a follower."

"Now with no one to follow?" Winifred asked.

"We can only hope he chooses a better way." He rose to leave, then hesitated and looked at Justine. "I'm sorry, miss. In all the commotion, I didn't introduce myself." He held out a hand. "Dr. Bevin."

"Justine Braden," she said. "It's very nice to meet you."

"If I may ask, how do you come to be in Piedmont? You here with family?"

She smiled. "In a way." *If he only knew.*

He winked. "We welcome you then. Good bye, ladies. Rest now, Winifred. We'll take care of Ned."

**

With all the men gone from Granny's house, a silence fell between the three women.

"Well then," she said, pointing at the chair the doctor had vacated. "We have some talking to do."

Goosie shook her head. "Doc said to rest."

"I will, in due time. Make us some tea, please. This young lady and I need to have a chat."

Goosie eyed them both, then reluctantly walked back to the kitchen.

Winifred adjusted her body as though trying to get comfortable in the chair, giving Justine a chance to study her. Although decades younger from the grandmother Justine had known, she could see that the Granny in her memories evolved from this young Winifred sitting before her. She could also see a resemblance to herself—for she was also twenty and had dark hair with a bit of a wave to it, and hazel eyes set above strong cheekbones.

Winifred got settled but a moan escaped.

"You must be hurting."

"I'll heal, and God help me for saying this, but I'm looking forward to a life with little threat of more wounds. I don't know who you are, but I appreciate your help. I never shoulda married that man. But when a Piedmont sets his sights on someone . . ."

"You said you were lonely?"

"My parents died last year from the fever."

"Both of my parents recently died too. My mother just a few . . ." She was going to say "days ago" but opted for, "Recently." *My mother. Your unborn daughter, Mavis.*

"I'm sorry for your loss. Our losses." She glanced toward the andirons. "And now I'm a widow."

"As the doctor said, you'll find someone." *And his name will be Ross Tyler.* Justine thought of something. "Do you have children?"

"No, thank God."

"Don't you want children?"

"Of course I do. But I didn't want Ned's children."

"How long were you married?"

"A month."

Justine gasped. "Only a month?"

Winifred touched her bandage. "There's no *only* to it."

Her words implied pain. "Of course."

"Where are you from, Justine Braden?"

"New York City."

She nodded. "I like that name of yours. Justine. It denotes justice. And strength. Are you a strong woman?"

She hesitated. "I hope so. I'm trying to be."

Winifred eyed her green dress. "Your fashion stands out."

She suddenly felt self-conscious. "I apologize. I wore what I had." *What was yours.*

Winifred touched the sleeve. "Green is my favorite color." She shook her head, dispelling the subject. "New York City is many days' ride from here. Why are you in Piedmont?"

Her mind swam with answers. "I'm . . . I'm not sure."

"You mentioned you were with family?"

She chose the truth. "Actually . . . no. I'm alone."

Winifred eyed her suspiciously. "Never seen a woman come through alone. You must have a story behind that."

"Not really. As I said, my parents died."

Luckily, it seemed to be enough of an explanation. "How long are you staying?"

Goosie saved her from having to answer by bringing in a tray that held three cups and a tea pot. She poured and served.

Winifred's question about the length of her stay, and Justine's total ignorance of how to respond — or how long she *would* be here — spurred her to ask her own question. "I couldn't help but overhear your argument. Your husband didn't want you in the cemetery, and then you said you'd gone back into Isaac Piedmont's life?"

Winifred studied Justine's face before answering. "I believe I did say that."

"What did you see there? You said he . . . wasn't himself? Who was he then?"

Granny's eyebrows rose. "You ask questions about what I saw?"

"I'm curious."

"It means you believe me."

"I . . . I do."

"It's not something easily believed."

Justine thought fast. "Your husband and his brother believed you. It scared them. They mentioned others think you are a witch."

Winifred set her cup and saucer on a nearby table. "Do you?"

"Not at all. But I'd like to understand the whys and hows of it."

Winifred laughed. "As would I, miss. As would I."

Should I tell her I am from 1878? Justine kept it simple — for now. "I don't think you're a witch, and I do believe you."

Winifred laughed. "Will you listen to that, Goosie? Our new friend believes my wild talk of traveling back in time."

Goosie sipped her tea noisily. "Ned believed you too. That was the problem."

Winifred brushed a hand through the air, scattering her husband's memory. "He believed because he saw me go once." She studied Justine as if sizing her up. Then she said, "When I travel I disappear. Poof."

So that's what it was like when I left? I suddenly wasn't there?

"How do you . . . do it?"

Winifred nodded toward the cemetery. "I trace my fingers across the name on a headstone. Then I end up back in their lives."

Justine remembered doing just that on Granny's grave. And the words in Granny's letter had stated the same. And here she was, in Granny's life.

A huge question loomed. "How do you get back to the present? Do you have to return to the headstone and trace the name again or —"

Winifred shook her head. "It just happens. Unbidden, as though the visit is declared over and I am suddenly back home."

Justine didn't like the sound of that. "You can't choose when?"

"I cannot."

Justine certainly didn't like the sound of *that.*

"Though actually, *not* having control is probably best."

"Why?"

"Because whatever takes me into the past has a reason for it beyond me. I'm just a vehicle. When its purpose is served, I'm brought home."

"So who . . .?"

"God. I assume. As the Creator of time only He has the power to bend it."

Which led to, "Why does He send you back?"

"I'm never quite sure. I wish I could ask my mother, but she died."

"She could go back too?"

"I assume so."

"She didn't tell you about it?"

Winifred shook her head. "When I was fifteen or so, she told me there was something that would happen when I turned twenty, something that could be amazing or frightening." She paused. "That's all she would say. And then she and my father died when I was nineteen. I discovered my ability by accident a few months ago."

"You visited Isaac, but did you visit your parents? Abigail or Joshua?"

Winifred looked taken aback. "You know their names? You are a stranger in town. How do you know—?"

You told me about them when I was little. She moved on to another important question. "What can you tell me about the Ledger?"

Winifred gasped, then knelt beside Justine's chair. She set aside the cup and saucer and held Justine's hands. Her hazel eyes were fervent with emotion. "I don't understand what's happening, but I feel the need to speak quickly, so listen to me. Do you have this gift of travel?"

The gift. Justine only hesitated a moment. "I do."

She studied Justine's eyes. "Oh my . . . your eyes are my eyes. . ." Her gaze fell to the cameo. She touched it. "That's my mother's cameo! How do you come to have it?"

Goosie gave it to me.

Winifred stood and drew Justine to standing, squeezing her hands. "God is doing a mysterious work here, one I don't understand. There's so much to say, so much you should know."

"Tell me."

"The Ledger is a book filled with large thoughts." She looked at Goosie. "It's safe, isn't it?"

"Always. I'm good at keeping secret things safe."

"Is it the book Ned was after?"

Granny nodded. "He saw me writing in it."

"Does it have something to do with why you go into the past?"

"Partly. And now you . . . You need to learn from the Ledger, add to it, and pass it on. And stand up for what is right, no matter the cost, Jussie."

Granny and Goosie were was the only ones who ever called her—

Suddenly Justine felt an inner pull, one she had felt recently.

No, I want to stay!

In seconds, she found herself back in 1878. She stood before Granny's grave and looked around. The new flowers she'd just placed there were still fresh. She looked down at the headstone and remembered how it had all started when she'd traced Granny's name.

She knelt to do it again. She had so many questions, and she hadn't even had a chance to ask more about Isaac Piedmont not being Isaac Piedmont. She held out her hand, ready to trace—

"I wouldn't do that if I were you."

She looked behind her and saw the caretaker, Simeon. She stood. "Do what?"

"It appears you have it too. You have the gift."

"You know about it?"

"I know your grandmother had it." He glanced at the new grave. "And your mother, though she didn't like it much. A wasted gift is a wasted chance. It's good you're here. I can tell you won't let it go to waste."

"Who else knows about the gift?"

"Not many."

"Who? Please tell me."

"Myself and Goosie. Arnold Piedmont knows of it, but he chose to forget."

She'd seen both Arnold and Goosie in the past. It made sense. But Simeon? "How did you come to know about it?"

"I'm the caretaker here. I see things."

That also made sense. Justine ran a hand over her brow and took a cleansing breath. "I'm not sure what to do with it. I don't really know . . . what *is* the gift exactly?"

He smiled. "You tell me."

Justine was hesitant to tell him about her visit to the past. Surely he'd think she was crazy.

Was she crazy?"

But he urged her on, nodding at her grandmother's grave. "How was she?"

"You saw me go?"

He made a motion with his hands. "Poof."

All right then.

"Granny's husband just died." *She pushed him.*

"I'm sorry to hear that."

"Did you know Ned Piedmont?"

"Can't say as I did." He looked to the sky. "I know he died in 'twenty-six."

1826. At least she knew the year now.

Justine remembered her grandmother's final words before Justine was whisked back to the present. "Granny said to stand up for what is right, no matter the cost."

Simeon nodded. "Can't argue with that. Make sure you write it in the Ledger."

"You know about that too?"

He shrugged.

"Does it still exist?"

"Goosie would know."

Yes, she would. "And I don't know what 'right' she's talking about."

"You will. Give it time." He chuckled. "Give it time." He reached down and plucked some weeds. "It's important for you to know that you can't change things in the past. You're not there for changing, but for observing."

She was shocked by his words. "You know this how?"

"Just do. I'm here any time you need me, miss." He started to walk away, then turned. "I'd appreciate it if you kept our discussions between the two of us."

"Of course."

"I'm just the caretaker. Giving advice is beyond my place. But…"

"But?"

"Do be careful. Bringing up the sins of the past can get a person in trouble."

"I don't plan on bringing up anyone's sins. That's not *my* place."

"Hmm."

"Is it?"

He put his hands in his pockets and walked toward the shack.

A sudden tiredness fell over her. Traveling through time was exhausting. But first things first.

She had a Ledger to find.

**

Justine burst through the front door. "Goosie!"

Goosie hurried out of the kitchen, wiping her hands on a towel. "Wrong?"

It took Justine a moment to reconcile the elderly Goosie with the thirty-something Goosie of the past. The senile Goosie of the present with the lucid Goosie. "There's nothing wrong." She took her wrinkled hands in her own, took a breath, and managed a smile. "I need you to give me something. Can you do that?"

Goosie nodded and her eyes seemed almost clear with understanding.

"I need Granny's Ledger."

Goosie shook her head back and forth. "No no no no. Secret."

"I know it's a secret and you've done a wonderful job keeping it so for Granny. But I just spoke with her about it and—"

Goosie's eyes grew large.

"I went back and saw her when she was young."

"Winnie?"

"I saw her. And you. On the day Ned Piedmont died in this very room."

Goosie looked toward the fireplace. "Bad man."

"He's gone now. You're safe. We're all safe."

She didn't look convinced. "Hide Ledger." She shook her head and said, "Piedmonts."

"You don't want them to find it?"

"Never!"

Goosie was a she-bear guarding her den. "You've done your job well. But Granny gave you that instruction decades ago, and she's gone now . I'm sure it's safe to let me see it. I won't show it to the Piedmonts. I promise."

Goosie clapped her hands over her mouth, shook her head, and retreated to the kitchen.

It was obvious Justine would have to do this on her own. She looked at the simple parlor before her. There was a small bookshelf. Surely the book wasn't hidden in plain sight. Granny had tasked Goosie with hiding the book from Ned and his brother—a task she still took very seriously. It had been hidden for over fifty years.

Goosie came out from the kitchen. "Dinner."

Task deferred. She'd continue to prod Goosie about it. One step at a time.

CHAPTER SEVEN

After breakfast, Justine sat on the front porch, planning her day. As her thoughts swirled around her alternatives, she had to laugh. "I am quite certain that no one in the entire world has the choices I do on this day."

For she was choosing whether to ask Goosie more about a secret Ledger, or whether she should visit someone in the past. God certainly worked in mysterious ways.

Should she go see Granny again? Or perhaps Ned Piedmont so she could discover what secret he was so desperate to keep. Yet the thought of visiting such a violent man — even if she would witness him at an earlier time — was not appealing. She closed her eyes and asked the spring air and the God who made it blow, "Whom shall I visit?"

"How about me?"

She looked up and saw Harland Jennings at the foot of the short walkway leading from porch to road.

She stood. "Dr. Jennings."

He came to join her and offered a little bow. "Miss Braden. I don't mean to interrupt your plans for a visit but—"

"No, no," she said. "I was just thinking aloud. I am very happy for *your* visit. Do sit down."

He sat in the other rocking chair. "You have an interesting view," he said.

"Though a cemetery view is not sought after, people don't know what they're missing. I couldn't ask for quieter neighbors."

He laughed. "It is noteworthy you see the bright side."

"I'll take the compliment, but I'm afraid I am more pragmatist than optimist."

He assessed her a moment. "You like facts?"

"I like understanding things."

"Such as?"

He spoke in challenges. "I like understanding how things work, why people act the way they do, and how everything fits together in some larger purpose."

"You are a pragmatist and a philosopher."

She didn't like the second label and shook her head. "Philosophers are stuck in their heads, drowning in vast ideas that have little practical application. I prefer to take an idea and act on it."

"A woman of action. I like that," he said.

She was surprised how much she enjoyed his approval. "What kind of person are you, Dr. Jennings? Pragmatist, philosopher, optimist, or . . .?"

He looked toward the road, as if searching his own character. "Like you, I believe I am all those things. But I am also a dreamer."

This surprised her. "What is your dream?"

"Not just one dream. I have many."

"Will you share?"

He considered the view again before saying, "I dream of changing things for the better."

"Of course. Healing people."

He shook his head. "More than healing the body. I want to help them discover their purpose."

"You sound like a preacher."

He shrugged. "Aren't we all, in our own way?"

"How so?"

He angled in his chair to face her. "I truly believe we are all here for a reason. A God-given reason. God didn't create us and then say, 'Hmm, what should I have Harland do now?' He had a reason for my life set in place before I was born."

"So everything is pre-destined?"

"I don't think that's true. For He's also given us free will. A brain and talents and opportunities and choices."

She thought of her recent loss. "And struggles."

"And struggles — which usually make us stronger and can be a part of leading us to the life we're supposed to be living."

She looked out on Piedmont. Piedmont was as different from New York City as cotton was to silk. There was a spot for both in the world, yet which one was she? Where did she fit in?

She caught sight of the trainmaster as he walked toward the house in a brisk manner, waving at her. "Telegram, Miss Braden."

Her heart beat faster as she took the message and thanked Mr. Beemish. "Telegrams bring bad news," she said under her breath.

"Not always," Harland said. "Good or bad, the news will not change between now and the reading."

She opened the envelope and read: *When are you returning to New York? Missing you. Morris.* She breathed easier.

"Good news?"

Justine looked down, "A friend wonders when I'm coming home."

He grinned at her. "I am curious about that too."

"I wasn't planning to stay but a day past the funeral."

"And yet here you are." He nodded toward the house. "What are you going to do with it?"

"I *was* going to have my lawyer arrange for me to move out."

"Was?"

She needed to clear her head. "Could I presume on your advice?"

"Of course."

"I think a walk would be perfect right now. I think better when I walk."

"Motion calms e-motion."

"Indeed."

They strolled down the road with Justine purposely turning to the right, away from the prying ears in the town *and* the chance of Mabel seeing them. Perhaps she could learn more about Piedmont—and the Piedmonts—from Harland.

Her swimming thoughts were interrupted by his compassion. "How are you faring since the funeral?"

Though only three days ago, it seemed like a lifetime. "I'm doing well enough. I've been . . . busy."

"I'm sure you have, facing difficult decisions."

"Yes. Those. But . . . it's complicated."

"If there's anything I can do to help, just ask."

"Actually . . ."

"Yes?"

"I was wondering about Piedmont. What is the town's history?"

He chuckled. "Not many people care."

"I do."

"Very well then." He took a deep breath. "It was founded in 1790 by Isaac Piedmont."

She remembered Quinn's boast. "Quinn said George Washington deeded the land to him as a reward for his loyalty during the war?"

"So they say."

"You don't believe that?"

He shrugged. "It's hard to believe that someone as great as President Washington would deed anything to people like the Piedmonts."

"Perhaps Isaac was more . . . "

"Likeable?"

"I was going to say 'honorable.'" *His son, Ned Piedmont, was anything but.*

"Hmm."

"How long have you lived here?" she asked.

"All my life. My father was a farmer and I was born here in 1855."

"I was born in 1857, which means you were here when I would visit my grandparents."

"Beyond rolling the hoop?"

"Beyond even that." She noticed some birds flutter out of a field. "Your father was a farmer, but you became a doctor."

"A very complex situation."

"Because?"

"He did not approve."

"How could he not?" she asked. "It's a very worthy profession."

"It is not farming. He thought I was being uppity and often begrudged me the time I spent with Dr. Bevin, even as a boy." He sighed. "I wish he'd been proud of my interest."

"Been?"

"He died during the war."

"I'm sure he was proud," Justine said, hoping it was true.

"I don't remember it that way."

She returned to her original question. "So you grew up around the Piedmonts?"

"An interesting trio."

"Trio?"

"Arnold and his two sons."

"Ah yes. One died."

Harland nodded.

"Was Quinn as charming then as he is now?"

"He's always been a bully. But his brother Thomas was as kind as Quinn is mean. *He* was an honorable Piedmont. He was the pastor here."

"You say Thomas was kind. And a pastor. How did he die?"

"He drowned in the river."

"How tragic."

"That, it was." He glanced at her. "Why would God let the nasty brother live and take the good one?"

"I don't have an answer to that."

He patted her hand. "No one does."

Justine needed to find out more about the good son, about Thomas. And the best way to do that was to go back and see him in the flesh. "I should get back."

**

Shortly after Harland left, Justine stood before the headstone of Thomas Piedmont: *Born 1832 Died 1860.* She looked down at her simple shawl, the green dress—Granny's clothes. Although she wasn't sure what year she would find herself, if the dress could get her by in 1826, it would work in the 1850s—for she assumed she would see Thomas as an adult.

She knelt down and closed her eyes a moment. "Help me, God. Keep me safe and show me what You want me to see."

When she opened them she saw Simeon watching her. He nodded an encouragement and she thought, *If Simeon wants me to go it must be all right.*

Realizing her reasoning was ridiculous considering she had only spoken to the man twice — she made the choice of her own volition. Drawing in a deep breath for courage she traced her fingers over his name.

But nothing happened.

She did it again.

Nothing.

Doubt raced forward. Maybe going back into Granny's life was all there was. Maybe there were rules she didn't know about.

She looked toward Simeon, but he was gone. Perhaps it was for the best. It was embarrassing to have the gift, then find it gone.

She stood and bowed her head. "All right, Father. You've said no to visiting Thomas. Now what?" She waited for an answer, but after receiving none, decided to visit her mother's grave.

The flowers she'd set there yesterday were wilted, and she knelt down to retrieve them. Perhaps she should bring over a vase of flowers, so they would last longer.

Suddenly, sorrow fell upon her. "Mother . . . what am I supposed to do here? Morris wants me to come home, and I'm torn between staying in Piedmont a while longer or going back to my old life — the life you created for me." She reached forward and touched the carving of her mother's name, and —

A wind swirled within her and when she exhaled she found herself kneeling in the cemetery with snow all around her. Snow?

She stood and brushed the snow off her skirt. The headstones of her mother and grandparents were gone. She was sitting in an open area, not yet used for burials. The trees in the cemetery were smaller, their branches bare and edged in snow. *The gift still works! I'm in Mother's life!*

She couldn't take long to enjoy the revelation, as the cold was bitter. She hadn't anticipated a change of season. She pulled the shawl tighter around her arms, despairing of its feeble warmth. The only place she could think to find shelter was home. But as she made her way in that direction, her attention was diverted to a building behind the church. She saw dozens of people walking toward it, each group carrying a plate or pot. Were they going to a supper?

She stood at the edge of the road. A couple looked up at her and she took note of their clothes in an attempt to know what year she had traveled to. The women wore hoop skirts, tight bonnets, and wool knee-length capes. The men wore long frock coats, and neckties tied in a knot at their throats. The only thing she could be sure of, was that she wasn't in 1878 anymore. She would guess it was the 1850s.

She saw two women who looked familiar coming out of the Tyler house, heading to the supper.

Granny! She was older this time, middle-aged, but still beautiful. And the woman at her side? It was a younger version of her mother! Gone was the stern countenance of recent years. This Mavis Tyler sparkled with life. And something else . . .

Mischief? Somehow the thought of her mother as mischievous was ludicrous. Yet the way she smiled at the young men who greeted d her, tilting her head, laughing . . . Her mother was flirting—and was very good at it.

Carrying a pot toward the venue was Grandpa Tyler. He'd died when Justine was very young so her memories were dependent on a small painting of him on Granny's night stand. His beard was full and more gray than brown, and he shared a brightness of eyes with his daughter, Mavis.

He was distracted by some men who called him toward a discussion. He handed the pot to Granny. "I will see you inside, Winnie."

Winnie? Justine enjoyed the nickname—one she'd heard Goosie use—for it suited Granny far more than the staid "Winifred." As she and Mavis walked by, Granny met Justine's eyes.

"Are you new in town, my dear?"

"I am."

"Gracious. You are not dressed for this weather. Come inside with us. We are having a community supper in the meeting hall. You are very welcome to join us to celebrate the new year."

And what year is that?

"Thank you. I'd be happy to."

"What's your name, dear?" Granny asked as they walked to the building behind the church. "And how do you come to visit Piedmont?"

Justine almost laughed at the last question. *If they only knew.* "My name is Justine Braden, and I'm passing through."

"Alone?"

"I'm meeting an aunt and uncle."

"What are their names? Grafton County is not that populated. Perhaps we know them."

Mavis slipped her arm through Justine's. "Enough inquisition, Mother. Miss Braden needs to get warm and eat some good food."

"I would enjoy both," Justine said.

They went inside the square clapboard building where Granny took the hot pot to a row of tables that were heavy with aromatic offerings. The room was set with tables and chairs, and had a lectern at one end, where those in charge probably oversaw meetings. Justine's memories flashed back to her childhood. She'd been here before with her grandparents and her mother, eating suppers just like this. To be here now — with them — before she was even born . . .

Granny moved toward some friends. Mavis took Justine's arm and drew her toward a table of young people. The two men stood.

"Hello there, Mavis," said a man with very black hair and eyes that hinted at an outgoing nature.

Mavis gave him a sideways smile. "Yes, Quinn. Good evening."

Justine felt her eyes grow wide. Quinn? Without a full beard she hadn't recognized him. Reluctantly she deemed him handsome — in a roguish way.

He turned his eyes on her. "Come sit by me, Miss-whoever-you-are. I'll take good care of you."

"This is Justine Braden," Mavis said. "She's just visiting. Be nice."

The other young man shook his head. "You're asking too much, Mavis. My brother has been introduced to 'nice' but has never shook its hand." He nodded at Justine. "Miss Braden, I am Thomas Piedmont. I am the pastor in town." He offered a bow. "It is very nice to meet you."

"And you, Pastor Piedmont." In these few seconds she had witnessed their character. Brash and bossy versus courteous and caring.

Quinn rolled his eyes. "I'm famished. Who wants to eat?" He offered Mavis his arm and the couple headed to the food table.

Thomas offered Justine his arm. "Shall we?"

As they made their way through the line, a mother in front of them led two tow-headed children. The four- and two-year-old nearly bobbled their plates. Justine saved one from ending up on the floor.

"Thank you," the woman said. "Dealing with Bee-bee and Harland makes it difficult."

Justine nearly gasped. "Your son's name is Harland?"

Her pale eyebrows dipped. "Is there something wrong with that?"

"No, not at all, Mrs. Jennings, I—"

"Have we met?"

Justine chastised herself for mentioning her name. "I'm with Mavis. She mentioned your name." She touched Harland's cheek. The boy grinned at her, and she noticed the widow's peak on his forehead. Then he reached for his plate. "Eat!"

"Soon, boy," his mother said.

I'll have to tell Harland I met him as a baby.

But as she had the thought, she pushed it away. She couldn't tell him that because she couldn't tell him she traveled in time. He would think she was crazy. Or worse.

An older woman came to the rescue, "Let me take the children to a table, Dorthea."

Dorthea relinquished responsibility with a sigh heavy with relief. "I thought I'd be glad when Harland learned to walk, but independence carries other problems."

"A stubborn will?"

They shared a laugh. When they reached the end of the line, Justine was tempted to spend more time with Dorthea. To get to know Harland's mother would be very interesting.

But then she saw Thomas waiting for her.

One quest at a time.

She and Thomas sat at the table with Mavis and Quinn. As they chatted something became very clear. Mavis was attracted to Quinn, but Thomas was romantically interested in Mavis. He kept gazing at her as though she was the most beautiful, amazing woman he'd ever known.

Yet Mavis only had eyes for Quinn. The two of them laughed and leaned toward each other as they spoke, and occasionally found a way to have their hands touch. Mavis even whispered to Quinn behind her hand.

Justine felt sorry for Thomas and was annoyed at her mother for being rude and blind to the better man. A good man. A pastor.

She'd known Thomas less than an hour and found him kind and thoughtful. He liked books and seemed interested in the world beyond Piedmont. But since he was not gregarious or flirtatious he was easily ignored. At one point Justine saw him watching Mavis and Quinn — for they drew attention like a flame drew a moth — and he looked at Justine, smiling sheepishly, as though resigned to love Mavis from afar.

Justine found herself getting angry at the doting couple. Reminding herself that Mavis hadn't married Quinn, her anger abated.

Keeping the balance of the future and this present that was in the past, made her head begin to hurt. She rubbed her eyes.

"Are you all right, Miss Braden?" Thomas asked.

"I am getting a headache. I will be fine."

"Would you like me to get Dr. Bevin for you?"

"I'll recover, I'm just — "

"*I* just realized how rude we've been," Thomas said. "We've chatted and laughed without once asking you about yourself. Please forgive us."

"Yes, yes, please forgive us," Quinn said with a flip of his hand. Then he leaned his elbows on the table and asked with a smirk, "Who *are* you and why are you here?"

Mavis swatted him on the arm. "Too direct, Quinn. Too direct."

He shrugged, exhibiting the same arrogance Justine had witnessed in 1878.

"I am merely passing through."

Thomas's forehead furrowed. "It isn't safe for a woman to travel alone."

"It's safe enough," she said. She remembered how her mention of an aunt and uncle had brought questions of their identity. She hoped they wouldn't ask for more details.

Luckily, Mavis intervened. "She's a long-lost cousin of my mother's mother's aunt, or some such thing. She's visiting." She pointed at each man in turn. "I expect both of you to treat her well."

"I will do my best," Thomas said.

"I am always eager to have another beautiful woman in Piedmont." Quinn winked.

Suddenly, Mavis stood. "With that, we will leave you gentlemen. I'm sure Cousin Justine is exhausted from her travels."

Justine wasn't ready to leave. She didn't know near enough about Thomas. He'd died in 1860. She didn't even know what year this was. But Mavis took her hand and led her out of the meeting house.

"Why are we leaving? I would have liked to talk to them more."

Mavis slipped her hand around Justine's arm and squeezed it twice. It was a familiar action, a very motherly action when Mavis Braden wanted to reinforce her opinion.

"When Quinn gets that way, it's time to leave."

"What way?"

Mavis glanced behind them.

"Are you upset he called me beautiful? And winked?"

"Let's get home."

Justine remembered she was supposed to be passing through. "Home?"

"You have somewhere to go?"

"Well, no."

"So your mention of relatives was a farce?"

"I . . . I don't know what to say."

Mavis shrugged. "I'm not one to question your honesty or motivation. Perhaps if you stay with us overnight you'll tell me all your secrets."

"Secrets?"

"Don't get flustered. I'm harmless enough. The point is, it's too late to leave town. I insist you stay with us. I know Mother will do the same."

Justine was excited to spend the night in Granny's house. With her grandparents. And her mother. Yet would she be allowed to stay? Or would she suddenly be yanked back to 1878?

**

"Did you enjoy the supper?" Granny asked Justine.

"I did. Very much. Thank you for inviting me."

Granny looked toward Mavis. "I am glad to see Mavis extended our hospitality to stay the night. Goosie will make sure you are comfortable."

Ever-loyal Goosie.

Grandfather sat by the fire and lit his pipe. "Are you meeting your aunt and uncle tomorrow?"

Granny sat nearby. "You never did tell me their names." She turned to her husband and explained. "I'm sure we know them in some manner."

He nodded. "Where do they live?"

Justine was overwhelmed by their questions—which had no answers. "It's . . . complicated."

Grandfather's eyebrows rose. "Where are you from?"

At least she could answer that one. "New York City."

"Really?" Mavis said. Her eyes took on a new luster.

Grandfather let out a puff of smoke. "Piedmont is a long way from there."

"You have no idea."

Granny looked at her with new interest. "What year were you born, my dear?"

Panic set in. Justine didn't know what year she was in, so how could she . . .?

Mavis once again came to the rescue. "How old are you, Miss Braden?"

That, she knew. "Twenty."

"I too am twenty! What a coincidence." She took Justine's hand, pulled her up and out of her chair, and led her to the stairs. "We're going to bed now. Tell Goosie we'll manage on our own."

The two girls didn't speak until after they entered Mavis's bedroom and closed the door. "I thought we'd never get away."

It was an overly-dramatic choice of words. For on the surface, her grandparents' questions were logical and innocuous.

Mavis pointed to the bed. "Sit."

Justine sat.

"What year is it?" Mavis asked.

It was a question Justine wanted to ask *her.* Should she guess?

"Your hesitation is your answer."

"What year *is* it?" Justine asked.

"Eighteen-fifty-seven."

The year I was born? I was born in November.

"What's your name?"

"Justine Braden."

"That's it? For sure?"

Justine felt a tightening in her stomach. Did Mavis know she had time-traveled here?

And then, like a slap, she remembered that the women in her family received the gift when they were twenty. Mavis was twenty. Had she . . . ?

She made a decision to tell the truth. If Mavis thought she was crazy she could run away, or perhaps her intense emotions would spur her to return to 1878.

"I'm waiting."

Justine took a deep breath. "My full name is Justine Louise Tyler Braden."

"Tyler." Mavis bit her lip.

"It's the surname on my mother's side."

"It's *my* surname."

Justine nodded.

Mavis paced up and back. Then she stopped in front of Justine. "I want to ask, but I don't want to ask. Yet I feel as though I know you."

What was she supposed to say? "I'm—"

Mavis put out a hand, stopping her words. "No! Don't tell me. Please."

Justine was taken aback. If the situation was reversed *she'd* be curious. But perhaps Mavis's desire for ignorance was for the best. Justine had no idea what effect such a reveal would have on her situation.

Mavis sat beside her. "Do you have . . . the gift?"

Justine felt her eyebrows rise. It felt a relief to tell someone. "I do."

"So you're not from . . . *here.*"

"No. I'm also not from . . . *now.*"

Mavis was up, pacing again. "I should get Mother. Tell her."

Justine stood. "I'm not sure you should do that."

"Why?"

"I . . . I don't know. And perhaps I shouldn't have told you."

Mavis pulled her back to sitting. "Do you like . . . it?"

"I'm not sure. I've only done it twice."

"One more than me."

"You've gone back?"

Mavis shuddered. "Mother made me. She said it was my duty. It was awful."

"What happened?"

Mavis grabbed a pillow and hugged it to her chest. "I touched the name of Isaac Piedmont, and suddenly I was in a dense forest and there were woods all around me. I saw the river. So it was here somehow, but way before the town was established."

"Did you meet anyone?"

"A man saw me and yelled after me. I didn't know whether I should show myself or not, but by the time I thought I shouldn't, he'd come up to me. He asked what I was doing there."

"Who was it?"

"He said his name was Samuel. He was *not* a nice man. He was gruff, accusatory. He looked like he would have rather bitten my head off than talk to me. He told me to come with him, but I wouldn't."

"Was he dangerous?"

"I didn't wait to find out. I ran away from him, into the woods. He followed me, but I hid well enough that he didn't find me. And then . . . then I was suddenly back here, in the cemetery." She shook her head. "That was enough for me. I'm never doing it again."

"Does your mother know that?"

Mavis shook her head. Then she smiled. "There is a lot she doesn't know." She stood. "Help me get undressed for bed. I'll loan you a nightgown."

That Mavis could move on so flippantly when she knew Justine was not of this time and knew they were probably related, indelibly linked her to the mother Justine grew up with. Neither Mavis wanted to deal with hard issues. Justine remembered when her father died and the lawyer was going over his will, giving Mother instructions. Mavis rudely cut him short. "I don't want to know the hows of it, I simply want to carry on my life in the manner I am accustomed. Can you arrange that for me, or not?"

At the time, Justine had taken issue with her mention of "my life" and not "our lives." And yet it was indicative of her mother's way. Mavis came first, and the rest of the world was there for her pleasure. Justine had gone through times of being angry about it, but had found it easier to carry on, accepting the truth for what it was.

When they were dressed for bed, Mavis peeled back the bedcovers and got in, rearranging the pillows. She gave one to Justine. Once settled, she said, "Don't you want to know the 'a lot' that my mother doesn't know about?"

"If you want to tell me." *Which you do.*

Mavis grinned. "I'm running away to New York with Quinn Piedmont."

Justine had heard this fact from the quilting ladies, but to hear it from her mother when the incident was imminent . . .

She addressed the most disturbing part of the news first. "Quinn?"

She nodded vigorously. "We're in love."

Justine doubted Quinn knew how to love anyone but himself. "Are you aware that that Pastor Thomas is fond of you?"

"Of course I'm aware."

"He seems like a very nice man."

"He is. But he's not for me. He's too quiet. Too kind for my taste. A pastor?" She shuddered.

You prefer crass and brazen? "Why New York?"

"Why not New York? It's exciting and new and *not* Piedmont." She looked at Justine. "You're from New York. You know what an amazing city it is."

I was born in New York — in November of this —

Justine gasped. Was Quinn . . .? No. Surely not. *Please, God, no!*

"What's wrong?"

Everything. "Shouldn't you think about this a while longer? Make sure Quinn is the kind of man you think he is before you run away and . . ."

Mavis took her hand. "I know what kind of man he is. He is my kind of man. I want someone with fire in him. I don't want a bookworm, Bible-quoter like Thomas. He'd smother me with politeness, fawning over me 'til I'd want to scream."

"You'd prefer a man who cares nothing for manners and kindness?"

Mavis leveled her with a look. "That's a harsh assessment of a man you've just met."

"I'm . . . I'm a good judge of character. Thomas seems like a man who could love deeply. Quinn . . . does not."

"My, my," Mavis said. "You have them all figured out."

"I know what my intuition says."

Mavis studied Justine, making her uncomfortable. *Was she considering her opinion?* Justine remembered Simeon's comment that she could not change the past.

But with a blink and a shake of her head Mavis said, "Quinn wants to leave Piedmont — as do I. He wants to get away from the family store. He's tired of working with his father."

"Why do you want to leave?"

Mavis pointed out the window, toward the cemetery. "I don't want anything to do with *that.* If I stay here, Mother will pressure me to use the gift." She harrumphed. "I want to live *my* life and not be saddled with the sins of the past."

Sins of the past? "What do you mean by that? What are you supposed to do in the past?"

"Don't you know?"

"Something about justice?"

Mavis scoffed, then faced her on the bed and took hold of Justine's hands. "We're supposed to right the wrongs of the past and facilitate justice." She flipped a hand and returned to her place, smoothing the covers around her. "As if *I* could make such a difference. As if I'm interested in dealing with other people's drama."

You create enough of your own.

She examined her fingernails. "What's done is done, I always say. I see no benefit, dredging up the past. Whatever happened, people have adapted and moved on."

"I'm sure it must be important if we've been asked to do it."

"By whom?" Mavis asked loudly. "Who is asking us to do this bizarre thing?"

She remembered Granny's answer to this question. "I believe God is behind it."

"If God is so concerned with justice, why didn't He arrange things differently in the first place?"

"Maybe it wasn't the right time then."

"There's a right time for *injustice?*"

"You're asking me to explain the ways of God?"

"It would be helpful." Mavis leaned over and blew out the oil lamp, then slid down until her head was on the pillow. "And why the women in *our* family? Answer that one, Justine. And if this is so important why doesn't Mother go?"

"Have you asked her that?"

"She says she made a promise." She harrumphed.

Justine slid down onto her own pillow. Maybe sleep would give her answers.

She prayed for those answers, as she also prayed that God would let her stay in 1857 a little while longer.

CHAPTER EIGHT

Justine awakened to the sounds of soft movement in the room. Was Franny bringing her breakfast?

She opened her eyes, anticipating a good meal, only to see that it wasn't her maid, but Mavis. Her mother. And she wasn't in 1878, but in 1857.

Mavis was trying to tie a crinoline cage around her waist. "Oh, good. You're awake," she whispered. "Help me. Goosie usually helps, but I dare not risk it."

Justine noticed it was still dark. "What time is it?"

"Five. Quinn is meeting me at 5:15, at the depot for the 5:30 train. I have to hurry."

Her mother's plan came back in a rush. "Don't go with him. Stay here."

Mavis shook the ties at her. "You won't talk me out of it, so stop trying. Are you going to help me, or not?"

The knowledge that her mother *had* moved from Piedmont to New York City before Justine was born caused her to get out of bed to help. She may not approve of Quinn, but as Mavis had said, there was no other way she could get away from Piedmont. If Justine was to be born in November of this very year, she needed her mother to get to New York so Mavis could meet Noel Braden. Their anniversary was March 15. It was now January 2. Much had to happen in the time between.

The hoop was tied, a petticoat placed over it, then a navy skirt and matching bodice.

Mavis sat on a bench and pointed across the room. "Be a dear and help me with my boots."

The fact Mavis needed so much help getting dressed begged the question of how she was going to manage it in New York. Justine didn't want to think about it.

She helped put on the high-top shoes and laced them. "Do you have a place to stay in the city?"

"Quinn said not to worry, he has it managed. He and Thomas often go there on buying trips. I assume we'll stay where they stay."

"Separate rooms, of course."

She gave Justine a annoyed look. "Of course. Quinn knows I am a lady and will treat me as such."

Did "a lady" run away with a man in secret? Quinn—not being a gentleman—would expect . . .

Mavis took a final look at herself in the mirror. "The hair is not as well-done as Goosie does it, but it will have to do." She turned to Justine. "How do I look?"

Justine remembered all the other times when her mother had asked the same question. She gave her usual, sincere answer, "You look lovely."

"I hope Quinn agrees." Mavis took up a carpet bag, then looked panicked. "My cape, gloves, and hat. They're down on the coat rack in the parlor. I'd planned on bringing them up last night and forgot."

"I'll go get them."

"You're a dear. Quiet now. Take note that the third stair from the bottom creaks if you walk in the middle of it."

So you've snuck out before. Justine slipped downstairs barefoot, avoiding the center of the squeaky stair. She gathered the items and hurried upstairs.

"There now," Mavis said, putting on her second glove. She took a deep breath and let it out. "I guess this is goodbye."

"For now."

Mavis gave her a questioning look but did not pursue the truth. She kissed Justine's cheek. "I wish you the best in *your* travels. Don't let the past dictate the present."

"But doesn't the past always influence the present?"

Mavis flipped the question away. "I stand by my words." She moved to the bedroom door. "Ta, ta, Justine. Wish me luck."

"More than luck. I wish you love. Open yourself up to *true* love, Mavis. Don't settle for less."

"Don't be such a romantic."

And then she was gone.

Justine stared at the door. Knowing the type of man Quinn had become, she wished she could have stopped her, but she was there to observe and find the truth, not alter events. And though she knew her mother didn't marry Quinn, that didn't mean she didn't suffer under his power in some way. It was painful to watch, like seeing someone running toward a cliff wearing a blindfold.

Justine heard the slightest sound of a door closing and rushed to the window in time to see her mother hurry down the road.

Toward Quinn.

And toward Justine's father.

Yet what would happen to Mavis between the first man and the second?

**

After Mavis ran away, Justine was rather surprised she wasn't pulled back to 1878. She'd continue with her visit — for as long as it would last.

When she entered the dining room for breakfast she purposely looked at the wallpaper where she and Granny had signed their names. They weren't there. She touched the spot that *would* contain their autographs one day.

"You like my wallpaper?" Granny asked. "I love roses."

"It's very pretty."

"Please sit, dear." Granny led her to the place at the table that would remain hers, her entire life.

She sat at the table with her grandparents and exchanged morning pleasantries. They kept looking toward the stairs, waiting for Mavis to appear.

"Where is that girl?" Grandfather asked.

Justine looked down at her empty plate, avoiding their question. *I know! I know!* But should she tell?

The truth was, Justine wanted her mother to get to New York where she would meet her own father — so *she* could be born. She wanted Mavis to have a head start before anyone went after her.

Granny stirred sugar in her coffee. "Justine, go upstairs and get her."

The glaring fact that Justine and Mavis shared a room made it impossible to hedge any longer.

"She's not there."

"Then go to the privy and check on —"

"She's not in the privy. She's not even in Piedmont."

"What are you talking about?"

There was no easy way to say it. "She packed a bag and ran away."

"Where is she going?" Granny asked.

"New York City."

Grandfather pushed back from the table. "That girl. I'll go after her." He looked at Justine. "When did she leave?"

"Before dawn."

Her grandparents exchanged a look. "If she gets to the city we'll never be able to find her."

Granny hurried to the foyer and held up Grandpa's coat. "She has to be freezing in this weather. She can't walk to New York."

"She's not walking. She . . . she took the early train."

Grandpa froze. "She's never traveled alone."

The way they looked at her . . . she couldn't keep the full truth secret any longer. "Someone is with her."

"Who?"

"Quinn Piedmont."

They seemed to be struck dumb. Finally Granny said, "He forced her to go?"

"She went willingly," Justine said.

"Why?" Grandpa said. "Do you know?"

"Partially."

"And?"

"She wanted to get away from Piedmont."

"Why?" Granny asked.

"She wanted to see New York City." Her voice wavered.

"That can't be the only reason."

Justine suddenly realized she didn't know if her grandfather knew about the gift. "May I speak with you in private a moment, Mrs. Tyler?"

Granny nodded and they went back to the dining room. "Be swift about it."

Here goes. "She doesn't want to use the gift."

Her eyebrows rose. "You know about the gift?"

Such a complex question. "I do."

"Mavis told you?"

Justine decided to risk a more revealing answer. "She did, but I know about it from . . . personal experience."

"I guessed it!" Granny grabbed Justine's upper arm. "Justine Braden . . . who are you? Exactly."

"I don't think I should say lest it affect . . . things."

Granny bit her lip. "I suppose you're right. Tis an intricate thing we do."

"Indeed."

"Can you tell me what year you traveled from?"

"Do you think that's all right?"

She nodded. "No details. Just the year."

"I came from 1878."

Granny's eyes grew large. "Over twenty years in the future. My, oh my, I have so many questions."

"Which cannot be answered."

She let out a breath. "Which cannot be answered."

"Winnie? I'm leaving," Grandpa called out.

"He can't stop her," Justine said. "Shouldn't stop her."

"Why—?" Granny stopped the question and walked to the foyer. "Don't go, Ross."

He adjusted a scarf around his neck. "Don't be daft. Besides being her father, I am Piedmont's constable. I have to go. Our daughter left with Quinn. Unchaperoned. You know there can be no good in that."

Granny looked at Justine as if pleading for more information about what would happen in New York.

"She'll be all right," Justine said.

Grandpa shook his head. "With that scallywag? He's as untrustworthy as a broken hinge."

Granny looked at Justine again, her eyes questioning.

Justine repeated, "She will be all right. I promise." *In the long run. But in the short of it?*

The two women stood there, studying each other, until Grandpa said, "Gracious sakes, Winnie. Do I go or not?"

Granny shook her head. "You do not."

He removed his hat and hooked it on the coat rack with extra force. "You have some explaining to do, woman."

"You have to trust me, Ross. Trust Justine."

He eyed them both in a way that suggested he knew enough about the gift to respect it. Then he removed his coat and went back to the dining room. "Goosie, you can serve breakfast now."

The two women were left in the foyer. Granny stepped closer and lowered her voice. "He knows but he doesn't approve of the gift. Doesn't understand it."

"Do you still go back?"

"I wish I could, but I can't disobey him. He made me promise not to. As the town constable he can't have a wife who claims to travel through time."

"You wouldn't have to let him — or anyone — know."

She shook her head. "Ross saved me from a very difficult situation. When my first husband died during an argument—"

"Ned Piedmont."

Granny cocked her head. "You know?"

"I was there."

Granny put a hand to her forehead. "Gracious."

"It wasn't your fault. He was violent."

"He was. But other than myself and Goosie, the only witness to what transpired was Ned's brother, Arnold. He accused me of murder."

"It wasn't murder. You were defending yourself. Dr. Bevin said as much."

"You met Dr. Bevin too?"

Justine nodded.

She sighed. "If only it had been that easy. The townspeople were wary of me before Ned's death. A few had witnessed me disappear in the cemetery. Rumors spread that I was a witch."

"Which you're not. We're not. Are we?"

"We are not." She sighed. "I admit I said too much about my travels when I should have remained silent." She pointed at Justine. "Keep it to yourself unless you are certain you can trust the other person implicitly."

"I'll do that, Granny."

Granny's eyes grew large, and suddenly Justine realized her misstep. "Mrs. Tyler."

Granny bit her lip, then smiled and touched Justine's cheek. "To have a granddaughter as lovely as you . . . I look forward to the time." She repeated the word and chuckled. "Time." She looked toward the door — thinking of the cemetery beyond? Suddenly she drew in a breath . . . "Who is your father?"

"Noel Braden. He was a good man."

Granny let out the breath. "That's a relief. Back to my story then . . . With many in town already against me and Ned dead, they chose to believe Arnold over me. I was headed for a trial and jail — or worse."

"Gracious," Justine said, using Granny's word. "How did you get out of it?"

Granny looked to the dining room. "Ross and my father saved me. They were well-respected and made others see the truth of what happened. Without their help, I wouldn't be here. *That's* why I abide by my husband's wishes to ignore the gift."

"But what about justice?"

"I chose my husband over some wrong from the past. Call me a coward. . ."

Granny couldn't go back. Mavis wouldn't go back... whatever justice needed to be accomplished was up to Justine. "What can you tell me about Isaac Piedmont?"

Granny grabbed her arm. "You know about him?"

"Only because I heard what you told Ned."

"I went back and met him, but there was something fishy about him. He wasn't *him?* Plus, he wasn't a nice man at all. At. All."

"Mavis met a mean man back then too."

"So she *did* go back?"

"Once. It frightened her."

"Does it frighten you?"

"Terribly."

"How many times have you gone back?"

"Twice."

"To find out about Isaac?"

"Not directly. The times I've gone back I found out about you. And Mavis."

"Why?"

Justine hesitated. "I don't know."

Granny thought about this a minute, then said. "As I gave up my chance, I'm not one to give you direction. So follow your God-given instinct. The truth about Isaac will come out in God's time." She chuckled. "He's waited for me and Mavis to do it and we both failed Him. Don't you fail Him, Justine."

She felt the full weight of the task upon her shoulders. "What if I ignore the gift too?"

"I suppose you can. God gives us free will . . ." Granny lifted Justine's chin and peered into her eyes. "But I don't think you will ignore it. You're far stronger than the two of us ever were. You can do it. You *will* do it."

Grandpa's voice resounded from the dining room. "Get in here, both of you. Enough of this nonsense."

Granny squeezed Justine's hand and whispered, "We have more to discuss."

So much more.

As they moved to join Grandpa, they heard a knock at the door. Granny opened it. "Thomas. I'm glad you've come."

Just the man she wanted to see.

His face was haggard as he greeted them. "You know about Quinn?"

Granny nodded. "Come in."

He entered, glanced at Justine, then turned his attention to her grandfather who stood in the doorway of the dining room. "Thomas? What news?"

Thomas looked at each Tyler in turn. "Quinn was gone this morning. He left a note saying that he was leaving and warned us not to go after him. He stole money from the store. Father is furious and told me to come tell you. As the constable we need you to find him."

There was something missing in Thomas's comments. "Did he say anything about Mavis?"

Thomas looked confused. "No."

Grandpa shook his head. "I knew Quinn to be an rash fellow, but I never could have imagined he was a kidnapper and a thief."

"He kidnapped Mavis?" Thomas's forehead furrowed.

"Not exactly," Justine said. She knew Thomas loved Mavis. To tell him the truth would hurt him horribly.

Granny said, "Mavis left with Quinn of her own accord."

Thomas shook his head back and forth. "That's not possible."

"The excitement of New York City—"

"They've gone to New York?"

Granny answered. "They have. Didn't Quinn mention it in his note?"

"He didn't. We've been to New York, he and I. He probably didn't say because he knew I'd come after him." His face clouded. "Him. And Mavis."

Seeing his discomfort, Justine needed to speak with him alone. "I shared a room with Mavis last night. Can I speak with you a moment? In private?"

He glanced at the others. "If it will help."

Grandpa put on his coat and hat. "Too many secrets for my taste. I need to go after them, Winnie. Beyond the personal reason, he's a thief. It's my duty."

Justine raised a finger. "Can you wait until I speak with Mr. Piedmont, sir?"

Granny put a hand on his arm. "Please, Ross."

He expelled a frustrated breath. "Fine. I'll go talk with Arnold about what his son stole. And asked Beemish about seeing them leave on the train." He grumbled under his breath. "He should never have let them go."

Each minute delayed gave Justine's mother a better chance of blending into the mass of people in the city.

Granny pointed to the parlor. "Have your talk in there."

They each took a chair near the fire. "I'm sorry the situation pains you," Justine said. "The money—"

"Is unimportant. I am pained that Mavis went with him. Willingly." Thomas shook his head against the thought. "Quinn made no mention of her in his note."

"That seems odd. Does he know you care for her?"

His eyes flashed. "How do you know that?"

"I saw how you looked at her at the church dinner."

He scoffed. "*You* saw, but she was oblivious."

"Does Quinn know you care for her?"

Thomas nodded.

"Could he have done this to spite you?"

His face looked even more pained. "We rarely see eye to eye." He glanced at Justine. "We are very different."

She touched his arm. "You are a good man, Thomas Piedmont."

"Not good enough for Mavis." He stared into the flames.

"Good has nothing to do with her leaving with him."

He looked at Justine, his eyes sad. "I am not enough for her."

"Quinn is *too* much for her."

"He will hurt her."

"As he's hurt you."

Thomas took a cleansing breath and looked back at the fire. "There is much to atone for. Much to forgive." He looked back to Justine. "We must forgive others as we ask for forgiveness."

"What do you need forgiveness for?" Justine asked.

His eyes were sad. He shook his head, as though dispelling a painful thought. "We must forgive the hills."

"The hills? What does that—?"

With a rush of inner wind, Justine found herself sucked back to 1878.

She stood before the Piedmont's general store.

How appropriate.

One large question surfaced . . . she'd stayed overnight in the past. Was today the "next" day from when she'd left for the past? Or had time stood still for her here?

She smoothed her hair, uttered a "Help me" prayer, and entered.

The store seemed empty.

But then, "Hello."

She saw the elder Piedmont sitting in a corner. "Good morning, sir. Could you tell me the day, please?"

He looked at her askance. "Friday. Last time I looked anyway."

She nodded, glad that her time in the present had remained where she'd left it.

"You need to buy something?" Arnold began to rise as if to help her but lost his balance.

"Careful!" She rushed toward him, saving him from the floor.

As she eased him back into the chair, the sleeves of his shirt inched up, revealing bony arms marked with awful bruises on his wrists.

He saw the direction of her gaze and pulled the sleeves down. "I'm fine. Fine. Thank you for helping me, miss . . .?"

"Braden. Justine Braden. I'm Mavis Tyler's daughter."

"Sorry to hear."

"Thank you."

"I was always glad she got away."

"Away?"

At that moment Quinn came in with a sack of flour on his shoulder. He took one look at the pair and dropped it on the counter.

"Don't go jawing with Miss Braden, Pa."

"We were just chatting," Justine said.

Arnold set his jaw. "When do I get some pie?"

"There is no pie, Pa, and you know it." Quinn turned to Justine and made a circular motion at his head. "He's obsessed with pie today. My mother used to make pies, but our stupid cook can't do it. She burns everything."

Arnold nodded his head a few times and said forlornly. "Pie."

Quinn rolled his eyes. "Don't mind him. Pa needs to keep to himself." He looked toward his father. "Don't you?"

Cowed, Arnold Piedmont nodded and looked to his lap. Justine felt sorry for him. She vowed to speak to him again.

Quinn wiped his hands on his pants. "I wondered when you would come by and visit me."

"I am not visiting you."

He cocked his head. "Actually, you are."

It was difficult to keep her exasperation in check. She knew too much about this tyrant. Unfortunately, she needed to know more.

"I need to ask you a few questions. Alone."

Quinn spread his arms. "We are alone."

She nodded toward his father.

"Pa hears what I want him to hear. He's as silent as the grave, aren't you, Pa?"

Arnold kept his head down and merely lifted a hand and dropped it into his lap.

Poor man.

Quinn leaned against the counter. "What do you want to know, Miss Braden?"

"What happened between you and my mother in New York City?"

His face was blank.

"Twenty years ago."

He smiled the smile of the wicked. "I'm flattered she told you about that."

"She didn't tell me a thing. In fact, until I arrived to bury her I had never heard your name." *So there, you egotistical lout.*

He crossed his arms. "Then I guess you'll never know. Though since you do know we ran away together I'm sure you can guess." He lifted and lowered his eyebrows suggestively.

She had a card to play. "It must not have been very satisfying since she stayed *there*, and you came back to Piedmont."

He moved behind the counter. "My choice, not hers."

"Whatever you say."

He slammed his hands on the counter. "You have no right to come into *my* store and disparage me like this!"

Although she wanted to back away, she moved to the edge of the counter, her heart pounding. "How did your brother die?"

He blinked. "What do you know of my brother?"

"More than you think." But not near enough.

In one split-second Quinn reached across the counter and grabbed her wrist roughly. "Mind your business, Miss Braden, or better yet, take yourself back to New York where you belong."

She yanked her wrist free, but the pain of his grip remained. "At the moment staying here *is* my business. I owe it to my mother." She gave him her own grin. "What did you do to her, Mr. Piedmont? Whatever it is, I *will* find out."

With that, she turned and left the store, accompanied by a cacophony of Quinn's threats and interesting epithets.

He doesn't scare me.

Actually, he did. But that didn't mean she would ease up on her quest for the truth. She'd surprised herself with insinuating Quinn had something to do with Thomas's death. She had no reason to say that. Yet the words had come out. Was there any truth to it?

"Justine!"

She turned to see Rachel Moore coming out of the jail house next door. Her face was drawn and long strands of hair had escaped her bun. She ran toward Justine, taking her hands.

"I need your help. I don't know what to do."

She hadn't seen Rachel since the quilting bee. "What's wrong? What do you need?"

With a glance toward the store, Rachel drew Justine past the jail, and into her family's butcher shop—which was empty of customers and her husband.

Rachel leaned against the counter, a hand pressed to her forehead. "I don't know what to do," she repeated.

"Tell me the problem."

Her face grew hard. "Quinn Piedmont is the problem."

Again? "What did he do?"

"He arrested Frank." She clarified. "My husband."

"How can Quinn arrest your husband?"

She blinked. "He's the constable."

"I thought Quinn was the mayor."

"That too."

It was wrong in so many ways. "Why was Frank arrested?"

"We're behind on the rent for the shop. We had three pigs die, then Frank was feeling poorly and couldn't do the butchering, and . . ." She gasped for a fresh breath. "This morning Quinn came to the house and arrested Frank, right there in our parlor, in front of all the children. Like he was a criminal."

Quinn's the criminal. "When will Frank be let go?"

"When we pay the rent. Two months' worth. Quinn is threatening to evict us from our house too. Plus he won't extend us more credit at the store." She burst into tears. "How can Frank make money to pay the rent if he's in jail? How can I feed my kids if I don't have credit?"

All Justine could do was comfort her.

Or *was* that all she could do?

"How much is due?"

Rachel dabbed at her eyes. "Ten dollars." She shook her head, forlorn. "I don't know how to butcher meat. And with four children . . ."

She remembered the telegram Mr. Beemish had brought by. "The telegraph office is at the depot?"

"It is."

Justine squeezed Rachel's hands and peered into her eyes. "I will get you the money you need."

"How?"

"You leave that to me." She brushed the stray hairs behind Rachel's ears. "You go home and see to the children."

Rachel pulled Justine into an embrace. "I thank God for you, Justine."

The women parted on the street, and Justine made a beeline for the depot. She found Mr. Beemish inside.

"Good day, Miss Braden. You wanting to catch a train?"

"I wish to send a telegram."

"I can help you with that too." He moved to a small office and sat at a desk behind a telegraph machine. He handed her a pencil and pad of paper. "Here you go. Write down your message, then who and where it's going to."

When she was finished he read it over, lifting his left eyebrow. "I'll get this sent right away."

"Thank you." She strode home with a victorious spring in her step.

**

It was hard to sleep. Every time Justine closed her eyes she was faced with memories of her time in 1857. She'd slept in this very bed with her mother, sharing secrets like two girlfriends.

Yet upon further reflection, she realized she didn't have any close friends in the present. Back in New York she had acquaintances with whom she enjoyed conversation and laughter during social events, but no bosom friend who shared her heart with Justine, or who listened while Justine shared her own.

In truth, she was a loner who was quite satisfied with her own company—until moments like this when she needed advice. When her own counsel wasn't enough.

Pray.

She nodded and did just that. *Guide me in the right way, Lord. And perhaps give me a confidante? Someone who can offer wise advice about this wondrous situation You've placed me in?*

Who *was* there to talk to? Back in New York, her maid Franny was a friend for ordinary matters like hats and dresses, and a good listener for a chat after a social event. Here, Goosie had a kind heart, but her mind was littered with the events of a life spent in service, obviously causing some kind of breakdown in her ability to communicate clearly. Rachel was an acquaintance but had enough problems of her own.

And Mother was gone. Yet even when she'd been alive, their mother-daughter conversations were rarely of an intimate nature but more focused on the to-dos and should-dos—and should-*not*-dos--of society.

I have Morris. Yet . . . no. Her conversations with Morris were similar to those with her mother. *It shouldn't be like that with someone I might marry, should it? We should be discussing our hopes and dreams—beyond the goals of wealth, a nice home, and children.*

She sat up in bed. "I don't even know the details of what Morris does at his father's bank. Why don't I know that?"

She adjusted the pillows and leaned against the headboard. She knew Morris disliked game fowl, the color yellow, and "tedious" people, though Justine wasn't exactly sure what made them tedious in his eyes. Sometimes she felt as though he thought *her* tedious.

She scooted down in the pillows. "Lord, help me. My mind is a jumble with so much knowledge from the past and the present, and anxious about knowledge I don't know. I still don't know the details of how Thomas died or if that's even important. Bring me someone to talk to, who can give me wise counsel."

Harland.

Justine bolted upright. Harland had a listening ear. Could she—dare she—talk to him about her gift? Or would such talk destroy their friendship?

"I need to risk it. Tomorrow I will talk to Harland." She sighed and felt instantly relieved.

With that decided, she could finally sleep.

CHAPTER NINE

Justine approached the day on a mission: she needed to speak with Harland Jennings.

Her task was delayed as the morning was filled with chores: cleaning out a mouse's nest under a dresser, sewing up the end of a down pillow that threatened to fill the room with feathers, and then helping Goosie make bread.

The latter was quite enjoyable. Justine had never cooked anything. To measure and mix, knead and form . . . it was cathartic and just what she needed. She didn't even mind Goosie's odd phrases and half-answers. Their laughter eased over any awkwardness of speech—or position. Her mother was probably turning over in her grave seeing Justine associating with servants and doing chores. "Know your place as they know theirs, Justine."

It might have been—might have been—a logical bit of advice while living in a mansion in New York, but it sounded meaningless and rather insulting while living in a simple clapboard house in tiny Piedmont. To her parents everyone had their proper position on the map of life. Making bread with those who served the family was akin to spilling coffee on the map, or tearing off a corner. It was . . . messy. So be it. Life in Piedmont *was* messy. Yet Justine was finding satisfaction in sorting through the muddle and finding a rhythm here.

As they waited for the second batch to rise Goosie left to bring a warm loaf to Pastor Huggins.

It was the perfect time to go see Harland. Justine looked down at her floured dress and shoes, and felt her mussed hair. She sat on the bottom step, took off her shoes, and headed upstairs to polish and tidy herself.

The front door opened. Without turning around she said, "That was fast, Goosie. Did you run?"

Goosie didn't respond.

Justine glanced around and saw Quinn walk into the foyer and shut the door.

Justine's nerves tingled. She turned on the stairs to face him. "Have you lost your manners, Mr. Piedmont? You've forgotten how to knock?"

His face was tense, his eyes malicious. Without a word he captured the space between them, making her step to a higher stair. But her legs got caught in her skirt and she faltered, nearly falling.

He steadied her by taking hold of her waist. He pulled her toward him, against him. Tight.

"Let go of me!"

His breath was foul, his eyes dark as sin.

"Let go!" She pushed the shoes she held against him with all her might, but he held her tighter making it hard to breathe.

His breath was foul, his teeth rotten. "Stop meddling in town business. Or else."

Town business? Was he talking about her contact with his father? Or Rachel Moore and her husband in jail? Or did he somehow know about her quest to right a wrong from the past?

"Let me—"

Suddenly he released her. She fell back upon a stair. Pain shot through her lower back. She held in a groan—and tears. Ignoring the pain she used the banister to stand. She glared at him, letting the anger in her heart spill out. She pointed to the door. "Get out! And don't ever come into this house again!"

"You mean *my* house?"

Drat.

He casually walked down the stairs and paused at the door. "Just trying to be neighborly."

And though she knew she shouldn't say it, the words came out. "You are evil, Quinn Piedmont!"

He shrugged and ran a hand through his beard. "Your mother didn't mind." Then he opened the door and left.

Justine threw a shoe at the door. Then the other one for good measure. She sank onto a stair, shaking from what was, and worse, what could-have-been.

Suddenly the door opened. She tensed.

It was Goosie, back from her bread delivery.

Justine burst into tears and Goosie ran to her.

"Quinn was here. He grabbed me. He—"

"You hurt?"

She shook her head. "He just scared me. He told me to mind my own business—or else."

Goosie sat beside her. "Beast."

She lay her head on Goosie's shoulder and let herself be comforted.

**

After Quinn's assault, Justine postponed her plan to speak to Harland until after the midday meal. Although still upset, she was finally calm enough for the visit. She would *not* let Quinn beat her.

She put on a bonnet, wrapped Granny's shawl around her shoulders, and walked down Main Street toward the doctor's office.

Her stomach tightened as she passed the general store. She quickened her pace.

But she wasn't fast enough.

Quinn came out of the store to the edge of the porch. "Miss Braden. How are you this fine afternoon?"

He speaks as if nothing happened between us. She suffered an inward shudder. "Very well, thank you."

"You're still here."

Justine kept walking. "I am, Mr. Piedmont."

"Not much longer, I'd say."

Justine kept on walking. "As long as it takes."

She felt victorious when he didn't respond, though in truth, even she didn't know what she meant by her words. It wasn't like her to be so antagonistic.

She shoved the bite of nerves aside, and walked past the jail, depot, butcher shop, and livery until she saw the hanging shingle: *Dr. Andrew Bevin.* Dr. Bevin had been the doctor in Piedmont for over fifty years. Justine had proof of it, for the doctor had given Granny aid at least that many years ago. His sign confirmed the passing of the decades. It needed a good painting.

She was just about to knock when the door opened. An elderly man took a step back. "So sorry, miss. May I help you?"

Although more craggled and stooped, the eyes were the same. "I'm Justine Braden, Doctor. I've come to see if Harland is available for a chat?"

He didn't smile and hesitated. He studied her.

"Is there something wrong?"

"Have we met before, young lady?"

Fifty years ago. "I don't think so."

With a shrug, he let it go. "I was sorry to hear about your mother. Though we haven't seen Mavis since her mother died, in her younger years she was a pistol, that, she was."

So, I've learned.

He made room for her in the doorway. "Come on in. Go through the door on the left. It will lead you to the parlor of our living quarters. Harland is reading, I believe."

She stepped inside and the doctor left. The office was small, with a bed for the patient and some cupboards holding a myriad of jars. The door from the office to the parlor was open. She saw Harland sitting at a table, reading an opened book.

He looked up when she came in the room and immediately stood. "Miss Braden."

"Justine. Please." She saw colored pictures and took a look. "Plants?"

"It's a book about herbal medicines. *A Curious Herbal* by Elizabeth Blackwell."

"A woman."

"A very talented woman. Doc says I need to know the herbal cures as well as those I learned in school."

"Old knowledge can still be valid knowledge?"

"He says God put plants on this earth for a reason. Some reasons have been discovered, and others will be discovered in the future."

"How interesting."

He nodded, then closed the book. "I'm glad you came. I was going to come by and ask if you'd like to accompany me to church tomorrow morning."

"That would be very nice."

He solidified the commitment with a nod. "But you didn't come here to talk about plants or church. To what do I owe the pleasure of this visit?"

She sighed.

He stood. "You sigh indicates a need to be comfortable." He gestured toward two chairs in front of the fireplace. She removed her bonnet and set it on her lap.

"Would you like some coffee? Tea?"

"No, thank you." Her stomach was suddenly topsy-turvy with nerves. The desire for a confidante might have consequences.

"Justine . . . please say what's on your mind, for clearly it's distressing you."

"That, it is."

"Then tell me."

"What I say may change the way you think of me."

"I doubt it."

"It's strange. Bizarre. Absurd. Nonsensical."

"All that?" He laughed. "Now I *am* intrigued."

She smiled. "I need you to have an open mind about everything I am about to say."

He leaned back in his chair, closed his eyes, took a deep breath, then said, "It is now open."

"You tease me."

"I do. But that doesn't mean I don't want to hear everything you have to say."

It was now or never. She'd thought about where she would begin. "Yesterday I spent the day and night in 1857."

"1857 what?"

"The year 1857."

He sat forward. "How did you manage that?"

She told him about the gift the women of her family shared, how her grandmother's husband forbade her from using the gift, how her mother had refused to use the gift, and how she had just discovered the gift.

"I also visited 1826. But only for a short time. Not overnight."

"Heaven forbid."

"It is a valid point. I never know when I will be whisked back to the present."

"Time travel can be thoughtless."

She tossed her bonnet on a table. "I thought you'd be appalled and you're amused?"

His face turned serious. "Actually, I'm fascinated. Riveted. I have a tendency to use humor to deflect my unease and uncertainty. I am not making fun of you, or making light of the subject."

"So you believe me?"

He hesitated. "I don't *not* believe you."

That's a start. "I have one more detail that might help convince you. Maybe then you can see why I'm seeking your counsel."

He waved his hand, indicating she should continue.

"During the first trip back to 1826, I witnessed my grandmother—who was twenty, the age I am now—in an argument with her husband."

"Ross Tyler. I knew him."

"No. Not Ross Tyler. Ned Piedmont."

"Ned? Arnold's brother?"

She nodded.

"He was married to your grandmother? He's been dead for decades. I never met him but have heard tell of him. He was a mean cuss."

"Very mean."

"What were they arguing about?"

"About Granny spending time in the cemetery and going back in time—like I did. Or rather, I'm going back in time like she did."

"It *is* hard to fathom."

"Don't defend him."

"I don't. It's just . . . to use your words, bizarre. Absurd."

She finished the list. "Nonsensical."

"That too. I'm sure it frightened him."

Justine had never thought of that.

She needed to get back to the point. "They argued about it. There was violence. An accident. During the fight he ended up dead. He fell and hit his head on the mantel and the andiron."

"I never heard that part of the story. There's always been bad blood between the Piedmonts and the Tylers, but I never understood why."

"Arnold Piedmont wanted to hang Granny for murder. Called her a witch too."

"Obviously, he didn't follow through."

"Cooler heads prevailed. My grandfather, Ross Tyler, saved her."

He rubbed his hands on his trousers and took a deep breath. "You're saying that you were there to witness it."

"In the same room."

"How extraordinary."

"But I don't think that's the reason I was sent there. I was sent back because of something Granny said during the argument."

"Which was?"

"That *she'd* gone back in time and had found out that Isaac Piedmont—the father of Ned and Arnold—wasn't really Isaac Piedmont."

"Who was he?"

"I don't know. That's what I'm trying to find out. I thought of going back in the life of Thomas Piedmont, Quinn's brother, but that didn't work so—"

"Didn't work?"

"I didn't go back into his life."

"Why not?"

"I don't know. But then—quite by chance—I traveled into my mother's life, into 1857. There, I actually met Thomas Piedmont."

"I never knew him."

"Actually, you did." It felt good to be able to share something positive. "In 1857 I met you and your mother at a potluck. You were about two years old and bobbling a plate of food."

Harland froze. He stood and took hold of the mantel. He leaned his head on his hand.

Did he believe her? What bit could she share that she wouldn't know otherwise? "Your mother's name was Dorthea. She had very blond hair and eyebrows. As did you and a sister."

He turned to face her. "Now, you're scaring me."

She went to his side. "There's nothing to be afraid of."

"But how does it happen? Why does it happen?"

"I had—and have—the same questions. When I was talking to my mother about it in 1857, she said—"

"You spoke with your mother . . . before she bore you?"

"We shared a room. A bed. The same bed I'm sleeping in at the house how. She confided in me about running off with Quinn Piedmont."

He stepped away from her and waved his hands in front of his face. "Your mother ran away with Quinn?"

"I thought it was common knowledge. The women at the quilting bee knew all about it."

"Well, I don't."

Justine regretted bringing it up. "She married my father a few months later, so the Quinn-detail is something I'll have to look into. It must have been short-lived." She removed Granny's shawl, letting it drape over the back of the chair. "Forgive me. I led us off-point. You wanted to know why this is happening."

"Very much so."

"My mother told me that our gift is supposed to be used to right the wrongs of the past, and see that justice is done."

"By you."

She didn't like his doubtful tone, though she agreed with it. "I know. It's odd. But yes, by me."

He took a deep breath, then let it out. "Forgive me for acting as if you aren't capable—I'm sure you are—but it's just very . . ."

"Strange?"

"Sobering."

"An interesting word."

He led them back to their seats. "Think about it. The women in your family have been asked to expedite justice. That's a serious task that holds a great responsibility."

"Actually, I wouldn't *have* to expedite anything. Granny and Mother didn't."

He shook his head vehemently. "You have to. You have to finish what they started. Obviously it's important."

She agreed with him and felt the weight of the burden anew. She thought about the Ledger. Should that detail be saved for another time?

"And?" He pointed at her face. "I can tell there's more."

"I'm not sure I like how easily you read my face."

"So there *is* more."

She nodded. "Granny spoke of a very important book she called the Ledger. Ned was desperate to see it the day he died, thinking she'd chronicled bad things about his family."

"Had she?"

"I don't know for sure. I haven't seen the book. She asked Goosie to hide it."

"Where did Goosie hide it? Ask her where it is."

"She won't give it to me."

"Perhaps it's been lost."

"I don't think so."

"Maybe she's just being careful. You haven't been here that long. She barely knows you."

True. She drew the shawl over her shoulders though the air wasn't chilly. "Besides finding out the truth about Isaac Piedmont, I think there's something important to find out about Thomas. He talked about forgiveness and said, 'Forgive the hills.'"

"What does that mean?"

"I don't know.

"There are all sorts of hills around here. It makes little sense."

"I want to know more about his death. You told me he drowned in the river?"

"That's what I always heard. But again, it happened a long time ago."

"Eighteen years ago. His headstone says he died in 1860."

Harland was pensive. "Dr. Bevin was here then. He might know more."

"When will he be back?"

"It will be late. He went to check on a patient who lives far outside of town. He's staying for dinner there."

Patience, Justine. She wasn't sure if the admonition was from God or from her own knowledge of her shortcomings. Either way, what choice did she have?

Harland returned to his chair and absently traced the pattern of the brocade on its arm. "With the issue of both Isaac and Thomas relegated to a future time — pun intended — I must say I'm intrigued by your mother running off with Quinn."

"Until coming here I knew nothing about it. In fact, I find it rather shocking."

"It's out of character?"

Justine hedged. Once more the mother she knew and the Mavis she'd met were in conflict. "Who she was then is not who she became."

"Have you asked Quinn about it?"

She shivered when she thought about his invasion of her home and person just a few hours previous. "I have confronted him about it. I even asked him about his brother's death."

"In the past?"

"Yesterday."

His eyebrows rose. "How did he respond?"

Her arm was still sore from where he'd grabbed her, and her tailbone felt bruised. "He threatened me."

Harland let out a breath. "No one crosses Quinn."

Her stomach tightened. "Except me."

"You *can* cross him. But if you do, strange things tend to happen."

"Like what?"

He looked into the air, grabbing a memory. "For instance, the wheels of Mr. Steven's wagon were mysteriously loosened and it crashed after he accused Quinn of cheating him. He broke an arm."

It fit what she knew about him. "When Quinn left with my mother, Thomas said he'd stolen money from the store."

"From his own family's store?"

Justine shrugged.

"So he's a thief and a cheat," Harland said. "But he's more than that. The Miller's horse was found dead after Mr. Miller started a rumor that the feed from the general store was full of wood shavings."

She shivered.

"And then there's the Simmons' barn that burned down when he —"

"Dared to run against him. The ladies told me that one."

"Plus, more than one family has been evicted from their farm or home — some with cause, but many without."

"Frank Moore is in jail right now for nonpayment."

"Really?"

"Rachel came to me, upset about it."

He stood. "I could ask people to donate money to help with his rent, but —"

"I'm taking care of it."

"How?"

They'd gotten off track. "Be assured it is in process. The point is, Quinn bragged that he owned the entire town, but I didn't think he really did."

"He does. Or rather, his family does. We are all beholden to the Piedmonts. As you can tell, he wields supreme power. So don't cross him."

"I didn't directly accuse him of wrong doing. I just said I wanted answers to a few things — and assured him I would get those answers." *And I called him evil. . .*

Harland shook his head. "You are fearless, Justine. I will give you that."

"Fearless or foolish."

"That remains to be seen."

She was disheartened that Harland seemed to fear *for* her. "What about his father? I know he was angry after his brother Ned died and wanted to hang Granny, but now . . . he seems meek. Quiet."

"I think Quinn bullies him."

"More than that, I think Quinn might be hurting him," she said.

"Why do you say that?"

She told him about yesterday, seeing bruises when she'd helped Arnold and how Quinn had brusquely lifted him up to set him in his chair.

"He keeps to himself," Harland said. "We never see him around town other than on the porch. He's never complained to us."

"I wouldn't complain either if I was living with my abuser."

Harland looked pensive. "I'll check on him."

"That would be nice." Then she thought of a caveat. "Don't say I sent you."

"I know better."

Justine had an observation. "In a normal town the constable would intervene when people hurt each other."

"But not here because Quinn is the constable."

"It's not ethical," Justine said. "He can't be mayor *and* constable."

"He is."

"So Piedmont has no real measure of law?"

"None."

"My grandfather was the constable."

Harland shrugged. "The last honorable constable."

"Why don't people vote him out?"

"They need to preserve their barns and horses."

"That's not right."

"Indeed, it is not." He smiled. "Perhaps in addition to righting the wrongs of the past, you could work your justice in the here and now."

"I don't *work* justice."

"Not yet, but you will."

"You have far more confidence in me than I have in myself."

"God must be confident in you, to send you on this mission." His eyes lit up. "Your purpose is to bring about justice and your name is Justine. That cannot be a coincidence."

"Mother always said Granny was the one who named me. She knew our quest, so she chose the name?"

"Like it's your destiny."

Justine had never thought much about her name, only that she didn't particularly like it.

She pressed a finger between her eyes. "This is so daunting. What if I don't do the right thing? What if I make things worse?"

"You can do all things through God who gives you strength."

"Good. Because I don't feel very strong on my own."

"He wouldn't give you the task if you couldn't do it. He'll do it *with* you."

She sighed, then shook her head. "Do you work hard on developing your ability to encourage and reassure everyone you meet?"

His voice turned soft. "Not everyone. Only those who deserve it."

She didn't know what to say. She'd never met anyone so thoughtful and generous.

The clock on the mantel struck two. She stood. "I've kept you too long."

He stood with her. "Not at all. I'm very glad you've trusted me with your secret."

Which begged the question. "Do you believe me?"

He stared at the fireplace a moment. "Despite being a man of science, I am also a man of faith. I believe in miracles. I believe God acts in ways we can never imagine. 'The things which are impossible with men are possible with God.' Who am I to declare that He would never allow or never orchestrate what you've experienced?" He looked at Justine. "And though I haven't known you long, I have no reason not to believe you."

"And so you do?"

"And so I do."

Her relief was so great she wanted to rush into his arms. Instead, she held out her hand. "Thank you, Harland. For listening."

"I didn't solve anything."

"I'm not sure anything can be solved. Here."

"So you're going back again?"

"I have no choice."

"To what year?"

"I don't have a choice there either. I can only choose the person."

"So… who gets a visit?"

She had the Isaac issue to resolve—which would probably take her back into the last century. But also the issue of Thomas. He was such a kind man . . . "I'm going to try to go into Thomas's life again where I'll hopefully find some clues about who might have wanted to murder him."

"That's *if* he was murdered. He could have drowned by accident."

It came down to this: "I will be open to any and all information. I will let God lead me to the truth He wants revealed."

"A wise attitude. But be careful. If Thomas didn't die by accident, the killer will not take kindly to your meddling."

She managed a laugh. "Until coming to Piedmont, I can honestly say I never had an enemy. And now I have enemies in the present and will most likely gain enemies in the past. This is not the life I was raised for."

"Which was?"

"To be the wife of a wealthy New Yorker. A great hostess." She rolled her eyes. "A mother to many heirs."

"You can still do that."

She thought about Morris. Morris who missed her. Morris, who was currently solving a problem for her. "Perhaps. But not today."

**

When Justine started home from Harland's she saw Mabel walking toward her. The girl glanced toward Dr. Bevin's then at Justine.

She saw where I came from collided with *who cares?*

Justine took the initiative. "Good morning, Mabel."

"Are you feeling unwell?" Mabel said, glancing at the doctor's.

"Quite well. Fully well." She felt a wave of shame pass over her but didn't let it linger. "I won't keep you," she said, and continued her walk home.

Justine wanted to glance behind and see if Mabel stopped at Harland's, but kept her eyes straight ahead. She'd stirred things up quite enough.

She was pleased with her talk with Harland—more than pleased, flabbergasted. She had hoped he would be open to her fantastical talk of time travel and her mysterious gift but she had not expected him to be so accepting and encouraging. So much so, that she walked toward home with a spring in her step—and a plan. She'd eat an early supper with Goosie to fortify her for another trip into the past. One should not travel on an empty stomach. She giggled at the thought.

Just then she heard her name. "Justine!"

She stopped walking. No. It couldn't be.

Morris? He strode away from the train depot, with Teddy, the luggage boy, following behind, carrying two suitcases.

He's here. He plans to stay. I can't have him here.

Morris greeted her with an embrace and a kiss to her cheek. He smelled of cigars and bay rum cologne. "I have missed you," he said.

"And I, you." But had she?

He studied her a moment. "You look surprised to see me."

"I am."

"Did you not send me a telegraph at the bank yesterday, asking me to get you some money as soon as possible?"

"I did. But I thought you'd wire the money."

"I did one better. I brought it to you." He patted his breast pocket. "You never said what it was for."

She spotted many eyes assessing the stranger in town. "I'll get into that later. Come with me."

He looked up and down the street. "This is all there is?"

"It's a small town, Morris. You knew that."

"I was told I don't need to hire a carriage to get to your house."

There are no carriages to be hired. "It's just a block away."

"How . . . efficient." He drew her hand around his arm and began walking. "How was the funeral? Other than the telegram I haven't heard from you."

"The service was very nice. Simple but nice."

"How is the house situation progressing? When are you ridding yourself of the place?" He swept a hand from right to left, encompassing the general store and the church. "I suppose it will be difficult. I expect not many people want to move here. It is no more than a hamlet."

She felt her defenses rise. "Piedmont is a fine town. Do not disparage it."

He mocked her. "Well, pardon me."

She stopped in front of her house and turned him to face it. "This is the Tyler family home."

He studied it, then turned around and nodded at the cemetery. "Not a prime location."

Actually, very prime. "My family built this house. They have lived here for generations."

"Aren't you glad you got away?"

She pulled her hand free and felt harsh words rise. But she couldn't have this discussion on the street—or in front of Teddy who was waiting nearby with the luggage. "Come in."

They went inside, and Teddy set the suitcases by the door. Justine expected Morris to tip him something, but when he did not, she got a penny from a dish in the foyer. "Thank you, Teddy."

The boy nodded, then left with a less-than-friendly glance at Morris's back.

"Would you like a tour?" Justine asked.

He looked at the small parlor with clear distaste. "It won't take long."

He had to stoop to walk through the low hall that led to the kitchen. Once inside he said, "Low ceilings. And the floor tilts."

"The kitchen used to be a separate building. That was often the Colonial style—to keep the fire and smells of the cooking away from the house. At some time over the years an interior hall was built." She walked toward the stove. "Truly, I've never noticed any inadequacies."

"You *have* been away too long."

"Less than a week." *A lifetime.*

Goosie looked up from cutting bread. Justine stepped forward to make introductions. "Morris, this is Goosie Anders. Goosie, this is Morris Abernathy from New York City."

"Goosie. What an unusual name."

Goosie eyed him suspiciously. "Bread. More bread?"

"Yes, Goosie. Morris will be staying for dinner. He's spending the night."

Her gray eyebrows rose, colliding with her furrowed forehead.

"Goosie has been here most of her life, haven't you, Goosie?"

She nodded, then went back to cutting the bread.

As they retreated down the short hall to enter the dining room, Morris said, "A servant with no manners. How quaint."

"She's more than a servant. She belongs here more than I do."

"I agree with that statement."

He walked past the table and chairs, already set for the evening meal with pottery dishes. "A table for only six. And no china? Alas, I guess you wouldn't do much entertaining here."

"Just because people in Piedmont don't use Waterford goblets, Crown Derby china, and Wedgewood tea sets doesn't make their hospitality any less pleasurable."

"Have you entertained here?"

She felt a wave of annoyance. "As you know, I've only been here since Monday." She led him up the stairs to the extra bedroom. "You can stay in my grandparents' room."

He stuck his head in the doorway, then nodded to a wash stand. "There is no indoor plumbing?"

Her exasperation grew. "There's a privy out back."

"Perhaps I should stay at a hotel."

If only it were possible. "Piedmont has no hotel or lodging of any sort that I know of. I'm afraid you're stuck here for the night."

"I'm here for more than one night, Justine."

Panic stirred her stomach. "I appreciate the visit, Morris. Truly I do. But I have much work to do here and—"

"I can help you with that work." He ran a finger along the top of a dresser, glanced at it, then clasped his hands behind his back. "The sooner we are finished here, the sooner we can return to the city and resume our lives."

Her old life seemed as distant as the earth to the moon. "I'm not ready to go back yet. I . . ." She came up with a viable excuse. "I am mourning my mother. It comforts me to be in Piedmont, in the family home."

With a glance to her green dress, he said, "Which you—or your mother—haven't visited since you were ten? Those are your words, Justine. The place can't own that much of a sentimental draw."

"You're right. It didn't mean much to me before, but it does now."

"What changed?"

She had just spent the afternoon explaining all that had happened to her in great detail—to Harland. The thought of sharing any of those details with Morris seemed impossible. Even unwise.

She thought of Frank Moore, sitting in jail. Before she spent more time with Morris, she had some business to attend to. "May I have the money I asked for?"

"I suppose." He reached into an inner pocket and took out an envelope. "*Now* will you tell me what you need it for?"

"A friend needs help."

"You're going to give it away?"

She held the envelope behind her back. "It's my money, Morris. I am quite sure I can use it as I see fit, and I see fit to help a friend."

"But—"

"In fact, if you'll excuse me, I will attend to that situation while you freshen up."

"You're leaving me here?"

"I will be back before you know it."

Justine closed the door and hurried out of the house before he could find a reason to call her back. She rushed down the street to the Moore residence and knocked on the door. She heard Rachel yelling at the children inside. The door opened.

"Justine."

"Afternoon, Rachel."

The woman smoothed her hair. "I look a sight."

"You look fine." She handed her the envelope. "For you."

"What's this?"

"Open it."

Inside were ten five-dollar bills. "This is fifty dollars!"

"It is. Get Frank out of jail, then pay off the rent *and* your bill at the general store. Keep any leftover for the future."

Rachel pressed the money to her chest and her eyes filled with tears. "You said you'd help, but I never . . . this is so generous."

"I want to give you some breathing room."

She kissed Justine's cheek. "You've certainly done that."

Justine felt her face redden. "Go free your husband."

"I will. Right away." Rachel untied her apron. "We'll pay you back, Justine."

"No need. It's a gift."

Rachel squeezed her hand, then closed the door. Justine heard her call after the children to tell them the good news.

Justine hurried back home. Morris was waiting.

**

Justine and Morris shared an evening meal. Before the food came, Morris picked up a fork and looked at its back, most likely for the sterling mark. Upon finding none, he set it back in place, straightening it just-so. Goosie brought in a plate of roast beef, boiled potatoes, and fresh asparagus. He remarked on the uniqueness of food being served family-style, as if it was below him to handle the serving plate. Everything he said was like a pebble in her shoe, annoying, hurtful, and impossible to ignore. Had he always been this . . . snooty?

He shared the latest gossip from back home: who had dared skip a Vanderbilt party, who was facing scandal over some nefarious affair with an actress, and news about Faye, their shunned friend from the opera whose betrothal had been broken.

"She *is* going to the occasional party," Morris said. "I saw her just this week."

"Are you being nice to her? Please be nice to her Morris. She's suffered enough."

"I have spoken to her."

"Try to speak with her every time you see her. Compassion, Morris. Our set needs more compassion."

His eyebrows raised and lowered, and he quickly changed the subject to a new brougham carriage he planned to purchase.

Once the dinner was over, they moved to the porch and each claimed a rocking chair.

Morris sat with his feet placed flat on the floor, his hands gripping the armrests. He was like a clock, too tightly wound.

"Take a rock up and back, Morris. You may enjoy it. Up and back."

"I'm fine."

"At least take a breath. Enjoy the fresh air."

He didn't even make an attempt. "Your view here, Justine. A cemetery? How gauche. How morbid."

"Everyone dies, Morris. And I don't mind it at all. Most of my family is buried there. I find their presence. . . comforting." *And convenient.* "Would you like to go for a walk?"

"Where? There?"

"It's quite lovely. Look at the newly budded trees, the grasses, and the wildflowers."

He shuddered. "What do you do in this town? Watch the clouds go by?"

"The world might be a better place if more people took time to do just that."

"We're missing a dinner party at the Astor's tonight."

She'd forgotten all about it and was surprised to realize such occasions seemed as meaningless as spending the requisite two hours dressing for such a dinner. Or waiting around the house in the mornings with Mother to receive callers who would regale them with polite but pointless chit-chat. Her life in New York had been filled to the brim with

139

such trivialities. Such niceties of nothingness. Which *had* been very important to her.

So much had changed.

Everything had changed. She had changed.

Which brought her to a question.

"How do you feel about change, Morris?"

"As in a pocketful of . . .?"

Really? "Change as in altering and transforming."

"Altering and transforming what?"

Was he really so dense? "Life, Morris. Changing one's life, making alterations, being transformed."

He looked at her, incredulous. "Surely you're not talking about this place? Making changes by keeping the house and visiting here more often?"

Or living here. She looked straight ahead. "Perhaps."

He shook his head violently. "I will not subject us to odd weekends in the dregs of the country, Justine. It's ridiculous. We don't have time for it. My father's bank is in New York, my friends are in New York. My life is in New York." He looked at her. "Our life."

Surely that wasn't another proposal? Justine hoped not. For months she had longed for a romantic, heart-felt proposal. But now? Here? Like this?

He looked forward. "You don't answer."

"I didn't know an answer was required."

He stood. "What's gotten into you? I take time to visit you — to surprise you — and find you obsessed with this place, with things that don't . . ."

He couldn't find the words, but she could. "That don't have anything to do with my life in New York?"

"Exactly."

She rose and moved to him, touching his arm. "Haven't you ever gone to a place that made you forget your ordinary life?"

"My life is not ordinary."

"Usual then. Regular. Normal."

"I suppose," he said, giving a tug to his vest. "I do enjoy Newport and the sea. The soirees there are quite extraordinary."

They are merely extensions of society in New York. "But what about a place that is nothing like New York?"

"You speak of Europe? "He took a cigar from his breast pocket and held it under his nose, taking in its aroma. "The opera is enjoyable in Paris, and the dinner parties in London..."

She tossed her hands in the air. "Parties, opera, dinners? There is more to living than socializing at such staid and stodgy events."

He pointed the cigar at her. "I did not come here to be insulted."

She'd gone too far. "I'm sorry, but—"

His neck had reddened. "A week ago you were nose high in those very same functions—and I will venture to say, you were enjoying yourself."

"Perhaps, but—"

He rose. "I should have stayed home. I gave up the Astors for this?" He went inside.

"Morris . . ."

He strode up the stairs to his room. "Good night, Justine."

He slammed his door. She stared after him. Why had she been so confrontational? Disparaging their life in New York was unfair.

She returned to the porch overlooking the cemetery. She rocked up and back, waging an inner battle against who she was, and who she could be.

CHAPTER TEN

"Let's go in," Morris said, pointing at the door of the church. "Why are we waiting?"

"I was meeting a friend," Justine said as other people walked into the church. She was nervous about Morris meeting Harland. The two men could not be more different.

Her worries were interrupted when she saw a beaming Rachel Moore walking toward them. A man—Justine assumed to be Frank—carried their toddler while Rachel held the baby. The other two children skipped behind. They made a beeline for Justine.

Mr. Moore removed his hat. "Good day to you, Miss Braden. I'm Frank Moore."

"Nice to meet you, Mr. Moore." She turned to Morris. "This is my friend from New York, Morris Abernathy. Morris, this is Mr. and Mrs. Moore."

He gave them a cursory nod.

"Good morning," Rachel said before turning her attention back to Justine. "We want to thank you for all you did."

"We do," Frank said. "You saved our family and we are beholden to you."

With a quick glance around, Justine said quietly, "Quinn should never have put you in jail. It makes no sense whatsoever."

"You were in jail?" Morris said, too loudly.

Justine squeezed his arm. "Shush, Morris. It was merely a rent issue."

"That money I brought to you was to get him out of jail?"

Justine was mortified. She let go of his arm. "Excuse Mr. Abernathy. I was very happy to do it." She smiled at the children, "It's nice to see all of the children again. You have a lovely family. You should be very proud."

"We are," Frank said. "Again, thank you." With a curt nod to Morris, the family went into church.

Morris grabbed Justine's arm and whispered harshly. "You do *not* apologize for me."

She shook his hand free. "I *will* apologize for you if you are rude and unkind."

"I would never have brought you the money if I'd known it was to be used to get a man out of jail."

Justine noticed people looking at them. It couldn't be helped. She wasn't done with him yet. She faced him and glared, but kept her voice low. "It's not your money, Morris, it's mine. And I can use it however I please."

His eyebrows lifted. "That was uncalled for."

Not really. She was about to go into church—alone if necessary—when she spotted Harland walking toward them with Dr. Bevin. He smiled and waved.

She nodded in his direction and whispered to Morris, "This is the friend I have been waiting for. Behave yourself."

"I beg your pardon?"

Dr. Bevin offered a brief nod then went inside, while Harland came over to them. "Good morning to you, Justine."

"And to you," she said. She gestured toward Morris. "Harland, I would like you to meet a visitor from New York, Morris Abernathy. Morris, this is Harland Jennings. Dr. Jennings."

Harland extended his hand. "Nice to meet you, Mr. Abernathy. I've really enjoyed getting to know Miss Braden."

Morris said nothing, shook Harland's hand, then looked to the entrance and offered Justine his arm. "Shall we go in?"

She grieved his latest rudeness and gave Harland a *please forgive me* look. Morris led her inside and asked, "Where is your family's pew?"

"I have no idea where they usually sat. This is the first Sunday I've been here." She spotted Goosie. "There's Goosie. Let's join her."

"We most certainly will not," Morris said under his breath. He chose an empty pew on the opposite side.

When they were seated, Justine whispered, "We're all equal in the eyes of the Lord, Morris. We should have sat with Goosie. She's like family to me."

He ignored her and looked upward at the rafters and at the simple altar at the front. She knew what he was thinking. This was a far cry from the grandeur of St. Thomas's Church in

New York. She knew enough about God's character to know He didn't prefer one to the other.

Looking around it was clear the presence of Morris had caused a commotion among the congregation. Though news of his arrival had surely run its course through the town, seeing him sitting beside Justine — in his finely tailored three-piece suit and top hat — added fuel to gossip's fire. He did look handsome, and smelled decidedly of bay rum. His only visible flaw was a small nick on his cheek, no doubt occurring while shaving himself this morning.

One of the congregation who took special interest was Mabel Collier. She sat with her family across the aisle and stared at Morris a good ten seconds before acknowledging Justine with a glance before focusing on something past her.

Good day to you too, Mabel.

Justine looked around to realize the subject of Mabel's interest, as Harland slipped into Justine's pew from the other side. He kept his distance but gave her a wink. Morris noticed and gave her his "This-does-not-please-me" face.

The service began, hopefully giving offering her a chance to settle her nerves. To be seated between these two men — perhaps the only significant men in her life — made it nearly impossible to relax.

The words of Pastor Huggins broke through her angst. "'Come unto me, all ye that labour and are heavy laden, and I will give you rest.'"

Please help me find peace in all this. She took a deep breath, closing her eyes. The heaviness of her burdens — immediate and future — slipped off her shoulders. In their absence she took a deep breath that cleansed her from within. Then another.

Morris must have heard her, for he cleared his throat. She opened her eyes to his disparaging look.

But then she glanced to her other side and saw Harland take his own deep breath in and out. His smile helped her recapture her peace. He was an ally who knew the depth and complexity of her situation.

Morris knew none of it. To him, she was merely a young socialite from the city, slumming in a remote hamlet until he could take her back to civilization.

Which led to the question: Should she tell Morris about the recent complications in her life? 'Complications' was too harsh a word. For though she didn't fully embrace the gift, she recognized its extraordinary, miraculous nature. Would Morris?

He was a man of facts and figures, black and white. Up was never down. He would never understand her world where *now* could be experienced in 1878, 1857, 1826 or any other year in the past where God chose to send her.

And her mission to bring about justice? *That* would make him laugh. *Really, Justine? Why would you ever think you could — or should — do such a thing? That God would use you to do such a thing?*

None of it would make sense to him. He would deem the entire concept illogical and fantastical. As such, he would discount it as impossible. She remembered Harland's recent words: "The things which are impossible with men are possible with God."

She was depending on it.

**

Upon exiting the church Justine was approached by Quinn Piedmont. He was scowling.

"Why the sad face, Mr. Piedmont?" she asked.

"You should not meddle in my business."

The rent? "I don't know what you mean."

"I know what you did."

"Can I assume you are speaking of Mr. Moore's situation?"

"Of course."

"Do you know why I did it — besides helping good people through a hard time?"

"I don't care why."

"I helped them because it is absurd and un-Christian that you jail a man for a rent issue *while also* threatening to cut off their store credit for supplies, which leaves them no way to earn money."

"That's not my problem."

Justine felt her ire rise. "Debtors' prisons were banned forty years ago."

He shrugged, glanced at Morris, then glared at her. "I am the constable in this town, the mayor, and the landlord of every single property from the river to the mountains behind us. I will not listen to the opinions of a . . . a . . ."

Before Quinn could find the right label for her, Morris extended his hand. "Morris Abernathy. It's good to meet a man of authority."

Quinn nodded toward Morris. "Introduce us, Justine."

She noticed Harland turning up the road toward home and called after him. "Harland? Wait, please." He waited nearby. Only then did she introduce Morris and Quinn.

They shook hands. "What do you do in New York?" Quinn asked.

"I'm a banker."

"How do you know Justine?" Quinn asked.

Morris hesitated. Then seeing he had an audience of people leaving church, he said, "We are betrothed."

Justine gasped.

Quinn grinned. "Betrothed? Why didn't you tell me you were marrying a banker?"

Should she deny it? Ignore? Accept? It was the look on Harland's face that helped her make her decision. "I didn't tell you—or anyone—of our plans because there are no plans. We are not betrothed."

Morris's face reddened and his chin grew taut. "Justine. Do not say such a thing."

"It is you who shouldn't say it." She glanced at Harland. "For it isn't true."

Morris must have noticed the direction of her gaze, for he took her arm. "Nice to meet you, Mr. Piedmont. I must get Justine home. We have much work to do, dealing with her family's belongings."

Although she wanted to break free of his arm, with so many people nearby she let him begin to lead her across the street. And yet she would not completely leave on his terms. "Harland," she called out. "I'm so glad you're coming for Sunday supper. Goosie is making something special."

To his credit, Harland went along with her ruse and caught up with them. "I've been looking forward to it."

Morris squeezed her arm tighter as Harland offered her an encouraging smile. She'd apologize to him later for corralling him into taking on the role of her buffer.

**

For once in her life, Justine was glad Morris was a talker. During the Sunday meal he talked about their missed dinner at the Astors' and proceeded to chatter on about the other social events he had attended — without Justine — while she was gone.

"It doesn't seem you missed me too much," she said.

"You belong on my arm, Justine." He glanced at Harland — who he'd effectively ignored. "You should not have contradicted my mention of our betrothal."

"You should not have said we were betrothed when we are not."

"A technicality."

"Not to me."

"You know I've been waiting to get that promotion to vice president." For the first time, he looked at Harland. "My family owns a very successful bank in Manhattan."

"How nice."

Morris frowned. "What does your family do, Mr. Jennings?"

"Dr. Jennings," Justine corrected.

Morris shrugged.

Harland pushed his dessert plate to the side and clasped his hands on the table. "My family are the salt of the earth. They were farmers in Piedmont. My father fought in the war and lost an arm at Gettysburg. He made it home but died a few months later from complications."

"I'm so sorry," Justine said.

"Thank you. Mother had a cousin come live with us and help with the farm until a few years ago when she decided to move out west. She and my sisters now live in the City of Kansas."

"What an odd name for a town."

He cocked his head. "There's New York City, so why not—?"

She thought about it a moment. There *was* a difference. "New York City has the state's name first, then the 'city' part," she said. "'Kansas City' sounds better."

"Actually, it does. Anyway . . . my family moved there."

"They weren't successful here?"

"They were successful enough. They had roots here. But the situation changed and became . . . untenable. So they decided to start fresh."

An untenable situation? Justine gave him a questioning look.

"There was a bad harvest that year and Ma got behind on the rent. Quinn evicted them."

Justine sighed. "He has no mercy."

"None."

"It was business," Morris said. "We have to call in bank loans all the time."

He presented this as an attribute?

"Why didn't you go with them?" Justine asked Harland.

"Ma wouldn't let me. She knew how much I enjoyed my apprenticeship under Dr. Bevin and that I had plans to go to Boston to study to become a doctor in my own right."

"It's wonderful she let you stay behind."

"She's a wonderful woman." He smiled. "If you have need of medical attention while you are in Piedmont, Mr. Abernathy, please do not hesitate to stop by."

Morris shook his head. "I have a personal physician in New York."

"Then let's hope you don't need medical attention here."

Morris studied him the briefest moment, then took a drink. "I like that Quinn fellow. Now there's a man with a pedigree."

"I thought you'd deemed Piedmont 'no more than a hamlet,'" Justine said.

"Hamlet or not, his family founded the town. He's the mayor and a businessman. He's also the law."

"Stay away from him," Justine said.

"Why?"

"He's cruel and can't be trusted."

He scoffed. "You sound like a child. Quinn Piedmont is the type of man you *should* associate with."

"Not some doctor?" Harland asked.

"I did not mean to disparage your position. Doctor."

He most certainly had. Justine knew Morris's ways. Belittling others was a hobby he'd finely honed. Suddenly, she wondered how she'd ever been able to tolerate him. He'd always been like this. Why hadn't it really bothered her before now?

Because I've changed.

Morris set his fork across his plate and pushed the vanilla cake aside. "Enough chittery-chatter. I need to return to New York on the afternoon train. I expect you to come with me, Justine. Enough dallying here."

"I am not dallying. I am working."

"At what? If you wish to keep renting the house—though I can't imagine why you would want to do such a thing—then keep it. It's gone on decades without your mother's involvement, it can go on decades more without yours. Its monetary outlay does not affect your wealth. In the larger scheme, it is a triviality. The point being, it's time to return to your old life with your friends. And myself, of course."

The arrogance and flippancy of his opinion was a slap to her soul. With a flash Justine saw the situation clearly. She shoved back her chair and stood. The men immediately stood with her.

"So you're ready to leave now?" Morris said. "Capital. My suitcases are already packed."

"Go get them," she said. She was surprised at the evenness of her voice.

He left the dining room and his footfalls could be heard on the stairs.

"What are you doing?" Harland asked her quietly.

She smiled with utter certainty and raised a finger, signaling he should wait and see. When she heard Morris's feet descending the stairs, she met him in the foyer.

He set his luggage on the floor. "Are you going to have your things sent after you?"

She handed him his hat and overcoat without saying a word.

"Justine?"

She opened the door and moved his suitcases to the porch.

When she came back inside he was staring at her. "What's going on?"

"I'm cleaning house."

"What do you mean by that?"

She felt a strength well up inside her, giving her a boldness that hinted of a great victory. "Good bye, Morris."

"Good bye?"

"Go back to New York."

He blinked twice. "When will you return?"

"I won't."

A groove appeared between his eyebrows. "Surely you're not staying here."

"Surely, I am."

He glanced at Harland who stood nearby. "Does this have something to do with him?"

She shook her head. "This has everything to do with *me*. At this moment I am where I belong—perhaps where I've always belonged. I have purpose here. I have a job to do."

"Job?" He laughed.

She stared at him, setting her jaw as he had earlier set his.

Morris's eyes flit this way and that, as he tried to grasp what was happening.

She leaned forward and kissed him on the cheek. "I wish you well, Morris."

"This makes no sense. You're being ridiculous."

"It makes perfect sense. To me. Go."

Morris stepped through the doorway, placed his hat upon his head, tilted it just so, then gave her one last look before picking up his suitcases and walking down the steps to the road. He turned left toward the depot. She enjoyed the fact he was carrying his own luggage.

Justine closed the door behind him. The click of the lock echoed in her mind and added finality to the moment. *What did I just do?*

"Are you all right?" Harland asked.

She stood with one hand on the door and tried to keep her breathing steady. "I think so."

"Do you want to go after him? The train doesn't come for—"

"No." She was reassured by the certainty of her answer. She let her hand fall away, but found it shaking. "I need to sit down."

They moved into the parlor and shared the settee. Justine appreciated how Harland let her sit in silence. She let out a breath she hadn't realized she'd been holding. "To think I was going to marry him."

"But you said you weren't betrothed."

"I was eager for him *to* propose." She added under her breath, "Though now I wonder why."

Harland shook his head. "He is not good enough for you. And . . . he doesn't suit you."

With total clarity Justine replayed the year they'd spent courting. Yes, Morris had been charming and she'd attended many a soiree or social event on his arm. He was generous with gifts too. For her twentieth birthday he'd given her a beautiful sapphire bracelet. She cringed when she realized she had been bought so easily, that baubles and attention had caused her to ignore his impatience, condescending ways, their lack of meaningful conversation, his selfishness and lack of charity... Plus, there was his insincere expression of sympathy for her mother's death that had been tinged with greed.

She looked at Harland's gentle eyes. "Why was I so blind?"

"Do you love him? Love often blinds us to truth."

She smoothed her hands against her skirt. "In hindsight I realize no. I don't. Didn't."

"Then why did you stay with him?"

The image of her parents came to mind. "Our fathers were in business together. And after Father died, Mother took up the cause."

"It was an arranged match?"

She thought of her friends. "It is not unusual in our set."

"So there must be an external benefit to a match? Money? Status?"

His words nudged her to standing. "I don't appreciate your tone, Harland."

He stood beside her. "Forgive me. It's not my place to disparage the ways of your friends and family."

Even though they are flawed. Her anger left her. "I'm not implying your words are wrong, but it's hard to hear them said aloud, so succinctly."

He nodded and motioned to the settee. They both returned to their places.

"I'm glad you're staying," he said.

"I didn't know I was until he pressured me."

"Do you miss New York?"

"In some ways, most certainly."

"How so?"

"There is always something to do."

He smiled. "So traveling back in time is not enough *to do*?"

She returned his smile but had a serious thought. "I wonder if my gift can be used anywhere, in any cemetery."

"If so, your task could be never-ending."

The thought of traveling back in time beyond Piedmont overwhelmed. "I can't think about that now. I have to finish what I started here."

"Which involves . . . what next?"

"She thought a moment, weighed her mental and physical stamina, and found them lacking. "I should travel back into Thomas' life—if I'm able."

"Why wouldn't you be able?"

"I tried before, but nothing happened."

"That's odd."

"It is, but . . ." She took a cleansing breath. "I have to try again. But not immediately. I need to recover from this crisis in the here and now before I seek out another crisis in the past."

"A wise choice."

They sat in silence — something Morris never appreciated. She didn't feel compelled to speak, to make small talk, or be polite. Once again, Harland knew silence was what she needed.

She was surprised how little Morris' exit affected her. Shouldn't she be in tears, mourning the loss? Was she so cold she could send him away and move on to the next to-do in her life with little to mark the transition? She took a moment to pray. *Father, I feel such peace about it. Does that mean it was the right decision?*

At that moment the mantel clock chimed the half-hour. She laughed.

"What's so funny?" Harland asked.

God. She didn't say it aloud, but let a new idea fully form. "I think what comes next is finding the Ledger. Somehow it is intertwined with my travels, but I'll never know how until Goosie gives it to me."

"We've already asked. Are you sure she still has it?"

Justine remembered how adamant Goosie had been when she'd made inquiries, something she wouldn't do if it didn't exist. "I believe she does."

Goosie came into the room. "Fancy man gone?"

What an appropriate description. "Yes, Morris is gone. For good."

Goosie's gray eyebrows rose. Then she nodded at Justine. "Stay?" She looked expectant, even eager.

"For now. It seems clear that in New York I was rich in money, but poor in people."

"But here in Piedmont?" Harland asked.

She looked at him. And Goosie. Two people who had touched her heart in a very short time. "I'm staying."

Goosie beamed.

Feeling the bond between them solidify, Justine took Goosie's hand and spoke softly, but with urgency in her voice.

"I really need you to give me Granny's Ledger so I can properly continue her work. Please, Goosie?"

The old woman studied Justine's eyes a long moment. Then she nodded once and went to the fireplace. She stooped down with a groan and shoved the andirons holding the wood back six inches. She pointed to an ash-covered stone in the floor of the fireplace. "Knife."

Harland pulled a pocket knife from his pocket and displayed the blade. Goosie moved aside. Harland brushed the ash away. "The grout is missing on one side." He pressed the knife in the gap until the edge of the thin stone was lifted. He removed it and looked inside. Then he stood. "There it is! Justine, you do the honors."

She peered down at the space beneath the stone to see a small black-bound book. She plucked it from its hiding place and held it reverently. "I can't believe I finally have it." She hugged Goosie. "Thank you."

"Open it," Harland said.

Goosie began to leave, but Justine said, "Stay, please. You're a huge part of this. You've been a part of this since the beginning."

Goosie stood nearby and watched as Justine untied the black ribbon that held the book closed. The pages were delicate and yellowed, and filled with the neat cursive of more than one hand.

She opened to the first page and read the heading. "'Wisdom Gathered by Siobhan O'Dea.'"

"Does it say a year?" Harland asked.

"Not in the heading, but the first entry is dated 1586 and gives the name, Angus Fitzmorris: 'Abide by the wisdom of the past.'" Justine looked up. "That is entirely appropriate for this moment."

"Nearly three hundred years later," Harland said. "Read another one."

She paged through until the handwriting changed. "Wisdom Gathered by Hester Doogan.' Her first entry is from 1607 with the name Leonardina Teague. 'Family ties bind beyond death.'"

"Another timeless truth."

As Justine carefully turned the pages, a note fell out. She opened it and gasped. "It's to me from Granny. It's dated a few weeks before she died."

"What does it say?" Harland asked.

Justine's heart beat in her throat as she read it aloud. "'Dear Jussie, I am happy that Goosie has given you this letter, for it means you received the letter I wrote for you on your twentieth birthday.'"

"You got a letter?" Harland asked.

"I did. Back in New York." She turned her attention to the note. "'I die with grief in my heart that your mother refused our gift. Yet I am far from blameless. But you, dear girl . . . please continue our family's work in a way your mother and I could not. I wanted to bring down the Piedmonts, but after your grandfather saved me from the noose and married me, he forbade me from using the gift. Plus, there is another reason I did not fulfill my duty. When I saw Thomas grow into a good man, I couldn't hurt him with the shame of his grandfather's crime—whatever it is. Then after Thomas died, I grew tired, and perhaps complacent. Be strong and courageous for me, Justine, my champion of justice. Do your best to bring out the truth of the ages. Set it free, Jussie! I love you dearly. Love, Granny.'"

Justine fell into a chair. "This is too much. I'm neither strong nor courageous."

"I think you are," Harland said.

She shook her head. "I'm not an adventurous person who enjoys mysteries or the unknown. I liked my life in New York. I liked knowing what each day would bring. I don't want to be responsible for deciphering the past. It's not fair."

She felt Goosie and Harland's eyes and was ashamed for her weakness. But she couldn't take any of it back.

Harland pointed to the Ledger. "Read some more. Maybe the words will help you understand."

Justine perused the entries and chose a few to share. "Fanny Lees notes this from 1627: 'Marry only for love.'" She looked up. "As if it's meant for me."

Goosie nodded vigorously and pointed to the door where Morris had left. Justine felt a wave of certainty that telling Morris to leave had saved her from future pain.

Then she continued. "Caisa McCraig from 1530 shares that 'Bitterness kills.' Seamus Grady in 1700 says, 'God provides.'" She kept turning the pages. "There are scores of others, calling out from the past, offering wisdom to all who come after: *Avoid foolishness, Embrace the work, Trust and obey, Love Jesus.* . ." She closed it. "I thought the Ledger would be a chronicle of events like a diary, but instead it's a chronicle of wisdom," Justine said. "It's full of life lines."

"Oooh," Goosie said.

"You like that term?"

She nodded.

"What's the last entry?" Harland asked.

"It's from Winifred Holloran Tyler."

"Your grandmother."

"It's dated 1801 and is quoting Joshua Holloran. I think he was her father. He says, 'Look beyond what you see.'"

"That's cryptic."

It was. "Did my great-grandfather know something fishy about Isaac Piedmont? I assume they knew each other."

"Maybe. There's no way to know," Harland said.

"Actually, there *might* be a way to know." She stroked the book, trying to focus on the wisdom inside. "This ledger . . . It's as though the barriers of time have faded and all of mankind is linked."

"You are the link, Justine."

She shivered at the immensity of it. Yet the poignant words of people who had long ago passed away had touched her deeply. "I don't want to do anything with all this and yet I can't ignore it."

"You could. Your mother and grandmother did."

She *did* have an out. She could be on the afternoon train and never return to Piedmont. She could take up her old life and relax in its . . . its mediocrity. Its insignificance.

Discover your gift. Discover your purpose, Jussie.

She let the words from Granny's letter sink into her pores. "I have to do it. Somehow I *will* do it." Suddenly, she remembered Ned yelling at Granny about some book, warning her not to write in it. She turned to Goosie. "Was Ned afraid of this book? It's a book of wisdom. Did he think it was a diary?"

Goosie nodded.

"How ironic Ned was afraid of being damned by a book that only contained wise sayings."

"Proving him unwise," Harland said.

"Thank you for showing me this, Goosie. I want to read all of it. It will inspire me and help me get to know my family better."

"It's a wonderful legacy," Harland said.

Oddly, Goosie's forehead furrowed, then she sighed deeply.

"What's wrong?" Justine asked.

Goosie finally said, "You need to add your wisdom to the book. Wisdom gathered in the past. And the present."

Justine and Harland stared at her, not for the content of her words, but for her use of full sentences. "What did you say?"

"I said you must continue to go into the past and bring back the wisdom you find there. As often as it takes."

"You're speaking normally."

She blinked a few times. "I trust you now."

Justine was incredulous. "But . . . why did you speak so oddly?"

Goosie sat down, her hands keeping each other company. "I wanted to tell you before but with you planning to go back to New York I didn't think there was reason to — nor that it was wise. But now that Mr. Abernathy is out of your life — good riddance. Now that you're staying here . . ." She took a breath. "I'm ready to help you in any way you need me to help."

It was like a door had been opened. "The ladies in the quilting group said you used to be very talkative, very involved. Why did you change?"

"When you obviously *can* talk," Harland added.

Goosie looked toward the window. Justine gave her a moment to gather her thoughts.

Finally, she said, "Once your grandmother died, I was here alone. Not speaking was my protection against the Piedmonts and their prodding." She shuddered. "Quinn scares me."

"Me too," Justine said.

"He's a bully," Harland said. "Everyone tries to stay out of his way."

Goosie continued. "He kept wanting to evict me, and even came inside a few times, saying he was the landlord and had a right to search the place."

"*He* was looking for the Ledger?"

"He was. His father must have told him it was something to be feared. He kept asking me about 'the book', even grabbing me and shaking me, demanding to know where it was. That's the main reason it was best for me to play dumb."

Justine hated the thought that dear Goosie had endured such abuse. "The first time I met Quinn, he grumbled about the rent we pay for the house, saying it was going to be raised now that I was here." Then she thought of something else. "Why did Mother pay the rent all those years? She never came back after Granny died."

"Sentiment was part of it, I suppose," Goosie said. "And she did it for me. This is basically the only home I've ever known."

It was nice to hear something positive about her mother. "Quinn said he couldn't get a hold of her and you wouldn't tell him where she was."

Goosie nodded. "Your mother sent me money to pay the rent and get supplies. I went over to Haverhill to cash the check because she made me promise not to ever let Quinn know where she was. If he found out the location of the bank she used, it would give it away."

Morris's bank.

"I suppose I could have packed up what little I had and moved away. But I'm too old. I've lived here since I was ten. Besides, I didn't want Quinn to win."

"Good for you," Harland said. "I'm sure it wasn't easy."

Goosie shuddered. "I've been praying God would bring you here. I knew you were nearly twenty. I prayed you'd feel a sense of duty and responsibility to take over where your grandmother left off."

Harland leaned forward in his chair. "So you truly think there's something serious in the past, something that would fall badly on Quinn and his family?"

"I do. But I know very little."

Justine had a different question. "Do you know more about why Mother ran off with him?"

She flipped a hand. "A whim. A chance to get away."

"She told me as much." Justine remembered Mavis telling her about her plan. "It could be that simple. She was never a small-town girl. She wanted adventure."

"Quinn would give her that," Harland said.

Goosie nodded. "Mavis was a fickle one, out for herself more than others. Never thinking things through."

Justine found it interesting that the mother she knew hadn't changed much from the girl Goosie spoke about.

Goosie continued. "Soon after they ran off together Quinn came back alone."

"So she rejected him?" Harland asked.

Goosie shrugged.

"Do you know what happened between them in New York?" Justine asked.

"The next time we heard from her, she'd fallen in love with your father, had eloped. Later in the year, she had you."

"So she stayed in New York. But she *did* come back here when I was little."

"She came back for Thomas's funeral, and after that a few times because your grandmother insisted on seeing you."

Harland shook his head. "She must have felt safe then, being happily married and a mother. Quinn couldn't bother her anymore."

"Quinn can bother anyone if he chooses, without logical reason," Goosie said.

Justine looked down at the book of life lines. So much wisdom, chronicled by so many women of her family.

Goosie interrupted. "If nothing else, Quinn has Thomas's death to atone for."

Justine was taken aback. "Quinn killed him?"

"I've always thought so. Winnie thought so. A lot of people thought so."

"Then why wasn't he held accountable?"

"There wasn't any proof. Drownings are hard to prove. And nobody around here would dare go against Quinn or they'd find the rent raised or find themselves evicted."

Justine felt the weight of duty. Justice was up to her. She ran a hand over the book.

Goosie noticed her movement. "Quinn, looking for the book . . . they still think we have something written up against their family."

"But we don't, do we?"

"There's nothing to write up—nothing we really know. Winnie went back a few times and said that Isaac Piedmont wasn't Isaac but no other details. Then Ned died and Arnold tried to get her hanged. Ross saved her. She never went back after that, but Arnold and Quinn must've thought she did. I'm thinking Mavis must have told Quinn more about the gift. Maybe that's one reason he got her to run away with him. To charm her into telling family secrets."

"She only went back the one time."

"But he'd expect her to go back more—or knew she *could* if she wanted to."

Harland walked to the window. "But what does something that happened to Quinn's grandfather matter to the Piedmonts now? Even if Isaac did something wrong, it's not Quinn's fault. Or Arnold's."

"That's what I told Winnie," Goosie said. "And we wouldn't have thought about it for another minute if not for Quinn's unnatural interest in Winnie and the book. That's why I decided it was best they believed I couldn't communicate, so they wouldn't press me for information that was none of their business."

Justine began to laugh. "It was a brilliant idea. But I'm so glad you can speak. There's so much I need to know."

Goosie took a deep breath, in and out. "I've been silent so long—ten years. It's hard to go back to speaking. In fact, I'd like my ability to remain between us. I will speak to the two of you. But to the rest . . ." She nodded toward town. "Maybe someday, but not yet."

"Your secret is safe with me."

"And me, "Harland said.

Justine added, "As the secret of my travels are safe with you?"

Goosie crossed her heart and Harland followed suit.

Justine glanced through the rest of the book. "This is an amazing piece of history."

"Priceless," Goosie said. "Wisdom you can add to."

"I don't know anything especially wise."

"Didn't anyone in the past share anything that inspired you, stuck with you?"

Justine stood and studied the air between them. Then she remembered something Granny had told her back in 1857. "Granny said to stand up for what is right, no matter the cost."

"There you go," Goosie said. "Write that in the Ledger and note when and who said it, just like the others did."

She returned to her seat, needing the chair's strength to supplement her own. "What a day this has been. Closing the door on one life and opening it to another." She looked at Goosie. "I have so many questions."

Goosie took a seat. "Ask."

"If Granny was supposed to right this wrong in 1826 and didn't, that means whatever injustice we're supposed to discover has gone on for 52 years past the proper time of its reckoning."

"All the more reason for you to make it right."

She felt a heaviness in her chest. "I don't know if I'm up to it."

"You are," Harland said.

Goosie nodded. "You are. I've been around four generations of your family. You are the strongest of the lot."

Justine was heartened by her confidence. "I hope so. Let's go back to what you know about Isaac Piedmont not being Isaac Piedmont?"

"I don't know any more than you do. When Winnie came back the day Ned died, she was sorely shaken to the core about what she'd seen, but then was consumed with Ned's death and her being blamed. Ross saved her before we had a chance to talk. He made her promise not to speak of it and to leave the past alone."

"But surely she told someone."

"Not that I know of. And if she didn't speak to me or Ross, she wouldn't speak to anyone."

"How frustrating to have knowledge but not be able to share it or use it," Harland said.

Goosie took out a handkerchief and blew her nose. "I don't think she knew that much, more of a notion than a knowing."

"So maybe there's nothing amiss at all."

"And yet you are here. The gift is active," Harland said. "There must be something to it."

"I agree," Goosie said. "Then there's Thomas. Such a nice man he was. Polite, kind, a good preacher, everything his brother is not."

"Can you tell me any more about his death?"

"Not much to say. He went missing and they found his torn coat washed up on the shore down river. His hat in another place."

"But no body?"

"Who knows how far it could have gone. There are tributaries galore. The Connecticut River runs 400 miles. Nobody ever reported it. Or even if they did find him, they wouldn't know who he was."

"Any sign of a struggle on shore?"

"Not that I know of."

"You need to find out," Harland said. "When are you going back again?"

She was fully exhausted. "Tomorrow. I still need to sort through my thoughts."

"Are you going to visit Isaac's time or Thomas's?"

She didn't need to think about it. "Thomas's death needs to be explored first. Isaac's mystery can wait a little while longer."

One mystery at a time.

**

Justine got ready for bed. She pulled out a drawer in a dresser to get her nightgown, and suddenly thought about clothes and her lack thereof.

She opened the other drawers and found underthings and neatly folded blouses, and even some skirts. Old clothes. Past clothes.

Past clothes?

She ran to the hall and called, "Goosie! Come here, please."

Goosie came out of her room in a nightgown, tucking her hair into a nightcap. "What's wrong?"

"Nothing's wrong, but I realized I need a travel bag."

"What do you mean?"

Justine retrieved a small carpetbag from under the bed. "When I went back into Mother's life, it was winter. I wasn't prepared. My clothes were wrong, and I only had Granny's shawl. In 1826 it was spring. Which means I never know into which year or season time will take me. I need to be better prepared."

Goosie's forehead "Will a bag go with you into the past?"

Justine had thought about this. "My clothes do. What I'm wearing here, I'm wearing there. So I assume if I'm holding it, it will go with me." She thought of another point. "When I suddenly show up in Piedmont, in another time, I'm a stranger. It's logical for me to be carrying a bag. In fact, it's illogical for me not to have one."

Goosie stood. "Then let's get one packed."

Justine laughed at her enthusiasm and pulled her into an embrace. "I'm so glad you're here with me, talking to me."

"Me too, Jussie." She let go. "What year are you going back to?"

"That's the thing. I don't really know. I have the parameters created by the birth and death dates of the person's life, but other than that, I don't know." She got out her fashion scrap book and opened it to the 1850s, the era of Thomas's adulthood.

Goosie studied it. "I remember this time, but don't remember the full hoops that are shown here."

"Probably because these are based on fashion plates for wealthy women and their dress designers. I remember helping Mother dress to leave for New York in 1857. She had a lesser crinoline. By some miracle is something like that still around?"

"She only had the one."

"Did she leave some dresses behind?"

Goosie smiled. "Your grandmother told me to leave Mavis's things alone. So I did. I have. All these years." She opened a trunk and picked out a sage-green skirt that Goosie deemed Mavis's favorite, and a matching buttoned bodice with long sleeves cuffed at the wrist. "Try it on."

Justine was relieved to find it fit.

"As if it was yours," Goosie said. "God's provision."

"It seems so." At least she had something to wear on her journey.

Goosie dug through a drawer and found what she was looking for. "Here's a white collar you can tuck in around the neck."

The white was a nice addition against the deep color. "Are there any stray petticoats around?"

Goosie took out a petticoat with ruffled layers.

With Goosie's help, the petticoat was added beneath the skirt. Justine swayed back and forth. "This is much better than the current fashion of flat in front and a bustle in back."

"I always thought so." Goosie pulled an apron from the trunk. "This was a nice addition. I remember tatting the bottom edge to make it nice."

Justine added it to her ensemble. "Would I wear the apron in public, or just at home?"

"More home, than out. But if you were just going to the general store, you could wear it. But not to church."

Justine smiled. "Not to church. Duly noted."

Goosie dug deeper in the trunk and came up with a slim dress of pale green. "Ooh. I remember this one. But it's earlier. About—"

"The early 1800s, I believe." Justine took the dress and examined it. "To think I spent my allowance buying vintage dresses, when Granny had a trunk full."

"They're yours now. If you dig deeper, you'll find your great-grandmother's clothes. Those Holloran women didn't like to throw out."

"Which is to my advantage."

Goosie retrieved a bonnet. "This would work."

The wide-brimmed bonnet was a bit smashed, and the silk flowers crushed. "If we remove the flowers and press the brim, it should work. And I could use Granny's shawl if it's chilly."

"That, you could," Goosie said.

Justine remembered the cold of January during her 1857 visit. "But if it's winter?"

Goosie dug deeper. "Here's a capelet that shouldn't take up much room." She unfolded a wool buttoned cape that covered the shoulders and arms to the elbow. "Again, a good press will do wonders. And there's gloves too." She glanced at Justine's bare feet. "Your boots are good enough. They're . . ."

"Timeless."

They exchanged a smile. Then Justine put a hand to her mouth, thinking of all contingencies. "I could pack my nightgown, a set of drawers, stockings, a brush, hair pins . . ."

"Toothbrush."

"With tooth polish if I am allowed to stay overnight."

"You only stayed over the one time, yes?"

"With Mother. Yes. The other time I came back rather quickly."

"So you don't know how long you'll be."

"I don't. I guess I'm allowed to stay as long as it takes for me to understand *why* I'm there."

"Only God knows."

"I'm at His beck and call."

"You're on His time table." Goosie laughed. "The Creator of time is in charge."

Justine found this comforting, if not incredible.

She noticed her sketchbook close by and packed it, along with some pencils. They might come in handy.

Goosie took up the capelet and the bonnet. "Let me press these. You'll be wanting to go first thing in the morning, yes?"

"Yes. Thank you for your help."

Goosie paused at the door. "I thank you for coming here, Jussie. You've brought excitement and purpose back into this old life. Now, to bed with you."

Justine got in bed, pulling the covers into place. She felt good about the travel bag and was pleased Goosie had found some pleasure in her presence.

The feeling was mutual.

Her thoughts sped back to the events of the day: Kicking Morris out, discovering the ledger, finding out Goosie could talk . . .

She turned over and hugged a pillow, letting out a soft laugh. "You certainly know how to fill a day, Lord."

CHAPTER ELEVEN

As the clock struck one in the morning, Justine threw the covers off. "This is ridiculous."

She'd tried to sleep, but the task of traveling back into Thomas's life kept her thoughts in a whirl. She may as well go now.

She quickly got dressed in the green outfit and petticoat she had chosen with Goosie. She brushed her hair into a low bun and collected her travel bag. She hoped they'd thought of every contingency but knew they probably hadn't. At least she was more prepared this time than the last.

Justine paused a minute to leave a note for Goosie: *Gone traveling. Be back soon.*

She put on the bonnet and Granny's shawl and tiptoed downstairs. She spotted a piece of paper that someone must have shoved under the door. She held it to the moonlight and read: *Stay away from Harland. He's taken.*

It wasn't signed but there was only one person who would have sent it: Mabel.

Justine didn't have time to ponder the girl's naiveté, acting like Justine wouldn't know who sent it? Harland had said the two of them were friends, only friends. Apparently, he needed to make Mabel understand his full opinion on the matter. Yet there was a hint of malice in the note, an unwritten *or else.*

Dealing with Mabel's jealousy would have to wait. She slipped the note into a pocket, left the house, and ran across the road to the cemetery.

It was eerie being there at night. Alone. Simeon's shack was dark. *Of course it is. The entire town is sleeping. As you should be.* Even the moonlight was hiding. She heard the howl of coyotes in the distance and the hoot of an owl close by.

Luckily she knew Thomas's headstone was near her mother's. She walked carefully around the other stones, only tripping once. *There you are.* She knelt down, held the carpet bag with one hand, and was about to touch the letters of his name with the other, when she paused.

Since she was "going traveling" again, and would probably do so many times, she needed to create a ritual. A tradition. She would feel better if she prefaced each bit of travel with a prayer. She bowed her head. "Father, protect me from harm as I travel back in time to right the wrongs of the past. Give me wisdom and strength to accomplish this task You have set before me. Amen."

Fueled by the prayer, Justine open her eyes and touched the cold letters of his name. *Thomas E. Piedmont.*

Nothing happened. Just like before.

She let out a breath and grabbed a new one. "What's going on? Why won't You let me go back into his life?" she whispered. "If not this, what?" She glanced across the dark cemetery and thought about going into Isaac's life, quickly discarding the notion. She was dressed for the 1850s or 60s. Not the 1790s. Who else had died around this time? Maybe she could see Thomas while in their life.

Suddenly she remembered Harland's mention of his father dying from his war wounds. The War Between the States was fought just after Thomas's death in 1860.

"Close enough," Justine said.

But where was Mr. Jennings buried?

She walked through the rows of headstones. *If You want me to use Mr. Jennings's headstone, help me find it.* A few moments later the moon broke through the clouds and illuminated the cemetery. She took it as a heavenly sign and kept searching before she lost the light.

And there it was: Private Jesse T. Jennings. Born July 30, 1830 - Died December 1, 1863. Thirty-three years old. Such a tragedy. So many dead soldiers.

She knelt before the headstone and took a moment to collect herself. "Lord, you said no to using Thomas's headstone, will You let me use this one?"

She traced his name and was relieved when the inner wind took her away. When she opened her eyes, she was outside Dr. Bevin's office. A boy of about five or six rushed out, nearly colliding with her. "Can you help, lady? Doc says we need help."

She gripped her travel bag and took a deep breath. "Of course."

How could she say no?

**

Justine followed the boy into Dr. Bevin's office — which looked much as it did in 1878. A younger Arnold Piedmont sat on the examination bed. He moaned as he supported his left arm with his right hand while Dr. Bevin examined the shoulder area.

"This lady said she'd help," the boy said.

The doctor looked up. "Are you squeamish?"

In her sheltered life . . . "I don't think so. How can I help?"

"Stand in front of Mr. Piedmont, facing him."

She set her carpet bag against the wall, stood in front of Arnold, and offered him a smile.

He tried to smile back, but his features were captive to the pain.

"What now?" she asked.

"Sing something."

"What?"

"It's important the patient is relaxed while I get his arm back in its socket. Arnold, you look at the pretty lady and focus on her." Dr. Bevin nodded encouragement to Justine. "Go on now."

She cleared her throat and began singing the first song that came to mind. "'My Jesus, I love Thee, I know Thou art mine. For Thee all the follies of sin I resign . . .'"

Dr. Bevin moved the arm down against Arnold's side.

Justine smiled and as she continued to sing, the boy sang with her. "'My gracious Redeemer, my Savior art Thou. If ever I loved Thee, my Jesus, 'tis . . .'"

Then suddenly, with a heave, a shove, and a scream, it was done.

Everyone took a breath.

"You made it through, Arnold," Dr. Bevin said.

He took a few deep breaths. "With the help of the pretty lady's singing."

"I sang too!" the boy said.

"Yes, you did. Now get me that cloth over there and we'll make Arnold a sling."

Justine helped with the sling, and in no time Arnold was standing.

"It's going to be sore for a while. You tell Quinn you can't do any lifting."

"He won't like that."

Dr. Bevin looked him straight in the eyes. "Tell him I said so."

"Won't matter."

"Want me to come back to the store with you?"

Arnold shook his head. "I'll be all right. Thomas will make sure of it."

Justine perked up at the name Thomas. *It has to be before 1860 when he died.*

"Where is Thomas, may I ask?" she said.

The two men exchanged a look. Then Dr. Bevin said, "Though I appreciate the help . . . who are you, miss?"

Without knowing the year, she didn't know if it was safe to use her real name. She'd been born in 1857 and *had* visited her grandparents in Piedmont. Though she'd used her real name while visiting 1857, it had been safe to do so because she hadn't been born yet, but now . . .

She chose a random name.

"I'm Susan Miller, a distant relative of the Tylers."

"They'll be glad to see you. Winnie gets pretty lonely with her daughter and granddaughter off in New York City."

The fact confirmed Justine's choice to use an alias. She pressed her question. "Do you know where I might find Thomas, Mr. Piedmont?"

"He's been gone all morning," Arnold said, heading to the door. "Walked off toward the river," he did.

River?

The boy stood at the foot of the bed. "What else can I help with, Doc?"

"Nothing, Harland. You need to get home to help with chores or your pa will have both our hides."

Harland?

"Don't pout now, boy," Dr. Bevin said. "On your way home why don't you show Miss Miller the way to the river."

"Yes, sir."

Heading out, Justine saw other ladies in town, making her glad for taking the effort to wear an appropriate dress. Except for her "stranger" status she fit right in. It was autumn and the trees were in brilliant color.

Walking down the main road with the boy Harland, after she'd recently walked down the same road with the grown Harland gave Justine an odd feeling. But a feeling not unpleasant.

He picked up a stick and dragged it behind in the dirt. "Good thing, you showing up like you did."

"I didn't know I'd have to sing."

"You sing pretty. Are pretty too."

"You're too young to give such compliments."

"I'm five-and-a-half."

She loved the *half.* "That old?"

"I know pretty when I see it. Hear it."

It was a pleasure to witness the root of the grown Harland's feistiness. "Do you help Dr. Bevin often?"

"Often as Pa will let me get away from chores. I have two sisters — one a new baby. You want to see her? She's pretty too."

"I'd love to." But then she thought of Thomas down by the river. Was he going to drown today? If so, she shouldn't be detoured.

Unless today wasn't the day . . . "This may sound odd, but with my traveling I feel a bit muddled. What's the date today?"

"September the fourteenth."

"And . . . the year?"

He turned around and walked backwards so he could see her. "You don't know the year?"

"Do you?"

"Eighteen-sixty."

Thomas died on September fifteenth.

He turned forward. "I'm only five but I know what day it is."

"I thought you were five-and-a-half."

They reached a fork in the road and pointed left. "If Mr. Thomas is at the river, he's probably down that-a-ways."

She nodded. Knowing he was safe — if only for today, she'd find him soon. Her immediate desire was to visit Harland's family. To be able to go back to 1878 and tell him she'd met them all — and had met *him* as a boy, would bring both of them much joy.

"I'll meet your family first, if that's still all right."

"Ma will like the company. Down this way." He took the right fork, then turned down a narrow road. He pointed ahead. "See? That's our house." He looked to a field and saw his father motioning him over. "I gotta go help Pa. Go see my new sister and meet Ma and Bee-bee. Her name's Phoebe but we call her Bee-bee." He waved and raced into the cornfield to his father, the height of the corn quickly making Justine lose sight of him.

Justine held in her disappointment. She didn't care much about meeting the females in Harland's life. She wanted to spend more time with *him*. But there was no turning back now.

She spotted Mrs. Jennings outside, stirring a pot on a fire. A seven-year-old girl with curly blonde hair sat on a bench, holding a bundled baby.

The mother looked up as Justine approached. "May I help you?"

Justine recognized Dorthea Jennings from their short interaction in 1857 at the church dinner. Would Dorthea recognize her?

Justine saw there was laundry in the boiling pot. She introduced herself as Miss Miller. "I'm a friend of the Tyler's."

"Nice to meet you," Dorthea said.

So she doesn't recognize me.

Justine explained how she'd met Harland at Dr. Bevin's.

"Arnold's hurt again?"

"Again?"

"That man has more injuries than are likely."

"He's prone to accidents?"

"He's prone to making Quinn mad in some way or 'nother."

Justine thought about Arnold's arm injury. It was totally possible his shoulder had come out from a good yank or twist.

"If people know Quinn hurts him, why don't they stop him?"

"Constable Tyler has tried. Even arrested him once. But nothing sticks, and then after . . . there's repercussions, you know."

Her grandfather Ross was Constable Tyler. He'd been a strong man. If he couldn't stop Quinn . . . Quinn was still a bully in 1878. If her quest was to facilitate justice, how was she supposed to stop him when no one else had been able to do so?

The baby began to cry, and Bee-bee said, "Ma . . . ?"

Justine stepped in. "I'll take her." She took up the child and bounced her until she calmed. "She's beautiful," Justine said.

"That, she is. Her name's Ellie and that's Bee-bee."

"Can I get my doll and play?"

Mrs. Jennings looked at Justine, who nodded. "I can stay a short while."

"Go get her but make it quick."

The older woman looked out at the field and heard father and son arguing. "Oh dear."

"What's wrong?"

She shook her head. "Those two are like oil and water. Jesse is impatient. He wants Harland to help, but he gets after the boy for things he doesn't know yet. I tell him, 'Train up a child in the way he should go: and when he is old, he will not depart from it.' But such advice doesn't give him patience amid the training."

Justine couldn't imagine Harland as a farmer. "It seems the boy has interest in medical things. I got the impression he spends a lot of time with Dr. Bevin."

Mrs. Jennings drew a few towels out of the pot with a stick and dropped them into a smaller pot of cold water. "That's a sore subject with Jesse, though I's proud of the boy."

Suddenly, they heard Harland scream. "Ma! Ma!" He burst out of a corn row, awkwardly supporting his stumbling father, whose head was bleeding profusely.

Mrs. Jennings rushed to his other side. "What happened?"

"I tripped and fell, hitting my head on the hoe. Let me sit."

Bee-bee stood in the doorway, her face worried. "Pa?"

Justine handed the baby to her sister, wanting to be free to help.

But Harland didn't need her. He saw the clean towels in the pot of rinse water and pulled two out, ringing them out, then handing one to his mother. "Clean the cut," he said. "And don't worry too much. Doc says head wounds bleed a lot."

She nodded and did just that as Mr. Jennings smarted at the contact.

Harland used his teeth to create a tear in the other towel and tore it into long lengths. "Let me look at it."

His mother made room for him, and he studied the wound. "I don't think it needs stitches but we need to press on it to stop the bleeding." Harland pressed a cloth on the wound, checked it often, then began wrapping his father's forehead with one, then two, then three bandages, tucking the final end in.

During all this, his father kept staring at him, as though amazed.

As was Justine. That a five-year-old boy would retain such composure in an emergency and truly be able to help . . . Harland was meant to be a doctor.

Harland helped him stand. "Come on. You need to lie down."

"I believe I do. I'm kinda faint," Pa said, walking toward the house with his wife's help. He paused at the door to say, "Thank you, son."

"Anything, Pa. I'll get you some water."

Ellie began to wail and Dorthea detoured to tend to her.

For the first time, Mr. Jennings seemed to notice Justine. "Forgive my manners. I'm Jesse Jennings."

"I'm Susan, a friend of the Tylers. Here, let me help you." She helped him inside. He nodded to a bedroom, then sat on the bed, getting settled, leaning against the wall.

He let out a long breath, then took another one. "My boy's something, ain't he?"

"That, he is." She decided to strengthen Harland's cause. "He has a distinct talent for medicine. It could take him far."

The man closed his eyes. "Dorthea says the same thing. She says I'm too focused on farm work. I push him too much." He opened his eyes. "I know I need to simply take time with him."

"Take time . . ." Justine repeated. "That is a good lesson for us all." *A life line.*

Harland came inside with a dipperful of water. He handed it to his father, who drank it.

"You feeling all right, Pa?"

"I'll be fine. You did good, son." He glanced at Justine. "You have a talent for healin'."

Harland's face brightened. "I like it, Pa. I like helping Dr. Bevin."

Mr. Jennings nodded. "I know. And I—"

Mrs. Jennings came in and stood beside the bed, holding Ellie. "You all right, Jesse?"

"I will be."

Justine and Harland left them alone and went outside.

But Harland's breathing was heavy. "When he fell and it bled so much, I panicked."

"No, you didn't," Justine said. "You knew exactly what to do. Dr. Bevin would be proud. Your father is proud."

Her words seemed to help calm him. "He is?"

"He said as much."

Harland cocked his head, taking in the compliment. "It felt good to help."

She put a hand on his shoulder. "You'll be a fine doctor."

He shook his head forlornly. "Not if Pa has his way."

"Today will help convince him."

He looked toward the house. "I gotta get back."

Justine hated to see him go. "It was a pleasure meeting you, Harland Jennings."

"You too, Miss Miller."

He went inside, pausing at the door to wave.

Justine headed toward the road. It had already been a good day in 1860. But she hadn't seen Thomas yet.

She hoped she wouldn't be pulled back to 1878 just yet.

**

When Justine reached the end of the Jennings' road, she heard commotion to her right, and saw Thomas running up the road from the river.

"Sir? Are you all right?"

He paused to catch his breath, leaning forward, putting his hands on his thighs. "Nothing to be alarmed about, miss." He found his manners and stood erect. "I am Thomas Piedmont. And . . . and you look familiar."

She wasn't sure which name to give, yet it had only been three years since he'd met her at Granny's—as Justine Braden. "I'm Justine Braden. We may have met a few years ago?"

"At the Tylers. Yes. Are you visiting again?"

"I am." She remembered the fact that he was going to die tomorrow. Drown. Was his agitation connected to his death? "Please tell me what's upset you so. I want to help."

He studied her a moment, then said, "Perhaps it would be advantageous—and wise—to have someone besides family know what I found."

The "besides family" was odd. "Found?"

He looked left, then right, as if afraid of being overheard. "Would you be willing to come with me to see? It's not far."

"Of course."

Thomas led her toward the river, and then left, into a field. A row of apple trees edged the corn. The ground beneath one of them was disturbed. There was a hole. A shovel sat nearby.

"You've been digging?"

"I didn't come out here to dig. Only to pick apples to sell at the family store. Though I'm the pastor, I still help out when I can. We keep a ladder out here, but with the rain lately, it sank into the ground a little, and then a lot. When I tried to pull it out, this came out with it." He picked up a bone—more than a bone. A jaw, complete with teeth.

"Gracious." She looked to the crude hole. "You dug up more?"

"I went back and got a shovel. I didn't tell my brother or my father what I was doing, because I want to know what's here first." He sighed deeply. "Now I know." He looked down at his discovery. "The grave must be old to not be a part of the cemetery. My grandfather, Isaac Piedmont, was one of the first people buried there."

He's just the man I need to meet next.

"At first I thought it could be the grave of Indians," he said, gently holding the jaw. "They were here long before settlers came."

"Perhaps you should just fill it in. It's a sacred place."

He raised a finger to make a point. "Agreed. But Indians didn't have . . ." He retrieved a doll with a painted wood head and strings of blonde hair.

Justine gasped. "A child is buried here?"

"And two adults: one female, one male. A family."

Justine put a hand to her chest, her breath leaving her. "How tragic."

"Indeed. The clothes are in tatters, but I looked around the gentleman to see if there was some identification, and I . . ." He pressed a hand to his pocket and shook his head, as if deciding he didn't want to say more. "The man has a wooden leg. Surely someone will remember that about some relative. I was running back to ask my father about it, to see if he'd ever heard any stories about a family being buried by the apple trees."

Justine peered into the grave and saw three distinct skeletons, and the remains of Colonial era clothing. "What happened to them?"

"You can count on me finding out." He turned toward the road. "Will you be my witness?"

"Of course."

But as Justine followed him to the road, she felt the now-familiar stirring inside. *No! Not now!*

When she opened her eyes she was standing on the same road. The sun was just coming up over the mountains. The apple trees were behind her, years larger, their white spring blossoms confirming that she was no longer in 1860, in the autumn when the apples were ripe.

She hurried to the trees and examined the ground beneath them. It was undisturbed, with wild grasses and yellow wildflowers scattered around the trunks to the edge of the unplanted field. There was no cross or any indication that three people were buried there.

Three bodies buried in a single grave under an apple tree? Why weren't they buried in the cemetery? Who was in the grave? Was it connected to the Piedmont's secret? Back in 1826, her grandmother had said that Ned Piedmont's father wasn't really Isaac Piedmont. Had Ned's father killed the real Piedmonts to assume their identity and possessions?

If so . . . Thomas's words returned to her mind: *"I was running back to ask my father about it, to see if he'd ever heard any stories about a family being buried by the apple trees."*

She put a hand to her chest. If he talked to Quinn and his father about it, and it was a family secret . . .

Had Quinn or Arnold killed Thomas to keep him quiet?

Justine was suddenly torn. She couldn't march into the general store and confront the men about something that had happened eighteen years ago. Not without revealing her own secret about her gift.

Not without putting herself in danger. If they—Quinn, Justine had to believe Quinn was the guilty one—killed his own blood to keep the secret safe, he would feel no compunction in killing her. He'd already threatened her about asking questions in regard to his brother's death.

She put a hand to her stomach and allowed herself a deep breath. *Lord?* Soon after the simple plea she felt a check to her emotions. *Take time.* She had to be wise about this. To speak too soon might have dire consequences and actually prevent justice from being done.

Justine walked toward home, taking a detour through the cemetery to clear her thoughts. She stopped in front of Thomas's headstone. "I wish I'd had more time to talk with you."

Simeon stepped into view. "You saw Thomas?"

"I did. I saw him the day before he died."

"Did you see who murdered him?"

"So he *was* murdered? For certain?"

Simeon shrugged. "That's for you to find out, miss."

"But you know something. Tell me."

He shook his head. "You don't reach your destination by standing at the river. You have to wade through it, one step at a time."

"What?"

He walked toward his shed and went inside.

"Justine?"

She looked up to see Harland walking toward her. She fell into his arms.

He held her tight. "You're shaking. Are you all right? I stopped by the house to say goodbye before you went on your journey and Goosie said you'd left a note saying you went back during the night."

"I did. I went back to 1860."

"Did you see Thomas?"

In a roundabout way. "I did. And . . . I saw you." It felt good to think of something positive from her travels. "Let's sit."

They sat next to each other on the bench near her mother's grave.

"You were five and were helping Dr. Bevin set Arnold's shoulder."

He stared out over the cemetery as if capturing the memory. "I remember that. A lady helped. She sang some song to distract Arnold. A Miss Moore, Miss . . ."

Justine gasped. "Miller." She grabbed hold of his hand. "That was me."

"I don't understand."

"I was there! I said my name was Susan Miller. It was me. I sang for Arnold."

"How is that possible?"

Her heart beat wildly. "I don't know." She pressed a hand to calm it. "Afterwards I walked with you. You took me to your house because you wanted me to —"

"See my baby sister."

"Ellie."

Harland put a hand to his chest. "Was that the day Pa fell and cut his head?"

"You took charge and got it cleaned and bandaged."

He looked to the ground. "I remember that day because after that Pa didn't argue as much about me helping Dr. Bevin."

"I have a life line for you. From him."

"What did he say?"

"He said he knew he was impatient with you, and admitted he was too consumed with the work of farming."

"It *was* a lot of work, and I wasn't good at it."

"But he also knew he pushed you too hard. He said . . ." she paused to remember Mr. Jennings' words, "he said, 'I know I need to simply take time with him.'"

Harland's forehead furrowed as memories came rushing back. "He *did* take time with me after that. He seemed more patient." He looked into the air. "I could have been a better son."

"We all could have been better to people in our pasts. *Could* be better to people still alive."

She wanted to cheer him up. "I met your mother, Ellie, and Bee-bee."

He laughed. "Bee-bee too?"

"Phoebe."

He laughed again. "To think you saw them, to think we met . . ." His face grew serious. "How can this be?"

"I don't know."

He squeezed her hand. "It's said that God's ways are beyond explanation. This proves it. I'm just glad you met my family." He changed the subject. "Did you see Thomas?"

She told him about the graves and the fact she had left Thomas on the way to tell his father and brother about it. "It was the day before he was murdered."

"So the rumors were true? He *was* murdered?"

Simeon said so. She remembered Simeon's direction to keep their conversations private. "Everything suggests it."

Harland put a hand on her shoulder. "Though all logic says I shouldn't, I believe you."

A sudden weariness washed over her. She needed rest. She needed home. Home is where she could figure out what to do next.

When to do next.

They headed there, but with her mind swirling with thoughts of the past and present she knew rest would be impossible.

They found Goosie in the kitchen. She was crying.

Justine ran to her. "What's wrong?"

She swiped her tears with her apron. "You have enough to worry about."

Harland came to her other side. "Tell us."

Goosie went back to rolling out a pie crust. "I went to get supplies and Quinn cheated me. Again."

Again? "Did you confront him about it?"

"How could I? I'm stupid. I'm not all there. I can't fight for myself without giving away the fact that I can talk and am perfectly sane."

Justine retied her bonnet. "I won't stand for it. I'm going over there this minute and tell—"

Goosie shook her head adamantly. "Please don't. I need to keep the ruse a little longer."

"Until when?" Harland asked.

"I'll know it when the time's right."

Justine put a hand on her shoulder. "Quinn cheats his brother out of life, cheats my mother out of her innocence, and cheats the townspeople financially."

Harland scoffed. "He's a peach." He held out a chair. "Sit down, Goosie. Justine has much to tell you."

She wiped her hands on her apron and joined Harland and Justine at the table. "What did you find out?"

Justine left the information about Harland's family for another time and focused on the main discovery. "I saw Thomas in 1860. He'd discovered a Colonial grave with three bodies—one was a little girl."

Goosie sat back with a huff. "Mercy."

"Exactly," Harland said.

"Whose grave is it?"

"I don't know. Thomas didn't know. The family could have died from some disease. Or an Indian attack."

"The Indians around here were on peaceful terms with the settlers. They didn't welcome us, but we didn't fight each other. At least not that I ever knew about."

"What makes it suspicious was that Thomas was upset. He was rushing back to talk to his father and Quinn about it."

Goosie absently picked at a dab of dried food on the table. "What if his family had something to do with it?"

Justine shook her head. "The clothes on the victims were Colonial. This was 1860. But according to Thomas's headstone, he died the next day." She thought of what Simeon had said. "He was murdered."

"Do you know for sure?"

She didn't. Yet. Justine leaned back in the chair, spent. "Should I go talk to Arnold about Thomas? I tried talking to Quinn a few days ago and he threatened me."

"You need to get Arnold alone," Harland said.

"That's difficult," she said. "Quinn is always in the store, and usually Arnold is with him."

"Or on the porch," Harland said. "You could be on the watch for when he's alone on the porch."

"But even if I talk to him there . . . Arnold could be involved. And involved or not, Quinn could overhear." Justine noticed the pie crust waiting to be finished and remembered her first meeting with Arnold. *When do I get some pie?* "He likes pie."

"How do you know?" Harland said.

She turned to Goosie. "Can you make an extra one I could bring to him?"

"One rhubarb pie coming up," Goosie said. "While you wait you need to rest a few hours. The pies will be done by early afternoon. You can take one over then."

Justine felt the tensions of the day tighten around her as though she were bound by rope.

Harland stood. "I'll come back at one o'clock and go with you."

"That would be nice. I'll see you out."

At the door, he lingered. "Thank you for visiting my family—and telling me about it. It's made me miss them. I'm going to go write them a letter."

"Am I doing the right thing, questioning Arnold?"

"I think it's a much-needed step."

Justine got an idea. "What if you went inside the store and kept Quinn occupied while I talk to his father?"

"I could do that." His hand skimmed hers, making her remember the note from Mabel.

She took the note out of her pocket and handed it to him. "This was slid under the front door when I left in the wee hours."

He sighed and handed it back. "Mabel."

"Mabel."

"This is getting out of hand. I'm not sure what to do about it."

"Tell her the truth."

He nodded. "She's a nice girl, but she's obsessed. I will explain it to her as plainly as I can. In the meantime, rest well, Justine. I'll pray everything goes smoothly and all truth is revealed."

"Add a bit about keeping me safe from the wrath of the Piedmonts."

"I will."

She had a thought. "My grandfather was the constable in Piedmont, but I heard Quinn has that position—as well as being mayor."

"He is both."

"Is that even legal?"

"Since he's the law . . ."

"He has total control."

"Pretty much."

Justine pressed the space between her eyes. "What if I find out that Thomas was murdered and that Quinn and Arnold had something to do with it? He's not going to arrest himself or his father."

"If all that's true the people of Piedmont will rise up against him."

She scoffed. "Are you sure about that? They haven't so far."

His face was forlorn. "Discover the truth and I'll help you find a way to bring about justice."

**

Although sleep beckoned, Justine held it at bay. She had one more thing to do that would complete her experience of visiting 1860.

She sat on the window seat and got out her sketchbook and pencil. She closed her eyes and let her mind return to the past, to meeting Harland's mother and sisters. She'd met Dorthea twice. To give Harland a sketch of his mother . . . *make my memory clear. Let me see her.*

Then, there she was in her mind's eye. The light auburn hair pulled in a low bun, the narrow chin, the high forehead and thin lips. She had Harland's eyes, or rather, he had hers.

Justine opened her eyes and took up her pencil. Line by line Dorthea Jennings moved from her memory to the page.

Chapter Twelve

After a short rest from her excursion into 1860, Justine's stomach twirled with nervous knots as she thought about her upcoming talk with Arnold.

"You're not eating," Goosie said, pointing to Justine's bowl of soup.

"I'll eat *after.*" *Maybe.*

Goosie put a calming hand on Justine's. "You're bringing the man a pie. It's a nice thing to do."

"Quinn won't think so."

"Even men like Quinn enjoy pie." She removed her hand. "Your great-grandmother was the one who taught me how to bake pies. Did you know that?"

"I didn't. I never met her. Your connection to our family is so strong."

" *Your* family is strong. You are strong," Goosie said. "And brave."

"I wish." Justine wanted to believe it — and she almost did. It was as if strength and courage loomed on the edge of a ridge. She could see their impressive silhouettes, and sensed she could catch up with them — even embrace them — if she tried hard enough. Yet, there was always a chance strength and courage would turn their back on her and walk away, maintaining their distance. Or let her fall off the cliff? Since they had only recently been introduced she was wary of the protocol. Did she go to them, or did they come to her?

She gave her worries a voice. "What if Arnold isn't on the porch? Will Harland be able to distract Quinn inside? Will Arnold have anything significant to tell me? What if I only make things worse?"

"I didn't take you for a pessimist."

"I didn't take me as brave. Ever. In any way." She pushed her soup aside. "The most courageous thing I've ever done was wearing black gloves to the opera instead of white."

Goosie shook her head. "You exaggerate."

"Not really."

Goosie pushed the bowl close again. "It was courageous to come here alone after your mother died. It's courageous to embrace a bizarre and fantastical gift and travel through time—coming upon whomever, in who-knows-where, in who-knows-what year. It's courageous being nice to an old man who could use a friend. Mercy, Jussie. You're bringing him a present."

She laughed. "One of your pies does have the power to change the world."

"I hope it has the power to make an old man smile. I never see him smile."

"Did he used to?"

Goosie thought about this a moment. "Not really. But living with Quinn would wipe away anyone's smile. Other than his accusations against Winnie after Ned's death, I've never considered Arnold a bad sort."

"He's not like Quinn?"

"Not at all. A follower, not a leader. Quiet."

"Long-suffering?"

"It's been just the two of them a long time."

"Has Quinn ever been married?"

Goosie scoffed. "What woman would commit to a growling bear who likes to use his claws?"

My mother. "When did Arnold's wife die?"

"Soon after Thomas was born."

Justine felt compassion for Arnold, the father with two young sons. "How did one son turn into a bully and the other into a kind man—a pastor?"

Goosie shrugged. She picked up Justine's spoon and handed it to her. "Arnold still holds his wife in high esteem. Sally was a sweet woman. I think they truly loved each other."

"What was Arnold like back then?" Justine set the spoon down.

"Not like Ned, that's for sure. Arnold was more like Thomas. Or rather Thomas was like him. Quinn is cut from the same cloth as his Uncle Ned."

Justine did the math. "But Ned died in 1826. Quinn wasn't born yet, was he?"

"He was born in thirty-three or so. Thomas in thirty-four. I remember Thomas's birth because I nearly got married that year."

Justine gasped, then felt bad for it. "Sorry. Nearly?"

"I was in love with a man who worked with Dr. Bevin. George Drew."

"What happened?"

"George was the one who delivered Thomas, as Dr. Bevin was off on an emergency. A farmer had fallen from a hay loft. That man died, actually."

She was getting off point. "Why didn't you marry him?"

"Sally had the baby but died three days after Thomas was born. Arnold was beside himself with grief—and anger at George for letting her die."

"Did George do something wrong?"

"I don't rightly know. I never spoke with him again."

"What?"

"He ran off. Doc Bevin said it was for the best, that George didn't have a talent for doctoring. And honestly, if he would have stayed no one would have bet on his safety against Arnold's angry misery."

"So Arnold is a violent man."

She shrugged. "Any man can go crazy with grief. The loss of his wife was devastating. George should have stayed and dealt with it." Her eyes glazed with a memory, then cleared. "Yet I say, good riddance."

"You're glad George left?"

"I mourn it every day."

"But you said—"

"He's the only man I ever loved. But he showed a weakness of character by running away like that and not even saying goodbye." She shrugged. "So be it." Then she took a deep breath which seemed to close the door on her memories. "It will be nice for Arnold to have a smile today."

"It's just a pie."

"It's a very tasty pie."

"If he can't tell me anything, I am still doing a nice thing."

"That, you are." Goosie took Justine's hand and bowed her head. "Father God, create a dome of protection over

Justine and Arnold today. Give them time enough to have a productive talk without incident. Spur Arnold to share what he knows so Justine can bring about justice."

Justine chuckled. "Your prayer was far more eloquent than my usual 'Help me' plea."

"That works too." She pulled out Justine's chair and gently nudged her toward the front of the house. "Go now. 'Be strong and do the work.'"

**

Justine waved at Harland as they approached the Piedmont general store from opposite directions. He walked faster, past the store, so they had time to speak privately. He waved at Arnold as he passed — who blessedly *was* sitting on the porch.

"Thank God for a warm day," he said upon reaching her.

"Are you ready to divert Quinn?" she asked him.

He touched his pocket. "Dr. Bevin gave me a list of supplies we need, so there *is* a reason for me to speak with him." He glanced at the pie. "I see you're ready."

"As I'll ever be." She nodded toward the pie. "I even brought a fork so he can indulge right then and there."

"And strengthen your bribe."

She took offense. "It's not a bribe. It's a kindness. He's an old man who could use some goodwill in his life."

He bowed slightly, offering his mea culpa. "I did not mean to discredit your motives."

She felt a wave of guilt. "I *do* want him to talk to me."

"Come on now," he said, turning toward the store. "Let's do this before we scrutinize our intentions into inaction."

Justine's nerves did a final flip as she walked up the steps to the store. Harland gave her a nod, and she turned toward Arnold, who was sitting with a blanket over his legs. He perked up when she stepped toward him.

"What you got there?"

She lowered it so he could see. "I've brought you a pie, Mr. Piedmont. I heard you like pie."

"You heard right." His eyes were bright. "What kind?"

188

"Rhubarb."

"You make it?"

She laughed. "Me? I can't boil water. Goosie made it." She handed him the fork. "I thought you might like to have a taste right now."

He took up the fork. "Don't mind if I do." He dug into the pie and took a large bite. "Mmm," he said, his eyes closing. "Just like my Sally used to make."

It was the opening she needed. "Tell me about your wife."

"Sally? My pretty little thing. Had the boys too close together. Died after Thomas was born."

"I'm so sorry. It must have been difficult raising two little boys."

He took another bite and glanced toward the door of the store. "Got a mixed bag out of it."

Justine understood. "I hear that Thomas was a very nice man."

Arnold motioned for Justine to move to the right, and she realized he wanted her to block the view of him eating the pie from the doorway. "I won't let him take the pie from you," she said. "I brought it especially for you."

He studied her a moment. "Sitting here all day makes me think about the past — probably more than I should. I want to tell you I'm sorry 'bout what happened to your grandmother way back. Her getting accused and all. I should'na done that. Once I started it . . . people like to think the worst. And Ned *was* dead." He took another bite, pondering his words as he chewed. "Pa and Ned were a pair, always riled about something. I went along when I shouldn't have."

She was heartened by his confession. "It turned out all right. Granny married a nice man."

"*I* wanted to marry her."

"What?"

He whistled, fork in hand. "Winifred was a beauty — and let me tell you, they were few and far between in Piedmont. I liked her feistiness. She deserved better'n my brother, but he knew how to use the sweet talk." He shook his head. "Don't know where he found such words, cuz he was a mean cuss most a the time." He shook his head in a short burst. "When he was gone I missed my second chance by getting angry and blaming her." He looked down. "My life coulda been far different."

"Did Granny have feelings for you?"

"We'll never know now, will we?"

All the information about her grandmother was interesting, but Justine realized her time might be short. "Can you tell me about the day Thomas died? I heard he found something down by the apple trees?"

Arnold had just taken an enormous bite of pie. He stopped chewing and cocked his head. "What you talking about?"

"He was down by the apple trees and dug up something that upset him. He ran to tell you and Quinn about it."

Arnold set the fork on top of the pie. "How you know all this? You weren't there."

She thought fast. "Granny told me."

He eyed her skeptically. "Sounds made up to me. Thomas never told me nothing about no trees."

"Maybe he told Quinn?"

From behind her she heard, "Told Quinn what?"

A shock coursed down the full length of her body and up again. She turned to see him standing outside the door. Harland stood in the doorway, giving her an *I'm sorry* look.

"Told Quinn what?" he repeated.

Justine couldn't put two words together. "I . . ."

Arnold did it for her. He held up the pie. "Tell you that she brought me my very own pie. And you can't have any."

Justine's heart found its rhythm again. "If you'd really like one, I could have Goosie make another."

"I don't like pie."

She shrugged. "Then your father can have it all to himself."

"You bet," Arnold said. He took another bite.

Justine nodded to Harland. "Are you all done with your shopping?"

He moved to the top of the steps. "I am."

Justine put on her best smile for Arnold. "Enjoy the pie." She nodded at Quinn. "Have a nice day."

She took Harland's arm, needing support to keep her feet steady. They walked toward home.

"That was close," she whispered.

"Sorry. I kept him inside as long as I could."

"What did you hear?"

"…'told Quinn.' That's it."

"Good. If he'd come out a moment earlier, he would have overheard me ask about Thomas finding the grave."

"What did Arnold say?"

Justine glanced over her shoulder and saw Quinn watching her. "Let's get inside."

They sat in the parlor and Goosie came out to join them. "So?"

"I asked Arnold about the day Thomas died and he knew nothing about Thomas finding anything near the trees, much less, a grave."

"So Thomas didn't get to town?" Goosie asked. "You said he was running home to tell."

"He didn't tell Arnold."

"But he may have told Quinn," Harland said.

"And the next day Quinn killed him?"

"Killing his brother . . ." Goosie shook her head. "Why?"

"It had to have something to do with the grave—or rather, who's in the grave." Justine said.

"What would be so bad that brother would kill brother?" Harland added.

Justine looked out the window toward the river. "We need to find what Thomas found."

"You want us to dig up a grave?"

"If it still exists."

"If it's bad enough to kill for, Quinn might have moved the bodies," Goosie said. "I wouldn't put it past him."

"Maybe," Justine said. "Though he and Thomas were the only ones who knew about it."

"And Thomas isn't talking."

They all started when there was a knock on the door. Goosie answered, immediately taking up her odd persona, avoiding eye contact, flinching.

"Goosie."

Goosie backed away from Quinn and Justine took over. "May I help you?"

He carried the empty pie plate and fork. "I'm returning this."

"Your father ate the whole thing?"

He shrugged. "When he gets sick, you're to blame."

She took the utensils. "I hope he enjoyed it."

"That old man will eat anything."

Justine glanced at Goosie and saw a flash of anger that she quickly absorbed. "Then it's good he had the chance to eat something extraordinary. Goosie's an amazing cook."

He stroked his beard. "I'd appreciate it if next time you visit my father, you visit me too."

Justine felt her stomach grab. "I meant no disrespect."

Quinn's eyebrow rose. "We're a team, we two. Talking to both of us is my preference. In fact, I'm going to have to insist on it."

"It's an odd request," Harland said, stepping behind Justine. "I think your father can fend for himself."

Quinn glared at him. "You work anymore, Harland? Or do you just spend all your time chatting with the ladies?"

"You ailing?"

"No."

"Your father ailing?"

"Not yet."

"Be assured I'll be there for him if ever he needs me."

Quinn hesitated a moment, then tipped his hat and left.

Justine looked out the curtains to make sure he was truly leaving and not lurking behind. "I hope he wasn't sneaking around outside when we were talking." She let the curtains drop. "The sooner we find out the truth, the sooner Quinn's put away."

"Put away?" Goosie asked. "Where? And by whom?"

However could this work? Justine sighed. "He has total control."

Harland took Justine's hand and then Goosie's. "God has total control—even over Quinn Piedmont."

They prayed for a miracle of God's justice and said a final "Amen."

Justine felt better for the prayers, but knew she needed to do her part in bringing out the truth. "Where's a shovel?"

"We can't just walk toward the river with shovels in our hands," Harland said.

Goosie agreed. "We're getting close to a truth that was bad enough that Thomas was killed for it. Discretion is needed."

Justine didn't feel very discreet. She wanted to run down the road with a shovel, find the skeletons, and shout out the truth. Surely someone would know who was buried there. Surely someone—beyond the three of them—would see that the Piedmonts were guilty of Thomas's death. If not more.

She must have looked like she was ready to bolt because Harland put a calming hand on her shoulder. "Let's get Dr. Bevin's buggy and put a shovel in it."

Justine nodded. "We're simply out for a drive on a lovely day."

"Digging up graves," Goosie said under her breath.

**

Justine and Harland drove down the road leading to the river. "There," she said, pointing to the row of apple trees.

Harland pulled the buggy to the side of the road and helped Justine down. He took out the shovel. "Do you know where we should dig?"

She surveyed the row of trees, trying to remember where Thomas had taken her. She looked to the road and back, to the adjoining field and back . . . Then she walked to a spot. "Here."

"Are you sure?"

"No."

He handed her his hat and coat. "At least it's a ways off the road. What explanation could we have if someone saw us?"

"We're taking a walk in the grove?"

"And just thought we'd dig a hole?"

Point taken. "I'll wait at the buggy as a lookout." She walked to the buggy and looked in the direction where Harland was digging. It was over a slight rise, so you could only see his head bobbing up and down, *not* what he was doing. But it would still be suspicious.

It was excruciating to stand so far away and not be a part of it. Justine paced along the edge of the road, causing the horse to snort and get jumpy. "Shush now," she told him. She reached out a hand to stroke his head, hoping that was the right thing to do. Being a city-girl she had little experience with horses. "It's all right," she told him softly.

Suddenly, his ears perked up and he lifted his head. Within seconds she heard it too. Another horse was coming down the road.

She glanced toward Harland, wishing she could call to him to get out of sight, but there wasn't time as the rider came into view. Her heart skipped when she saw it was Quinn.

Of all people, Lord. Why him?

She stepped onto the road and put on a smile. She even managed a wave. He stopped nearby. "Hello again," she said.

He eyed the buggy. "This is Dr. Bevin's." He looked in both directions. "Is Harland with you?"

"He is." *Think of something!*

"Where is he?"

Why hadn't they thought of a reasonable answer to such questions. "He took a little walk—"

"Alone?"

"He—"

Suddenly, Harland came walking over the ridge, his coat and hat in place, carrying some branches of apple blossoms like a bouquet.

Justine rushed across the road to greet him. "They're lovely. How sweet of you." She took the branches and drank in the fragrance.

Only then did Harland acknowledge Quinn. "Where you headed?"

"I have some fishing lines in the river."

"I didn't take you for a fisherman," Harland said.

"I didn't take you for a pansy."

Harland shrugged and said, "Apple blossoms, not pansies."

"Those trees belong to my family," Quinn said.

"Sorry," Harland said. "I took small branches."

Justine made a show of enjoying the fragrance again. "It is much appreciated. He won't do it again, Quinn. Promise."

Harland raised a hand. "Promise."

Quinn looked from one to the other. Was he convinced? There was no way he could guess what they were doing. Could he?

"I'll leave you to your ride then."

"And you to your fishing," Justine said. She was surprised when Harland helped her into the buggy. They were leaving?

He climbed in after her as Quinn rode on.

"We're going?"

Harland chucked at the horse, and the buggy moved down the road. He patted his pocket. "I have what we need."

"What's that?"

"An arm bone. The radius to be exact."

"What's that?"

"The outer bone of the forearm that spans between the elbow and the thumb."

"Human?"

"No other animal has such a bone."

She pulled at his pocket, but he placed a hand over it. "Now is not the time." He nodded toward the river. Quinn was too close.

"I think it's best I turn us around." He pulled onto a side road that had a turnaround place. Soon they were headed back to town.

"What about the grave?" she asked. "How many were buried there?"

"I didn't dig that much. I didn't think it wise to disturb the ground more than I had to. Not until we're ready."

"But you found the bone."

"It wasn't very deep. Perhaps the freeze and thaw of the years drew it upward. Where there's one, there are many. I filled in my digging and covered the top with grasses as best I could."

Justine nodded. "We don't want to alert Quinn in any way." She admired the blossoms. "Fast thinking with the apple branches."

"I thought you would like them."

"You're a romantic."

"I could be, given the right inspiration."

For the moment, she stared at Harland, their dangerous errand forgotten.

For the moment. Because suddenly Justine had an idea. "Let's find a place to hide, to see if Quinn goes to the orchard to check on the grave."

"You think he will?"

"He might. He was going to the river—though I doubt he was checking lines. On his way back . . . if I were him I'd check."

Harland turned the buggy onto the next side road and drove far enough that they couldn't see the road—and couldn't be seen from the road. "Are you up for a run through the fields?"

Justine hopped out of the buggy and was glad she'd set aside her fussy, bustled New York dresses. She hiked her skirt above her ankles and they hurried over a freshly plowed field.

They slowed when they saw the tops of the apple trees. Harland led them to the far end of the orchard, where they found a hiding place behind one of the larger trees. The low spreading branches added to their cover. Justine leaned forward to check if she could see the place Harland had dug. "Where is it?"

"There," he whispered. "Eight trees down."

He'd done a good job with the cover up. She could see no obvious disturbance.

"If I'd had more time I would have done a better job—" He grabbed hold of her arm and pulled her back. "I saw him." They pressed themselves to the tree trunk.

Justine clapped a hand over her mouth to contain her fright, for there would be no feasible explanation for their present location. She heard a soft rustling, like feet through grass. Then silence.

Harland squeezed her free hand. Hard. He was as nervous as she.

The footsteps started again. Faded. The next footsteps they heard were a horse trotting away. Toward town.

Justine slid to the ground, using the trunk as support. "I feel sick."

Harland knelt beside her. "It's all right. He didn't see us."

"Are you sure?"

"Pretty sure."

"Did he see where you'd dug?"

"Let's go see what he saw." He led her to the spot, which was well covered but for some loose dirt in the grass nearby. He scattered the offending dirt with his hand. "Unless he knew exactly where to look and looked closely . . ."

Justine's nerves took hold again. "Oh dear."

"Yet it proves he knows about the grave. Why would he come into the grove otherwise? To clip some apple blossoms for his father?"

"You're right. He knows."

"It will be all right, Justine."

Or not.

**

They returned the buggy just in time for Harland and Dr. Bevin to go to the Connor's farm to help with a birth.

Before he left, Harland repeated his reassurance. "It will be all right."

She tried to believe him but returned home knowing what she had to do.

Goosie met her at the door. "Did you find the grave?"

"We did." Justine headed upstairs. She paused on a step. "And we nearly got caught." She told Goosie about the close call with Quinn—the two close calls. Then she went to her room and took up the travel bag.

Goosie followed her there. "Where are you going?"

"Back."

"Into . . . ?"

"Into Isaac Piedmont's life. It's all connected. I need to find out how." She paused a moment to think. "When did he die?"

"The early 1800s, I think. When I was young."

"Then I need to wear something that suits the time." She thought of the gorgeous Regency gown she had in her room in New York. It would be appropriate, yet far too fancy. She remembered Goosie pulling out her great-grandmother's dress. "I need that green—"

Goosie took over. "I know the one. She opened the trunk and retrieved a pale green dress with a slim silhouette and a high waist. "This should do. I remember Abigail making it soon after I first came here."

"When was that?"

"When I was ten. Eighteen-hundred was the year. They took me in."

"As their servant?"

Goosie shrugged. "More than that. They told me to call them Aunt Abigail and Uncle Joshua. They were newly married and building this house when I came. I was here when your granny was born a few years later."

Justine squeezed her hand. "You are the rock of this house, its foundation. I don't know what I'd do without you here."

Goosie squeezed back, then helped her on with the dress. It felt odd to have nothing between the fabric and her body.

"Don't I need a petticoat?"

Goosie had already found a slim one in the trunk. "It has a few holes in it, but no one will see."

The dress had a low scooped neckline. "I need a scarf of some kind. I feel too exposed."

"A fichu," Goosie said. She pulled a sheer scarf with a collar attached out of the trunk and wrapped it around the neckline. "You can wear it out, tied in a knot, or overlap it and tuck it into the bodice."

Justine tried it both ways and preferred the tuck. "I'll use the same shawl, capelet, and bonnet I've used before."

Goosie gave her a good look-see. "You're all wrinkled. I should press the dress."

Justine shook her head. "It will have to do. I don't want to wait."

"Maybe the trip through time will do the pressing for me."

"Very funny." She took up the travel bag along with a breath. "Here I go."

Goosie gave her a hug. "Be careful. We don't know who's in that grave, but everything points to Isaac Piedmont being someone you wouldn't want to cross."

Like his grandson.

"God be with you."

Justine hurried across the street to the cemetery, hoping she wouldn't be seen.

She looked for Simeon. She would have liked to ask him more questions but it was not to be.

She walked to an old section of the cemetery and found Isaac's grave. Born 1755. Died 1810.

Justine was just about to touch his name, when she remembered her vow to say a prayer first. "Father, keep me safe from harm as I travel to right the wrongs of the past. Give me wisdom and strength to accomplish this task You have set before me. Amen."

With her travel bag held tightly in one hand, she traced his name.

And was gone.

**

Justine looked around and panicked for a moment. She was on a winding dirt road, surrounded by dense woods. Where was Piedmont? The position of the sun didn't help her with directions as it was directly overhead. She looked to the right, then to the left. *Which way, Lord?*

She heard the nicker of a horse and smiled at God's immediate response to her prayer. She started walking toward the sound.

There, around the first bend, was a small wagon. A little girl was reclining in its short bed among various packed household items.

"Hello?" Justine called out.

The girl sat up to get a better look. "Hello."

Justine quickened her pace to catch up. She didn't see an adult nearby. "Are you out here all alone?" When she reached the wagon she saw the girl was about nine or ten.

"Nah. Pa had to do the necessary in the woods. Plus, I ain't feeling too well so he was finding me some catnip." She rubbed her stomach. "I's upset."

"I'm so sorry." Justine saw some blankets folded to make a makeshift bed for the girl. "You should lay down again."

"I don't feel too good."

Justine remembered what Mother used to do when she'd said the same. She put a hand on her forehead. "You're hot. You have a fever."

The girl lay down and pulled a patchwork quilt tight around her. She curled into a ball. "I'm freezing."

More proof she was sick. Justine looked to the woods, wishing the father would appear.

"Where are you headed?"

"Piedmont."

Perfect. She looked down the road. "Is it far?"

"Not too. Pa wanted to stop before we got there because he has business to attend to right away."

"What kind of business?"

The girl closed her eyes as soon as she answered. "Justice."

Justine was taken aback.

Just then a man walked out of the woods, saw Justine, and tipped his hat. "Afternoon, miss."

"After—" Justine couldn't finish the greeting. For standing before her was Simeon, looking exactly as he did when she talked with him in the cemetery. How could this be? She suffered an involuntary shiver.

He must have noticed. "You feeling poorly too?"

"No, sir. I'm fine. But your daughter . . ."

He reached over the side of the low wagon and touched his daughter's head. "I got you some herbs, Goosie. As soon as we get to town I'll get some tea made with 'em."

What? Goosie. And Simeon. Goosie was Simeon's daughter? Justine quickly accepted the fact and mentally moved on. If Goosie was eighty-eight years' old in 1878, then the year had to be around 1800.

"You heading to Piedmont, miss?"

"I am."

"Climb in." He helped Justine onto the driver's seat beside him. "The name's Simeon Anders, and that there is my daughter, Augusta."

Augusta?

"Goosie," said the girl from the back.

"How did you get that name?" Justine asked.

"Pa, you tell . . ." She snuggled into the worn quilt.

Simeon took the reins and they headed to town. "When she was a wee thing, not even walking yet, she was outside and before I knew it, she was surrounded by dozens of Canadian geese. I don't know if you're familiar with geese . . ."

"Not at all."

"They can be mean creatures and will attack a person, flapping, hissing and biting."

"But they liked me," Goosie said.

"They liked her. She'd crawl around on the ground and they'd walk around her, or even sit nearby as though she was one of them."

"They knew I wasn't going to hurt them."

"Who's telling this story?" her father asked.

"Sorry, Pa."

He continued. "Anyway, that's why I call her Goosie."

Justine couldn't wait to tell the elderly Goosie that she'd heard the source of her name—from her father, himself.

"And who are you, miss?"

"Justine."

"Nice to meet you."

"And you. Thank you for the ride. Your daughter said you're going to Piedmont for justice?"

Simeon glanced over his shoulder at Goosie, then looked ahead. "Old business. Overdue business."

"May I ask what it pertains to?"

He looked at her, then shook his head. "What's *your* business in Piedmont—if I may ask?"

She thought about saying "justice" too, but felt it was best to keep that fact to herself. "I have family there." *Hopefully.*

"Traveling alone, are ye?"

"I'll be with them soon."

"Sorry," he said. "I shouldn't pry."

She grabbed onto his courtesy. "Are you from around here?"

"We haven't been there in ten years, since before it was even a town. But when I heard there was a town named Piedmont . . ." He shook his head as if it disgusted him. "I had to come back and make things right."

"Right?"

The twitch in his cheek revealed he hadn't meant to say so much. "Goosie and I left back in ninety. Made a good life up north."

"Then why come back?"

He chucked at the horses.

"Justice," said Goosie, from the back.

"It's complicated," Simeon said.

If the Simeon she knew in 1878 looked like this man seated before her now . . . did he die at this age? Was he in danger? If he had come for justice . . . not everyone would want justice.

"You should be careful," she said, without planning to say it aloud.

He glanced at her sideways. "You know something I don't?"

I know too little. "It's always good advice."

"That it is," he said. "Looks like we're almost there." He pointed up ahead, at some buildings.

They were entering town from the north and she saw the area she knew as the cemetery on the right. She couldn't see a single headstone, just trees and grass.

On the left was her family's home, looking brand new. A ladder was set upright beside an unfinished chimney.

Just as they reached the house . . . "Pa!"

They both looked back and saw Goosie hurling herself to her knees, leaning over the wagon, vomiting.

"Whoa!" Simeon climbed into the back of the wagon, steadying her as her body heaved.

Justine jumped down and ran up the front steps of the house. She knocked loudly. "Hello? Hello? Please?"

A young woman came to the door, looked at Justine, saw the wagon and Goosie's predicament and said, "Oh dear. Bring her inside."

"Thank you, ma'am." Simeon turned to Goosie. "You done for the moment?"

She nodded weakly.

Simeon swept Goosie into his arms and carried her into the house.

"Bring her upstairs." The woman led the way to a small room with a cot in it.

Simeon lay his daughter down. Her body was limp and done in.

The woman gave her a blanket. She looked to Justine. "There's a pump in the kitchen. Get her a cup of water."

Justine hurried down the stairs toward the kitchen and was surprised to find it was a separate building behind the main house. She pumped some water into a tin cup and hurried upstairs.

The woman took it from her and helped Goosie sit up. "Just a sip. No more."

Goosie managed it, then fell back on the cot. The woman felt her forehead. "She has a fever. How long has she been feeling poorly?"

"A day," Simeon said. "I got some catnip in the woods. I need to brew it up for her."

"I'll stay with her," Justine said.

Simeon held out his hand to the woman. "Simeon Anders."

"Abigail Holloran." She looked at Justine.

"I'm Justine and that's Goosie." Her thoughts were spinning. This woman was her great-grandmother!

The woman shoved a chamber pot close. "Just in case." Then the two left Justine alone with the girl.

Goosie opened her eyes and moaned. "Am I dying?"

Justine knelt by her side. "Not at all. I know for a fact you'll live a very long life."

Goosie gave her a questioning look before falling asleep.

Justine stroked her face. A question surfaced: She knew Goosie had been part of her family for most of her life, yet here she was with her father. Simeon must have stayed in Piedmont.

Goosie opened her eyes. "My quilt. I need my quilt. Pa told me to never ever lose it."

It seemed like a strange warning to a child, but Justine stood. "I'll get it. You rest."

She retrieved the quilt from the wagon but wondered why it was so important. It was well-loved and worn, with many patches to the various six-inch squares that created the simple pattern.

Once inside again, Justine met up with Simeon and her grandmother as they headed up the stairs with a mug of a steaming liquid. Justine immediately felt bad, for she'd promised to stay with the girl. She held up the quilt. "She asked for it."

"Good girl." Simeon hurried upstairs.

Justine looked down at the quilt. Why was it so important? Perhaps it was a family heirloom?

She heard Goosie vomiting again, and let the question go.

Chapter Thirteen

"Of course the three of you can stay," Grandmother told Simeon as all but Goosie sat down for a meal.

"Thank you, ma'am. Your kindness is much appreciated."

"It is," Justine added. She wanted to tell them how wonderful it was to meet them, that she was their great-granddaughter visiting from 1878. To be here, before Granny was even born boggled her mind. She loved hearing the Irish lilt to her grandparents' voices. She wondered how long they had been in America.

Justine's grandfather sat across the table from his wife. "We're sorry for your little girl's ailment. I hope she feels better soon."

"The chicken broth and the catnip tea has helped," Simeon said. "She's been calm for a few hours now. We thank you for your hospitality and care."

Grandmother nodded to Justine. "You and your husband can stay in the guest room."

Husband? She exchanged a look with Simeon, who said, "Thank you, ma'am," Simeon said.

Justine set aside her shock and added her own thank you to the Hollorans. Perhaps it was for the best. Most likely she wouldn't be here long. Yet as she eyed the two pies of meat and fruit, she hoped she would be here long enough to eat. How ironic that Goosie had just told her that she'd learned how to bake pies from Justine's great-grandmother — who sat at the table with her now. Would wonders never cease.

As the food was passed, Justine had to focus on the reason for her visit, *and* the possibility that her reason meshed with Simeon's. "I do appreciate you having us, Mr. and Mrs. Holloran," she said. "Can you tell us something about Piedmont?

Simeon nodded. "Yes. Please."

Grandfather took a slice of a meat pie and passed it on. "Not much to tell — yet. Was nothing more than a passing through place for travelers until Isaac Piedmont made it a town ten years ago."

"We pay him rent," she added. "And some farmers lease the land to plant, just outside of town."

Simeon blinked, then started shaking his head no.

"Is something wrong, Mr. Anders?" Grandfather asked.

"That's not the way it was supposed to work."

Grandmother's eyebrows rose. "You have other knowledge?"

Simeon seemed to struggle to find an answer. "Where does Mr. Piedmont reside? I'd like to speak with him."

Justine's insides stirred. *Was* Simeon's quest for justice linked to her own?

"He just opened a store down the road a bit."

"It's too late to go calling now," Grandmother said.

Grandfather nodded. "I can introduce you tomorrow if you'd like, Mr. Anders."

"I would like to meet him too," Justine said.

"As you wish." Grandfather patted his rotund stomach. "As usual this is delicious pie, wifey. My Abigail keeps me very well-fed."

"Too well-fed," Grandmother said.

He winked at her. That simple action warmed Justine's heart. It was clear they loved each other, which made her want to know more about *them*.

"You've recently moved here?" she asked.

"We have. Came over from Ireland a year ago. Landed in New York and tried to stay there, but—"

"We don't like the city," Grandmother said. "The conditions were deplorable, dirty, and there was no future there."

"Why Piedmont? It's a long way from New York."

Her grandparents exchanged a look and her grandmother continued the story. "It's because of me. When we were miserable in New York, I was praying about it, asking God where we should go." She glanced at her husband as if uncertain she should continue.

"Tell them the story, Abbie. There's no hedging on the truth of it."

She took a fresh breath. "I had a dream where God told me to go to New Hampshire."

Grandfather spread his arms. "And so we came."

Simeon had a question. "You came on faith?"

"We did," he said. "Abbie was so certain of it, and we had no other inkling, so we packed up what little we had, and headed out."

"But why did you stop here?" Justine asked. "It's barely a town."

Grandfather gave another nod to his wife, who said, "I know it sounds strange, but all of it is true. We were traveling north on the road out there, and I got a feeling. A knowing, that this was the place we should settle."

He chuckled. "By 'this' she meant, this exact place. I talked to the owner of the land, and said I wanted to build a house here. He told us the conditions, that we could improve it on our own dollar, and then pay him rent for the land."

Simeon shook his head. "That's not right."

"Again you say . . . what's not right about it? Are you questioning my telling, Mr. Anders?"

He backed down. "I mean no disrespect. Forgive me."

Grandfather cleared his throat. "We liked the proximity to the river and the abundance of woods and game."

"More so, we liked its beauty," Grandmother added. "It reminded us of Ireland, the lush greenness of it all."

But why across from the cemetery—wait, it wasn't a cemetery. Yet. "You have a beautiful plot of land across the street," Justine said.

Grandmother's face grew sad and Grandfather got up from his chair to go to her. "There, there, Abigail."

"I'm sorry," Justine said. "I didn't mean to upset you."

Grandmother took a deep breath and dabbed at her eyes. "You had no way of knowing."

Grandfather returned to his seat and explained. "We lost a child a few months ago."

"Three months ago," Grandmother said.

"Three months ago. Nathan was nine months old. Caught the fever and died."

Simeon and Justine spoke as one. "I'm so sorry."

"I was with-child when we left New York — being so was one of the main reasons we needed to leave. I would not raise a child in those deplorable conditions. He was the first babe born in Piedmont."

"And the first buried," Grandfather said quietly.

His wife nodded. "When Nathan died we wanted to bury him in a right proper place, in God's acre, but there was no cemetery in Piedmont."

Grandfather continued the story. "I went to Isaac and asked him to designate some land for it." He and Grandmother exchanged a glance. "He said yes, as long as we paid the rent on the land. " He grumbled. "He didn't want us burying him here, where we built the house, and we didn't want Nathan in the woods somewhere, away from us." He looked at his wife. "So we asked for the land across the street. I know it's odd. Most don't want a cemetery across from their house, but Addie — we — wanted Nathan close. Tis a wild land here . . . "

"It was a good decision," Grandmother said. "At least Nathan is close by. Right now he's all alone . . ."

"You wish to give him company, wifey?"

"No. Of course not. I'm merely voicing a mother's concern."

They continued eating. Justine was glad to know the reason for the home's location. She hadn't known Granny had a sibling. Granny herself wouldn't be born for six more years. Had Grandmother lost other children between Nathan and Winifred? Poor woman.

Simeon broke the silence. "This is mighty tasty, ma'am."

"Thank you. Or thank Joshua, for he is an expert at butchering and curing meats."

"Built a curing shed out by the kitchen," he said. "Trying to spread the word."

"We're up to ninety-eight citizens in Piedmont now," Grandmother said.

Justine noted that there were less than five hundred in Piedmont in 1878.

Simeon put his fork down. "I see you're finishing off the chimney on the house."

"Trying to," Grandfather said.

"Joshua doesn't like the heights of a ladder and roof."

He shrugged. "I figure if God wanted us to be higher than the back of the horse He would have given us wings." He stabbed a chunk of venison in the pie. "Makes me dizzy up there."

"I could finish it," Simeon said.

"You're not bothered by heights?"

"Not a bit. I did some masonry work in the last place we lived. It would be a way to repay your hospitality and kindness."

"It would be much appreciated."

Justine was glad they had a legitimate reason to stay. She just hoped her gift would abide by the extra time.

**

It was awkward.

Justine's great-grandparents had presumed she and Simeon were married. Now she and Simeon stood in the bedroom—which only had one very small bed.

"You sleep there," he said. "I'll sit up with Goosie in her room."

It was a good solution. "Thank you for saying what you did, taking me in, as it were, at least in their eyes."

"I thought it best because you'd seemed uncertain about sharing your reasons for traveling alone."

Justine busied herself with her carpet bag. "You deserve an answer."

He stood at the window, parting the curtain. "I'm curious, but will not press."

"Thank you." She sat on a wooden chair. "You wouldn't believe it if I told you."

He turned to look at her. "Now you intrigue me."

She thought of something she *could* say. "I feel like I've met you before."

His bushy eyebrows rose. "I think not."

She regretted her comment and smoothed the fabric of her dress over her knees. There was no benefit for her saying such a thing. "You're right. I think not."

He studied her a moment. "You look mighty pretty in green."

She jerked her head to look at him. The compliment was familiar. It had been said by Simeon when she'd first met him in the cemetery while wearing Granny's green dress. "You said that to me before."

He simply smiled at her. "We just established we hadn't met."

"But—"

He went to the door. "Sleep well, Miss Braden."

Before she could acknowledge his use of her last name— which she had never given him— he was gone and she heard him speaking with her grandmother on his way to Goosie's bedside.

She moved to the door wanting to ask, not wanting to ask, wondering how, while feeling frightened of that same how.

Justine retreated to the chair and bowed her head. "Father, I don't understand this. How—?"

There was a knock on the door and she rushed to it, hoping to ask Simeon how he knew her last name.

But it wasn't Simeon. It was her great-grandmother.

"May I come in, dear?"

"Of course."

Grandmother followed her into the room and shut the door. "If you'll forgive me, I overheard your prayer."

Justine let her thoughts backtrack. "That I don't understand all this?"

She nodded. "The prophet Isaiah wrote: 'For my thoughts are not your thoughts, neither are your ways my ways, saith the Lord. For as the heavens are higher than the earth, so are my ways higher than your ways, and my thoughts than your thoughts.'" She nodded once. "I don't know the details of your uncertainty, but I do know that there is no uncertainty in God, only confidence."

Had her great-grandmother just given her a life line?

"Thank you, Mrs. Holloran."

She studied Justine's clothes. "I commend you on your dress."

It's your dress!

She touched the trim on the edge of the sleeve. "I would like to make such a dress when I get a chance to purchase some fabric."

If Justine would have brought anything else to wear into 1800 she would have given her the dress. And yet . . . if the dress wasn't made yet? Confusion took hold.

"You seem tired," Grandmother said. "Is there anything else I can get you?"

"Not a thing. You've been very kind."

"Stranger helping stranger makes us strangers no more, yes?"

Justine smiled. "Agreed."

"I'll say good night, Mrs. Anders."

Alone again, she was officially overwhelmed. She put on her nightgown and got in bed. As she smoothed the covers she doubted she could ever sleep. She was sleeping in her mother's room—in the same room she was using in 1878. The same room she'd shared with her mother in 1857. Next door Goosie was recovering in the same room *she* would sleep in for the next 78 years. And with her, was Simeon, who Justine had met in the cemetery, looking the same as he did right now.

Then there was the whole "you look mighty pretty in green" comment . . .

She turned on her side, reveling in the miracle of it all. As Grandmother had said, God's ways were not man's ways. *Thank You for letting me experience this wonder.*

Suddenly she thought about the Ledger. She didn't remember seeing any entries from Abigail Holloran. Surely Grandmother was over twenty. Did she have the gift?

There are no headstones but that of her child's.

If Grandmother had the gift, she had no means to use it— which made Justine rather sad.

It also made her remember why she had come to this time and place: to bring about justice. She'd been so enamored with the personal experience she'd nearly forgotten.

Tomorrow she would meet Isaac Piedmont.

She prayed for protection and purpose until sleep finally found her.

**

When Justine awakened, it took her a full ten seconds to realize she was in the right bedroom, but in the wrong year.

I will never get used to this.

The sun was up. She heard people stirring and some commotion against the far side of the house. She heard a child's voice, and quickly got dressed so she could check on Goosie. She packed all her belongings, wanting them close at hand. Who knew what the day would bring?

She found Goosie sitting up in bed, being fed some broth by Mrs. Holloran.

Her grandmother turned around. "Good morning, Justine. How did you sleep?"

"Very well, thank you." She studied Goosie's face. "You seem better."

"I am. Only got sick once in the night." The little girl looked at Mrs. Holloran and pointed to the soup. "This tastes good."

"It's good for you, but you need to eat it slow."

There was a pounding outside, which made them look to the right of the house. "What's going on?" Justine asked.

"Mr. Anders is helping Joshua stone up the last of the chimney. I think they had to remove part of what Joshua did near the roofline because truth be told, he doesn't have masonry skills." She served Goosie another spoonful. "There is porridge in a pot and some scones if you'd like. And coffee."

Justine felt bad. "I'm sorry for missing breakfast. I hope you didn't wait on me."

"No need to be sorry. The men wanted to start the work early."

Their work would provide an excuse to be out of the house. Justine retrieved her carpet bag, went to the dining room, and took a scone from a plate covered with a towel. She went outside, leaving her bag on the porch. Around the north side of the house she saw Simeon, high on the ladder, next to the stone chimney which had reached the roofline. Black soot stained the roof around the chimney opening. It was a dangerous situation, as sparks could easily fall upon the nearby shingles. Justine was no stone mason, but even she could see that the chimney needed to be extended at least four feet higher.

Her grandfather had his coat off, and hair had escaped his queue in back. He looked up from stirring some mortar. "Mrs. Anders, good morning. I hope our noise didn't wake you."

"It did not." She looked up at Simeon. He had one knee on the roof and was setting a row of stones around the opening. "It appears you have done this before."

"I have, though that house was not near as nice as this one."

She commended his work ethic but guessed he would not be searching out Isaac Piedmont until he was through with the work. And so . . . "How can I help?"

Her grandfather stood erect and arched his back. "Really, Mrs. Anders? You are our guest."

"I have two willing hands and a strong back. What do you need me to do?"

He handed her the stick he was stirring with. "Keep stirring so it doesn't harden." He called up to Simeon, "Send down the canvas and I will fill it with more stone."

Simeon emptied a canvas onto the roof side of the chimney then lowered it down with a rope. Grandfather spread the canvas on the ground and began piling stones of different sizes in its middle.

"I need more mortar, please," Simeon said. They directed Justine to scoop some into a tin bucket, which also had a rope attached. "Toss me the end," Simeon said.

After two attempts he caught it and pulled the bucket to the roof.

Watching him work was fascinating and she admired his ability to fit one stone to another, trying a few to achieve the best fit. He would slather on the mortar and clean it off with the edge of a trowel, pounding down on the stones to make a tight fit.

Her grandfather must have seen the direction of her gaze for he said, "His craftsmanship surpasses my own. I'm afraid my attempt was a bit irregular and messy."

She couldn't argue with his assessment, for the lower part of the chimney was haphazard and rough.

He checked the mortar. "It's thickening. I'll go fetch more water from the pump." He took up a bucket and walked toward the back of the house.

Simeon looked down at her. "I don't mean to delay your business, Miss Braden."

"But what of yours?"

"Although I am eager for it, justice will wait a day until my daughter is better and my debt for the Holloran's hospitality is paid."

"That's commend—"

She was interrupted when she saw a man come around the front of the house. A man with black hair and a massive frame. A man who resembled two others she knew: Arnold and Quinn Piedmont.

This had to be Isaac. Shivers coursed up her spine and her nerves tightened to full alert.

He nodded at her, then looked up the ladder. "Well now. Who have we here? Simeon Anders himself."

Simeon stopped working but did not descend the ladder. He studied the man. "Samuel. Samuel Hill."

Samuel Hill?

"It's Isaac. Piedmont."

"So you took his name and—"

The man stepped past the ladder to look at Justine. "Are you the second Mrs. Anders?"

"No, sir. The name is Justine."

"And what is your business in my town?"

She took note of his ownership. But how could she answer?

Isaac sidled up to her, imposing his heft next to her slight build. He smiled smugly. "A woman traveling alone then? Don't you know that's not safe?"

"She's with me," Simeon said.

Isaac's eyebrow rose. "An interesting arrangement. I didn't think you had it in you, Simeon."

"Leave her be. Though it's been ten years, you and I have business."

Isaac shook his head, taking a random stir of the mortar. "It's too stiff."

Simeon ignored him, glanced at Justine, then seemed to make a decision to speak openly. "After your atrocity I ran away with my daughter, but when I heard there was a town with the Piedmont name I knew it was time for the truth. So I'm back to let the world know you are not Isaac Piedmont. You killed the Piedmonts. And it's time you were brought to justice."

"Were they buried by some apple trees?" Justine asked.

Both men looked at her. Then Isaac grabbed her upper arm and shoved her, pushing her to the ground. "Watch yourself, little lady."

"Leave her alone!" Simeon got on the top rung of the ladder to descend. But Isaac rushed toward it and yanked the ladder backwards. It—and Simeon—fell.

He hit his head against the pile of stones.

Justine ran to him. His head was bloody, his eyes rolled back.

He seemed to focus for a moment. "There is proof. Truth *is* proof."

"Go get help," she yelled at Isaac.

He just stood there. "You go."

She touched Simeon's arm. "I'll get help." She ran to the front of the house and was just going inside when she heard a commotion and ran back. She saw Isaac standing over Simeon with a rock in his hand, bashing it over and over into his head.

"Stop! Stop!"

She ran and grabbed Isaac's arm. And he did stop. But not before he'd finished his evil work. Simeon Anders was dead.

Grandfather came running from the back of the house with grandmother close behind. "What happened?"

"He fell off the ladder," Isaac said. "I tried to save him."

"You did not. You hit him with this stone!" She picked up the bloodied rock, but as soon as she did, Isaac lunged for her. *Can I die in the past?*

She didn't wait to find out, but ran around to the front of the house, grabbed her bag, and bolted down the road.

"Get back here!" he yelled.

As she ran. . .

She was carried away.

Suddenly she found herself in front of her house. She ran around the side and saw the finished chimney. No Simeon. No grandparents.

She was back in 1878.

**

Justine noticed the rock in her hand. The rock that was wet with blood. In the other hand she held her carpet bag.

It was unnerving being in one year one second, then being in another, in another.

"Justine?" Goosie came around from the front of the house. "You're back. What are you doing over here?"

She held out the rock as all the revelations from the past met the present.

"Your father is Simeon Anders."

"Yes."

"Why didn't you tell me?"

"Why would I? He died when I was ten."

Justine rushed to the place where she'd just seen Simeon die. "He died right here! I went back to 1800. I saw you and your father when you came back to Piedmont. You were sick and my great-grandparents took care of you. And—"

Goosie looked at the rock. "Come inside. You know I can't talk freely out here."

Justine shook her head, then pointed at the cemetery. "Come with me." She pulled Goosie along.

"Not so fast. I'm an old woman!"

Justine slowed down. She needed to regain her composure. Once they were in the cemetery, she said, "Where is your father's grave?"

"Over here."

They moved to the oldest part of the cemetery. There, was a small buff-colored headstone. Justine knelt beside it and peered at the inscription: *Simeon Anders. Born 1760 Died 1800. Beloved Father.*

Goosie pulled a weed nearby. "The Hollorans made the stone for him and buried him near the baby they lost." She nodded toward another small stone. "They took me in."

Justine sat back on her heels. She still had the rock in her hands. "He didn't just die. He was murdered by Samuel Hill." She showed Goosie. "This is his blood."

"But how . . . ?"

Justine told Goosie the whole story.

Finally Goosie said, "After your grandmother did her traveling to the past, she said Isaac wasn't Isaac, so the man who everyone thought was Isaac killed the real Isaac?"

"And buried him in the grave in the grove—with the entire Piedmont family. Samuel Hill must have killed them all."

"But why?"

That answer was less clear. "To become the leader of the town?"

"He could have done that without murdering them. To kill an entire family . . . there has to be more to it."

Justine placed the bloodied stone next to Simeon's headstone. "It was so hard to be there, knowing he was going to die fairly soon and not being able to do anything to stop it."

"How did you know Pa was going to die?"

Justine stood and looked toward the shack—Simeon's shack. What if he was in there? What if he wasn't?

"Something else is bothering you," Goosie said.

"I can't say . . . it's too preposterous."

"And traveling back in time isn't?"

She had a point. "When I went back to 1800 and saw you and your father, I recognized him."

"So you saw him in one of your other visits?"

She shook her head. "I saw him here. In this cemetery. I spoke to him as clearly as I speak to you now. He looked like he did when I saw him in 1800."

Goosie looked at his headstone. "But that's impossible."

Justine's heart beat faster. "It happened. He was the one who told me Thomas was murdered."

Goosie bit her lip. "And now you say Pa was murdered."

"By the same family."

Goosie sighed. "Evil begets evil."

Justine gazed at the shed that Simeon had always entered after his visits with her. She had to see inside. She hurried through the headstones to the shack and knocked. When there was no answer, she opened the door. It took a moment for her eyes to adjust to the dim light, but soon enough, it was clear it was nothing but a storage shed. Rakes and hoes and buckets. No bed. No signs of a man living here. Not even a chair.

"I don't understand."

Goosie caught up with her. "Pa came from in there?"

"He did."

Goosie shook her head back and forth twice. Then paused. "When you saw him . . . how was he?"

"How was . . . ?" Justine looked at her, incredulous.

"I was ten when he died. We were very close, as my mother died soon after I was born. It was always just him and me."

Justine wasn't sure what Goosie wanted to hear. "He was a very kind man. I met you two on the road outside of town and he gave me a ride and included me in your group when the Hollorans let us stay at their house."

Goosie nodded across the street. "Your house."

The entire thing was so absurd. Justine stared at the shack. "Why did he speak to *me? Here?*"

"Did he give you guidance? Information?"

"He did."

"Would you have received that guidance and information any other way?"

"There's no way to know, but probably not."

Goosie slipped her arm through Justine's. "God sent him to help you on your quest."

Justine gasped as she remembered something Simeon had said the first time they'd met. "He warned me: 'Bringing up past sins can get a person in trouble.'"

"He spoke from experience." Goosie looked back to her father's grave. "I wish I could speak to him one more time." She shook her head against the thought. "But it's not my gift, it yours."

"Seeing Simeon is a part of the gift?"

"It happened to you and only you, didn't it?" She turned them toward home. "'Be not forgetful to entertain strangers: for thereby some have entertained angels unawares.'"

Justine scoffed. "An angel in the guise of your father."

Goosie shrugged. "Do you have a better explanation?"

"None."

They walked across the road, into the house. Once inside, Justine said, "In 1800 your father came back to get justice for the Piedmonts."

"And was killed for it." Goosie touched her arm. "Who knows how far the Piedmonts will go to keep that secret. You have to be very careful."

"I need to know the whole truth of it. The real Piedmonts are dead, your father is dead, Thomas is dead . . ." Then she remembered something. "Your father's last words were, 'There is proof. Truth *is* proof.'"

"What truth? What proof?"

Justine felt the fight go out of her and sank into a chair. "I thought you might know."

"I don't."

She looked up into Goosie's eyes. "Somehow I have to finish what your father started."

"How are you going to do that?"

There was only one way. She pressed her hands to her forehead. "I have to go back into your father's life and see what he saw, see the horror of Samuel Hill's evil." Her hands started shaking and she made fists to calm the tremor.

Goosie drew her to standing and held Justine's hands between them. "The truth can wait a while longer. You're trembling."

"The sooner I know, the sooner this can be over."

"You need to rest. Think things through. And pray."

"I need to make a plan. I . . . I need to talk with Harland."

"Not in that dress you don't."

219

Justine looked down at Granny's slim-fit gown. "I need to change."

Goosie slipped her hand around Justine's arm. "And rest."

"But—"

"I insist."

**

Justine did as Goosie had asked. She changed into her blue day dress and rested, but only for fifteen minutes. And yet even that short respite had helped her feel more in control and rejuvenated. She checked her hair in a mirror, and tucked in some stray wisps. She smiled. "All in all, not too mussed for traveling seventy-eight years and back."

She noticed the sketch of Harland's mother on the dresser. She'd wanted to give it to him before this, but yesterday had been a bit busy—being in 1800 and such. She rolled it up and tied a ribbon around it, told Goosie she was leaving, and walked toward Dr. Bevin's office.

To see Harland would help organize her thoughts. For a fleeting moment she thought of Morris and realized he had no such ability. Harland was a sounding board, allowing her to speak all that was on her mind before returning comments or answers steeped in compassion and logic. The only time she'd spoken of deep issues to Morris had been after Mother had died. In return, he'd given her solutions that lacked compassion and spoke of logic that benefited himself above all else.

Thank You for helping me break free of him, Lord.

As she walked past the general store she noticed Arnold wasn't outside. The day was warm and she expected to see him. She'd check on him later.

She found Harland in the office with Dr. Bevin. She didn't want to intrude, so said hello, then retreated to wait outside.

Harland immediately came to the doorway holding a pencil and paper in his hands. "We were doing an inventory of medicinals. We're almost through."

From the office Dr. Bevin said, "I can finish without you, Harland. Go talk to the pretty lady."

Harland took the pencil and paper back inside and grabbed a hat. "It appears I am at your disposal."

"I have much to tell you." She raised the rolled sketch. "And show you."

"Tied with a pretty ribbon. You have my attention." He led her to the bench under an ancient maple.

She handed him the scroll and he untied it.

"Mama." He looked at her. "You really did meet her."

"You doubted me?"

"No, but . . ." He sighed. "To see her as she was when I was a child . . ."

"I'm sure it's not a great likeness as I drew it from memory, but I thought you would like it."

"I do." He kissed her cheek. "I will cherish it always." He looked at her, cocking his head to the side. "But this is not the only reason you've come to visit."

"It is not. I need a willing ear and wise advice."

"You have the first, and I will attempt the latter." He tied the ribbon around the drawing and set it beside him. "Before you continue, let me say I am glad to have you safely back again."

"As am I."

"So what did you discover in Isaac's life?"

A torrent of words spilled out. "I went back to 1800 and met my great-grandparents and actually stayed in the room I'm staying in now, but it was far different then because they were just building the place. In fact, there was an unfinished chimney and Goosie was there, and she was sick, and Simeon was back in town to get justice against Isaac."

"Who's Simeon?"

"Goosie's father." She wanted to tell him that she'd seen Simeon in 1878 but didn't dare. Yet.

"What justice was he searching for?"

"As I've heard all along, Isaac wasn't Isaac at all. Simeon called him Samuel Hill. Samuel wasn't too keen on Simeon being back and yanked his ladder back so he fell, and then he hit him with a rock over and over until he was dead." She took a deep breath, clearly exhausted from the telling but also from recreating the hitting motion.

"That's horrible."

"I had the rock in my hand and said I was going to tell, and he ran after me, and would have caught me too, but I was whisked back to this time. I have the rock. With blood on it. It's proof."

"A bloodied rock won't convince people seventy-eight years after the fact."

The air went out of her. "I was so relieved that it came with me."

He put a hand on her arm. "I'm sorry to stifle your enthusiasm."

She popped off the bench. "How is any justice going to come from this? We have the murder of the Piedmonts in the grave, and—"

"It's the Piedmonts?"

"That's what Simeon said. Samuel killed them."

"Why?"

Her thoughts collided. "To take over the town?"

"There was little town to take over back then, was there?"

She pressed her hands to her forehead and paced in front of him. "We have their murders, the murder of Thomas by Quinn, and now the murder of Simeon Anders, Goosie's father. But how does it fit together? Why does it matter? Samuel is long dead. Quinn and Arnold can't be held accountable for what he did."

"People are dead by foul means, Justine. That always matters."

She stopped pacing. "I need to go back into Simeon's life and see what started all this." She took a step toward the road. "I need to—"

He grabbed her hand, stopping her. "That is *not* what you need to do. At least not right this minute."

She thought back to Goosie's words. "Goosie told me to pray about it. I haven't prayed."

He drew her hand around his arm. "All in good time." He started walking, taking her with him.

"Where are we going?"

"There's something I have to show you."

"I don't have time for a walk, Harland."

"The justice for Piedmont and for *the* Piedmonts can wait a little longer."

"But—"

"Hush now. Do you trust me?"

"I do." *More than anyone else.*

"Then let your mind clear as I take you up the mountain." He nodded toward the mountain on the east side of town. "We won't go all the way up. Just far enough."

"Far enough for what?"

"You ask too many questions."

**

Justine wasn't used to exerting herself. Although she often strolled in Central Park, the walks were leisurely, the terrain flat.

Hiking up a mountain trail was a new experience. She had to hold up her skirt and watch every footfall lest she trod upon a rock or slew of pebbles that would cause her to turn an ankle.

Harland helped her when she needed it and let her pause to catch her breath often. At one point, she stood with her hands on her hips, feeling the burn in her lungs and the pounding of her heart in her chest. It took a few minutes for her to be able to speak. "Not to be indelicate about it, but you have the advantage, Mr. Jennings. Trousers, sturdy shoes, and no petticoats to trip on, nor a corset that rebels against deep breaths."

"I had not thought about that. Would you like to go back down?"

She shook her head. "We've come this far. Now it is a matter of pride. But is it much farther?"

"Not much. I promise it's worth it."

"And what exactly is *it?*"

"A surprise." He winked at her, held out his hand, and they continued on.

Five minutes later they stopped in a clearing in the forest. There was a meadow of spring wildflowers, and even a small stream.

"It's lovely," she said. The water enticed her. "Can we drink?"

"Of course." He positioned himself on the bank, squatted down, rinsed his hands in the water, then cupped them to hold a drink. He brought it to her.

She maneuvered his hands to manage a drink and found the water cold and refreshing. "Thank you," she said, wiping her mouth with the back of her hand. "Now, you."

He repeated the process, then returned to her side. Their thirst quenched, he led her to a specific place on the low grasses. "There," he said, pointing. "Behold God's handiwork."

The beauty took her breath away. For as far as the eye could see trees sprouted with lush spring greenery, layers and layers in all directions. She could spot the rooftops of Piedmont far below, and a break in the greenery beyond. "Is that the river?"

"It is. Vermont lies on the other side."

She drew in a deep breath, closing her eyes, letting her mind empty and her body revitalize.

"You like it? Was it worth the hike?"

"Yes. And Yes." She kept her eyes closed. "When I go back in time it's like being carried away." She opened them. "But here . . . I am also carried away."

"That's a lovely way to put it. This has been my special place since I was a boy."

She was touched. "Thank you for sharing it with me."

"There is much I wish to share."

His words made her tingle inside. She turned to look at him directly. "My thoughts always fall into place when I'm with you." She took his hand and gave it a squeeze. "Thank you for bringing me here, and for. . . being you."

"It's all I know how to be."

She laughed. "I think you are the most genuine person I have ever met. You have no artifice. No deception. No manipulation."

"I thank you," he said. "But you are wrong about the last."

"Manipulation?"

"I manipulated you up this mountain, didn't I?"

She didn't like the word, even though it had been her own. "You *invited* me. You saw what I needed when I couldn't."

His voice grew soft. "I want what's best for you, Justine. Surely you know that."

"I do and am fully grateful for it." She turned her gaze to the breadth of nature spread before her. A hawk soared over the tops of the trees, tilting, compensating against a draft of wind, taking advantage of it. The clouds in the western sky undulated slowly, being in no hurry to change, yet changing nevertheless.

"As do I."

"What?"

She hadn't meant to say the words aloud. She nodded toward the clouds. "They change slowly, but they *do* change. As do I."

"I know you've been burdened with change."

"It's not just that." She stood and took two paces from him, needing space to say what was in her heart. "My life was set, as constant as a plain blue sky. I was supposed to marry a rich man, live in a luxurious house, and have many fine children."

"Those are not bad things."

"No, but that life . . ." She looked at the clouds. "It did not allow for clouds, for life to be ever-changing, re-forming itself."

"Yet it did change. Your life *was* re-formed. And now you are here."

She touched a new maple leaf that hung low on its branch, half unfurled. "Circumstances changed, leading me here. I'm not sure I would have changed if not *for* the circumstances."

"You will never know."

That truth bothered her. "Did I need to be pushed?"

"Again, you will never know."

"Mother's death started it all. I hate to say that something so awful could create something good, but there's no denying it."

"God always makes good come from bad."

"Always?"

"We don't always see it right away, but the Bible says it's so."

"As such, you choose to believe it?"

"I don't think the Bible should be read with an attitude of pick-and-choose."

She felt inadequate. "I'm afraid I read far too little of it."

"A point that is easily remedied."

She made a silent vow to do just that. Then she went back to watching the clouds change. "Circumstances made my situation change, but it's more than that."

He went to her. "*You* have changed?"

She put her hands to her chest, her emotions heavy. "When I think about the Justine Braden of New York City, it's like I'm seeing another person, as though I'm in the audience at the opera, watching an actor portray a character."

"You were more than a character. The person you were has led you to become the person you are." He took her hands in his, then touched her cheek. "I see the *after* Justine and I care for her very much. All of her. All she was before, all she is after, and all she will come-to-be."

His words caused her throat to tighten. "Why are you so good to me?"

"Because I'm falling in love with you."

Her heart skipped. "You are?"

He nodded. "The question is, are you falling in love with me?"

She looked into his eyes that matched the blue of the sky. As she'd told him, there was no artifice there, no deception or manipulation. Just . . . love. She took his hand that lay upon her cheek and kissed its palm. "I am, Harland. I am falling in love with you. In fact, I am quite carried away when I am with you."

He smiled, then kissed her.

It was not Justine's first kiss, but she knew it was her last, first kiss.

**

226

"You've ruined me," Justine said as they walked from the trail to the road in Piedmont.

"I don't think so," Harland said. "If I offended you in any—"

She laughed and stopped just before the road to face him. "Not like that. You have ruined me because *now* is such a delightful time that I wonder why I would ever go back to another."

"Our delight is quite mutual." He tipped her chin back and kissed her gently.

They heard a gasp and turned to see Mabel on the road.

"Good afternoon, Mabel," Harland said.

Her face was a mask of pain as she scurried away.

"Oh dear," Justine said.

"If you don't mind, I need to go speak with her."

"Please do."

He ran ahead and called her name. Thankfully, the girl stopped.

Justine walked toward home and passed them as they stood in front of Dr. Bevin's. Mabel shook her head no while Harland talked. Justine had just reached the store when she heard a female cry of agony. Mabel ran by her, clearly distraught. Justine turned back and saw Harland. He spread his hands, shaking his head.

It was done. That was a good thing.

Wasn't it?

"There are consequences to stirring up trouble, you know."

She turned to her right and saw Quinn standing in the doorway of the store. She ignored him and walked home, the implied threat nipping at her heels.

**

Although it had been an eventful day, there was one more thing Justine had to do.

She knelt before the fireplace in the parlor, pushed the andirons back, swept the ash away, and used a knife to pry up the stone that covered the hiding place of the Ledger.

Just as she was taking it out, she felt a presence behind her. "Goosie. I was . . . I hope it's all right to . . ."

The old woman smiled. "You have something to say now?"

"Other people do."

"Very good. It's time you added their wisdom to the book."

"It's not my wisdom, and it's not really theirs. I truly feel it's God's wisdom."

"Which is a very wise thing to say." Goosie put a hand to her heart. "I'm proud of you, Jussie."

I hope I deserve it. She headed upstairs, then paused. "I'll put everything back when I'm through."

Goosie shook her head. "There's no need to hide the Ledger anymore, now that it's found its rightful owner."

Justine took the book to her room, feeling the responsibility of the ages. She'd been to the past four times now. She'd heard wisdom there. But would she remember it?"

Ask.

Of course. She sat at the desk and bowed her head. "I'm sorry for taking so long to write in this book. I will be more diligent in the future. Help me remember what You want me to remember."

She forced herself to relax, trying to clear her mind of its muddle.

Then—as if a heavenly hand swiped the slate of her thoughts clean, Justine began to remember. At the top of a new page she wrote: Wisdom Gathered by Justine Tyler Braden. Then she began her list:

~ *Winifred Holloran Tyler 1826: "Stand up for what is right, no matter the cost."*

~ *Mavis Tyler Braden 1857: "Don't let the past dictate the present."*

~ *Thomas Piedmont 1860: "We must forgive others as we ask for forgiveness."*

~ *Jesse Jennings 1860: "Take time."*

*~ Simeon Anders: 1878: "You don't reach your
destination by standing at the river. You have to wade
through it, one step at a time."
~ Simeon Anders: 1800: "Truth is proof."
~ Abigail Holloran 1800: "There is no uncertainty in
God, only confidence."
And: "God's ways are not our ways."
And: "Stranger helping stranger makes us strangers no
more."*

She thought of something Harland had said today. Should
current wisdom be included?

"I don't see why not."

So she added one more entry: *Harland Jennings 1878: The
person you were has led you to become the person you are.*

"There now. All finished." Though she knew she wasn't.
There would be more additions. Hopefully many more. Justine
paused and looked over her entries. Each one had helped her.

As they can help others.

She should not have been surprised by the thought, but
she was. The Ledger contained wisdom of the ages, life lines
that were eternal.

Life lines that were meant to be shared?

But how?

She nodded her agreement to God's nudge but knew the
"how" would be answered another day.

Rest, Justine. Rest.

Chapter Fourteen

The next morning, Justine readied herself to go back into Simeon's life. Although she had no control over what year, because there was a purpose to her travel she had to believe she would be going back to pre-1800, when Piedmont wasn't even Piedmont.

She chose a plain skirt and simple bodice with the squared neck of Colonial times, and packed a fichu scarf in her travel bag along with a mop cap she found in a trunk. And Granny's shawl, of course. She found it interesting that a piece of clothing could be so timeless. Skirts, bodices, waistlines, sleeves, collars . . . everything else changed, except for the simple shawl.

She stopped in the parlor where Goosie was dusting the knick-knacks. "I'm going now."

Goosie put down her cloth and drew Justine into an embrace. "Do be careful, child. I've not been fearful before now. If Samuel Hill is the cause of four people's deaths, he won't think twice in killing a wayward girl who suddenly appears and interferes."

Justine felt a sudden wave of unease. "Do you think I can get killed in the past?"

"Do you want to test it to find out?" Goosie put a hand on her shoulder and bowed her head. "Keep watch over our Justine. Show her the truth You want her to find, then bring her home safe to us."

Amen.

**

Justine took a step outside and paused. She preferred to walk to the cemetery without the eyes of the town upon her. She looked right and saw no one on the road. But to the left people crossed and crisscrossed, going about their business. She spotted Rachel and Mrs. Beemish having a chat with Pastor Davies in front of the church.

She'd waited an entire day for this trip. Her patience had grown thin. And so she wrapped the shawl around her shoulders, hid the carpet bag on her far-side, and hurried across the road, quickly weaving her way between the trees and headstones until she reached Simeon's grave.

She was about to kneel down to touch the name, when she heard movement to her left. She turned to find Mabel, standing with some flowers in her hand.

"Justine."

"Mabel."

The girl eyed her old clothes. "What an interesting . . . ensemble."

"Yes, well. They were my grandmother's."

"You carry a carpet bag to a cemetery?"

Justine couldn't think of a single explanation. "Why are you here?"

"I'm bringing flowers to my grandfather's grave," Mabel said.

"How nice of you. I'm visiting the graves of my mother and grandparents."

"But their graves are over there." Mabel pointed to the newer section of the cemetery.

Oh dear.

Mabel wasn't through, "I don't like you and Harland. Being together."

Gracious. Would this girl never stop? "I'm sorry if you were hurt. We had no such intention."

"Now you're lying."

"Ly—?"

Just then Simeon walked toward them. Justine was surprised to see him, especially when she wasn't alone. Did Mabel see him?

"Good morning, ladies," he said.

"Who are you?" Mabel asked.

So she could *see him.*

"I'm Simeon, the caretaker here. And you are Mabel Collier, I believe?"

Mabel put a had to her chest. "You know my name?"

"I know many names."

Justine smiled at his cryptic answer. "I was just about to... visit you," Justine said with a glance to his grave.

He laughed. "I'm sure I could use the company." He looked at Mabel. "And you? I haven't seen you here before."

"I . . . I don't particularly like cemeteries."

"Most don't." Simeon took a deep breath. "Me? I find them enlightening, don't you, Miss Braden?"

She loved their banter. "Completely. You never know who you might run into."

"Alive or dead?" Simeon asked.

"Either will do." Justine leveled Mabel with a look. "Don't you agree?"

Mabel fumbled the bouquet, clearly flustered. "I don't like this conversation."

Justine shrugged. "Talking to the dead isn't your cup of tea? How unfortunate."

Mabel's head shook a quick *no,* then scooped up the flowers, set them on the nearest grave, and ran toward town.

Simeon raised a hand to wave. "I'll tell your grandfather, Horace, hello for you, Miss Collier."

She ran faster.

"Is her grandfather named Horace?" Justine asked him.

"That's what the headstone says."

"You don't know him?"

"Never met the man."

Justine took in the moment. "You're not really here."

He pressed his hands against his body. "I'm not?"

"You know what I mean."

"You witnessed my death."

"I'm so sorry. I wish I could have stopped it."

"That's not allowed."

She nodded and pointed to his grave. "I was just going back to finally get the whole truth of things — unless you can save me the trip."

Simeon shook his head. "It is better you see things firsthand." He gazed at his headstone. "I would have liked to spend more time with my daughter."

"My great-grandparents took her in." She pointed back to the house. "She still lives in their house. She's an old woman now."

He stared across the street. "I know."

"You do?"

"The Almighty occasionally lets those who've passed see glimpses of their loved ones. He is very generous."

"She's become a dear friend."

"She has no husband? No children?" He looked toward the house. "I've never seen her with anyone."

"She has neither. But she's remained loyal to my family for many generations."

"Including you?"

"Including me."

He took a breath in and out, looking at the house where his daughter dusted the parlor.

"Would you like to see her? I could go get—"

"No," he said adamantly. "It is not allowed."

"But I see you. I speak with you. Mabel saw you."

"That served a purpose."

"What purpose?"

"You will see."

"Seeing your daughter would serve a purpose. It would make both of you happy."

He shook his head, looking forlorn. "Tell her I love her dearly and we *will* see each other someday, in heaven."

"I will do that."

He blinked and seemed to return from his memories. His forehead furrowed. "Be wary of Samuel Hill. Do not believe anything he says."

She thought of something Simeon had told her in 1800. "You mentioned there was proof against him. What is that proof? Or where can I find it?"

Simeon suddenly looked up toward the morning sky. Then he nodded. "God wants you to go now, see for yourself."

Justine looked heavenwards too. "He just spoke to you?"

"I'm here according to His will, not my own. I will not come again."

She was disappointed at the thought. "I thank you for your direction and advice."

He pointed upward. "His direction and advice. I am merely the messenger." He tipped his hat. "God speed, Justine Braden." He walked toward the shack.

"Thank you for handling Mabel for me," she called after him.

He didn't even turn around but raised a hand in acknowledgment before disappearing inside.

"Well then," she said with a sigh. "I best be going before anyone else comes along."

She took up the carpet bag and knelt before his headstone. As she traced her fingers along Simeon's name she heard movement to her left and saw someone behind a tree. Mabel?

But before she could stop the process, the gift took her away.

**

There was no cemetery, only a small clearing — though Justine thought she recognized a trio of young maples with a boulder between them. The trunks of the trees were a mere eight-inches across instead of their enormous girth in 1878. There were no headstones. Without those trees and that one rock, she would have no notion she was in Piedmont. Or a town of any name.

There were no intersections, no roads, no buildings. The location of her family's house was forested, the ground covered with low plants, ivy, and a carpet of autumn leaves. As was the majority of the land around her.

How far back did I travel?

She sat on the boulder, trying to collect her thoughts. A soft shower of crimson leaves danced around her. She held out a hand to see if one would land on it, but they floated by. She shivered in the autumn air and draped the fichu scarf around her neck, tucked it into her open neckline, and donned the mop cap.

When she'd previous been carried into the past, she had always seen something familiar, seen someone who'd been able to help her understand why she'd been brought there. But today she felt very alone. It was eerie, almost sinister. Nothing in her life as a city girl had prepared her to be in true wilderness. Even when she'd hiked up the mountain with Harland, there had been a trail, proof that others had gone before. *Lord?*

There was rustling in the woods. She stood and held the carpet bag close to her chest. *As if it can protect me from wild animals?*

A deer came into view and she relaxed. It lifted its head and eyed her as if *she* were the danger. Then it moved on.

"Calm down, Justine. God knows where You are."

And then, she heard a baby's cry.

She whipped her head toward the sound, which was coming from the north. She hurried into the woods. If *she* felt vulnerable in the wilderness, a child . . .

She came to an opening in the trees, newly cleared. There was a man holding a baby next to a makeshift tent set near the beginnings of a log cabin. Two horses grazed nearby. There was a fire going, with a small pot hanging from a three-legged stand above the flames.

The baby continued to wail as the man tried to soothe it. Justine moved into his view. "Excuse me?"

When he looked up she saw that it was Simeon. A slightly younger Simeon. Which meant the baby must be Goosie.

"I'm sorry for appearing so suddenly, sir, but I heard the baby's cry and—"

"She's hungry, but I can't do two things at once."

"May I?"

He handed over the child, and readied a bottle of liquid with a cloth stuck in its top. He handed it to Justine. "Broth from a venison stew. I was letting it cool but she got impatient with me."

Justine stuck the odd bottle in the baby's mouth, tipped it downwards and watched as Goosie eagerly gnawed and sucked on the cloth.

"There now," Simeon said. "I'm beholden for the help. I was just about to smash up some cooked apples."

Apples. From the apple trees down by the river?

"Go on and finish it up," Justine said. "I have her."

"I see that." Simeon smiled. "Augusta likes you."

Justine was glad she'd already heard Goosie's given name. "She's beautiful. How old?"

"Two months now. She was born August the first." He smashed some cooked apples on a tin plate, then paused. "Her mother died soon after."

"I am very sorry for your loss. And hers."

"Thank you. We're managing. Somewhat. I thought about taking her north to the next town, but it's a half a day's ride and my responsibilities keep me here."

"Responsibilities?"

He added a bit more water to the apple sauce. "My name is Simeon Anders. I'm here with Colonel Piedmont and Samuel Hill. We all fought together in the War of Independence."

Justine was surprised. They'd been comrades?

"I joined when I was young and learned how to fight under the Colonel. He was kind enough to take me under his wing and let me become his secretary and aide. Samuel works for him now too."

To know the Piedmont's fate was bad enough, but to know she could do nothing to stop it was excruciating.

"You all right, miss?"

"Yes." She adjusted the bottle so Goosie could get more of the broth. "Your loyalty to the colonel is commendable."

"There's no finer man. He was deeded six square miles around here and is to make a town of it. He brought me and Samuel with him, and even said we can each have a parcel of our own."

Have a parcel? Or rent a parcel? "That's very kind of him."

"Generous," Simeon said. "I'd follow him anywhere." He finished the applesauce. "Would you like to give it a go? She's just learning how to take from a spoon and I haven't had much luck. Maybe I'm doing something wrong."

"I'm sure you're not, but I'd be happy to try." She moved to a tree stump and sat down, setting the bottle on the ground. Simeon knelt beside them, holding the plate of applesauce as

Justine gave a spoonful to Goosie. The baby's tongue wasn't sure what to do with the texture, but as soon as she took it in, her eyebrows rose. "She likes it."

"Sweets for my sweet," Simeon said.

They continued the feeding until sleep became more important to Goosie than food. Justine rocked her gently, loving the feel of a baby in her arms. Someday . . .

Simeon took the plate away. "I am obviously no gentleman, for I have not asked your name. Forgive me."

"I'm Justine Braden."

"Nice to meet you, Miss — " Just then, Simeon stood erect and froze. "I hear a horse."

Justine's hearing was not as attune to such sounds, but within a few minutes a man rode up. A man she recognized from 1800. A man with raven black hair. Isaac —

No. Samuel Hill.

"Evening, Simeon," Samuel said.

"Evening," Simeon said. There was a wariness in his greeting. "Does Colonel Piedmont need something?"

"Not a thing. I just heard voices." He looked down at Justine and the baby and studied her a moment, like he recognized her. She moved behind Simeon.

"Finding a new wife so soon, Simeon?"

"She's just a friend passing through."

His smile was wicked. "You can pass through on my parcel if you'd like, miss. A man can get mighty lonely out here in the wilderness."

"Leave her be, Samuel," Simeon said. Justine saw his hands clench at his sides.

But then they heard a tree fall with a crash in the direction of the river.

Hill turned his horse in that direction. "Take care of yourself, miss."

Before he rode away, he pointed to a leather pouch. "Jerky?"

Simeon nodded.

Hill held out his hand. Simeon gave him a few strips of something that looked like leather. Then he rode away. Justine was glad to see him go.

"Pardon his manners. He's not the friendliest sort," Simeon said. "Not a good kind of friendly anyway."

"He has a cabin started too?"

"Of a sort. He's lazy. We're each supposed to be working a parcel, getting the town started. Then hopefully newcomers will want to settle here too."

"What's the name of your town?"

"Justice."

Justine was taken aback. "I thought . . . I mean sometimes people name towns after themselves."

"No, miss. That's not the colonel's way. Justice is very important to him so I think it's a fine name." He smiled. "I'm keen on justice too. The good book says, 'Every way of a man is right in his own eyes: but the Lord pondereth the hearts. To do justice and judgment is more acceptable to the Lord than sacrifice. A high look, and a proud heart, and the plowing of the wicked, is sin.'" He nodded, created a physical "amen" to the verses. "We're starting fresh here, and we're going to do it right."

"I commend you for your courage and your mighty goal."

He tied the top of the pouch and hung it from a branch. "Unfortunately we don't all agree on the goal—or the process."

She didn't have to guess who was causing the problem. "What does Mr. Hill want?"

"Everything."

Justine felt her stomach clench. "For himself?"

"He always was a selfish cuss, but since we got here, he's been complaining about the colonel having the land in his name, and him being in charge."

"Someone has to be."

"I agree. Isaac was the one to take it upon himself to get the land in the first place. He's being generous by asking us to go with him, not working under him, but as settlers in our own right. He's brought his wife and daughter and was glad to have me bring my Dottie." His face grew plaintive. "I shoulda waited until after Augusta was born to travel, but Dottie was excited and insisted we go. It was too much for her and she died soon after the baby was born." He looked to the right. "I buried her nearby."

"I'm so sorry."

"Life is short. Love now."

It was a wonderful life line. Justine vowed to remember it for the Ledger.

Simeon took a seat nearby. "I'll take her if you want me to."

"If it's all right. I like holding her."

He nodded and continued his story. "The colonel has grand plans for a church, a school, shops and stores, and houses everywhere, with people growing their families here, making Justice prosper."

"It sounds wonderful."

"It will be. I pray it will be."

There was doubt in his voice.

"You're worried?" He shook his head, but Justine persisted. "About Mr. Hill?"

"Lazy I can handle. Even selfishness is tolerable. But I've seen a mean streak in him. Saw it during the war, but let it slide because it *was* war. But now. . ." He visibly shuddered. "He's evil."

Justine suffered her own shudder, making Goosie twitch. "That's a strong word."

"An apt one." Simeon poked at the fire, making sparks scatter. "I just hope—"

He suddenly stopped, cocking his head to listen. Two men's voices could be heard arguing.

"Oh no," he said.

"Is that Samuel and the colonel?"

"Can't be anyone else."

They heard a woman's voice join the men's.

"Mary." Simeon's face contorted in worry. "I need to go. It sounds bad."

Justine stood. "I'll come too."

"No!" Simeon picked up his rifle and mounted his horse. "I know we've just met, but . . . will you stay here with Augusta? Please? I need her safe."

"Of course, but what are you going to do?"

"Stop things from getting worse."

But you don't stop him. Even though she knew the truth, Justine called after him. "Be careful!"

The knowledge of what was about to transpire roiled inside her. Most likely Isaac Piedmont and his family had only moments to live and she was helpless to stop it.

She paced in front of the fire with Goosie in her arms, then stopped and looked to the heavens. "Samuel is going to kill the Piedmonts and change the course of this entire settlement forever. How can I stay here and let that happen?"

A shot rang out.

And then another.

Justine held Goosie tightly to her chest. "Oh, dear God, what should I do?"

Suddenly Simeon came riding through the woods. Fast. "Come on! We have to go! Now!"

Justine didn't wait to hear details. She set Goosie on the ground and opened her carpet bag, shoving in the baby's bottle, a plate, fork, food stuffs, nappies…anything she could fit inside. Simeon dismantled the tent and stuffed packs that he placed on the second horse.

Was there time for this? "Should we just run?"

"I shot Hill in the leg. He'll be after us, so we need the horses." He took a length of cloth and wrapped it around Justine diagonally. "It will help you hold Augusta because I need to be able to shoot."

She nodded.

"Get on." He helped her mount his horse, then handed the baby to her. Justine tucked Goosie into the sling. She was awake now and fussing. Would her crying give them away?

He tied her bag to the back with some other supplies. "Go! I need to load my gun before I follow."

"Where to?"

He pointed. "There's a town a half a day's ride north. Now away with you. Don't stop. I'll catch up."

As Justine and the baby bolted through the woods, she had the thought that *now* would be a good time for her to be whisked back to 1878. Yet if that happened, would Goosie go with her? That certainly wouldn't work.

And it didn't happen. "It's all right, Goosie. Shh. Shh." Between holding onto the horse's mane and the baby, and dodging low branches, Justine didn't have time to think of anything except the moment at hand. She listened for gun shots but didn't hear any. Was Hill hurt bad enough not to follow? Was Simeon right behind them? Or was he waiting to confront the man? Surely he wouldn't risk it. Surely he wouldn't leave his daughter in her care — the care of a stranger?

Justine felt the baby slip a bit in the sling, so had to slow down to use both hands to adjust her. She took a moment to look into her innocent gray eyes. "It's all right, Goosie. We'll both get through this, and so will your papa."

She heard a horse coming. *Please be Simeon...*

It was. He caught up with them, riding astride the pack horse. "Why did you stop?"

"She was slipping in the sling."

"Keep going," he said, with a glance behind.

"Is the colonel dead?"

"Yes. As is his wife and daughter." His forehead furrowed. "I can't believe he killed them all."

"Why is Hill after you?"

"He knows I saw. I'm the only witness." With another glance behind, he said, "We need to ride faster."

"It's going to be dark soon."

"All the more reason to keep going. There's a cave an hour north. I found it while hunting. We'll sleep there."

**

If Morris could see me now.

Justine huddled inside the entrance to the cave, tucking her feet under the hem of her skirt. She'd put on the capelet she'd brought along and used Granny's shawl over her legs.

"I'm sorry you're cold," Simeon said. "But I can't risk a fire."

"I understand." She put a hand on a sleeping Goosie, who lay between them. Simeon tucked a patchwork quilt around her.

"I do have some candles, so we can at least have a little light." He set one in the crack of a rock and lit it. The low undulating light cast odd, disconcerting shadows. He sat between the light and the opening, blocking it from the outside.

He opened the pouch she'd seen before and offered her one of the leathery, aromatic strips.

"What is this?"

"Deer jerky. You eat it." He tore off a bite.

Again, Justine had a thought about Morris being appalled at the mere thought of eating dried venison. She bit into it — and with some wheedling — got some torn off. "It's salty."

"I salt the meat while it's drying."

As she chewed, it softened a bit and tasted like meat instead of leather. Simeon handed her a canteen of water.

"We should get some sleep while Augusta's sleeping," he said.

But Justine couldn't sleep. She had no idea when she would be pulled back into the future.

"Can I ask you some questions about the colonel and Hill?"

"I guess you're due since I've dragged you into the middle of it. By the by, where were you heading?"

"Haverhill. To visit a relative." It seemed like the best answer.

"Will they be worried about you?"

"It will be all right." She needed to get to the questions. "Are you sure Hill killed the Piedmonts?"

"I saw him. He and the colonel were arguing about the ownership of the land. Hill didn't just want to settle here, he wanted to be in charge."

"It's not his land."

"He wants it to be. When the colonel said no, Hill lunged at him. The colonel has a wooden leg, so he toppled back. Hill took advantage, slashing his throat. Mary screamed and went to him, and Hill . . ." Simeon struggled for composure. "He killed her, and then little Sophie who was right beside her." Simeon looked to the darkened sky outside the cave. "Lord, why?"

Unfortunately, there was no answer now. Nor would there ever be.

She gave Simeon a moment of silence and prayed for the souls of the Piedmonts. And for her quest for justice. God had sent her here. She had to trust He would work things through.

Finally Simeon spoke. "As you see, Samuel Hill *is* evil."

"He is."

"Today proves he's more evil than I thought. I shot at him and he shot back and missed me. I rode to get you and Augusta. If he's willing to kill the Piedmonts he'd think nothing of killing us."

Justine heard Granny's voice in her head, a young Winifred arguing with her husband, Ned: " *Your father wasn't called Isaac Piedmont. He had another name.* "

Yes indeed: Samuel Hill. "Samuel will pretend to be Isaac Piedmont, the deed holder."

Simeon cocked his head, considering her words. "With me gone no one can argue with him."

Her mind sped through the logistics of it. "Won't people wonder why the colonel looks different? Or ask after Mary and Sophie?"

Simeon spread his hands wide. "What people? We were creating a new town." His voice choked. "No one will know."

"Unless you tell them."

Goosie began to stir, and opened her eyes, seeking her father. He picked her up, and held her against his shoulder, embracing her, supporting her. Gaining comfort *from* her. "I have to keep her safe. Above all else."

The tragedy of the day fully took root. One family lost, another on the run. Seeing Simeon and his daughter provided the final tug to Justine's heart and she let tears fall.

He kissed his baby's head. "Sorry for the pain of it, miss. But even if I come back with the law, I don't have the deed. Samuel will find it in the colonel's possessions. It will be my word against his."

"But the Piedmonts . . . their bodies . . ."

Simeon sighed. "It's a large forest, a fast river." He handed Goosie to Justine. "I have to write it all down, everything I saw today. The complete truth. Will you witness it for me?"

Sign "Justine Braden" on a document that's from a time before I am born? Yet she couldn't deny him. "I will be your witness."

"Thank you." He hesitated. "Do you have any paper?"

She remembered her sketchbook. "Actually, I do." She ripped off a page and gave it to him, along with a pencil. "May I sketch you and Augusta while you write?" She opened the sketchbook to let him see other sketches and it landed on the one of Goosie—the old woman.

"Who's that?"

"A woman named Goosie."

"That's an odd name. She have a penchant for geese?"

"When she was little, she did. Or they did, for her." *You gave her the nickname.* "May I sketch?"

"Don't see why not."

She settled in to sketch as Simeon found a flat rock to use as a desk. He began to write.

As he did Justine had one thought: Where was this page of testimony in 1878? She had the feeling she'd need it.

**

"There," Simeon said. "I'm done."

Justine awakened from a doze.

"Will you witness it?" He extended his deposition toward her. It was just a page, but the writing was very small. "There, at the end. Put the date and your name after 'witnessed by'."

She hesitated. If these pages still existed in 1878, signing her name might prevent people from believing it was true.

"The date is October 1, 1790."

She filled in the date but paused before signing. *Lord, what should I do?*

"You hesitate," Simeon said. "Do you wish to read it first?"

"That's not necessary." She took the pencil and wrote her name, trusting God to make it work.

He folded the paper into fourths and set it aside. Then he pulled Goosie's small patchwork coverlet close, and with the tip of a knife began to rip out a six-inch by six-inch square.

"What are you doing?"

"Creating a hiding place." He removed the stitches from one side, slipped the paper beneath the square. "Now, I'll sew it shut."

Justine looked closer at the quilt. "I've seen this before."

"What?"

She was unable to explain how she'd seen Goosie's blanket. Was the deposition still there?

She moved her carpetbag to act as a pillow. "We should sleep."

"As soon as this is sewn," he said. "Good night, Justine."

He finished his work, blew out the candle, and settled in beside his daughter.

Only then did Justine close her eyes as the winds of time swept her away.

Chapter Fifteen

Justine opened her eyes in 1878. She was standing in the cemetery, facing Simeon's grave.

"There she is!"

Justine turned around to see Mabel Collier rushing toward her from the road.

Mabel was not alone. Behind her came Piedmont's finest: Pastor and Mrs. Huggins, Dr. Bevin, the Moores—with assorted children, the Beemishes, and others she had not met. And Quinn. Unfortunately, Quinn. None of them looked happy to see her. This was not a welcoming party.

She was glad to see Goosie and Harland. At least she had two supporters for whatever was about to unfold.

Justine set her carpet bag behind the headstone, letting Granny's shawl fall upon it.

She faced them, refusing to be intimidated. Yet her insides stirred. Had people seen her suddenly appear? She prayed for the right words but was uncertain what right words would accomplish or whether there *were* any *right* words.

Mabel stopped a short distance away and pointed. "I tell you, she disappeared! I was watching her from behind the trees. She knelt down by a headstone and then she was gone!"

So they didn't see me reappear just now. Justine scoffed. "I was gone?" She pressed her hands against her skirt. "It appears I am very much here."

Some of her audience snickered. "She *is* here, Mabel," Mrs. Huggins said. "You're talking crazy. People don't disappear."

"*She* did!"

Justine almost felt sorry for her. "Why is everyone gathered? Is there a town function going on that I'm not aware of?"

"Town function. Sure," Quinn said. "We're here because Mabel accused you of being a witch." He eyed her with a wicked grin. "Are you?"

She grinned back. "Not today."

Pastor Huggins stepped between Justine and the others. "Such accusations are ridiculous, and such gossip is un-Christian. I suggest everyone go home."

Mabel shook her head violently. "I am not going anywhere!" She pointed at Justine again. "Look at her clothes, the ones beneath the cape. They aren't from now, they're from past times, times when witches were all over New England."

Oh dear. Justine removed the mop cap. "I wear my grandmother's clothes. When I came to Piedmont I never planned on staying so long, so I'm having to make do. I'm sorry if they aren't fashionable enough for you, Mabel."

Mabel ran behind the headstone and pulled out the carpetbag. "Why do you have this in a cemetery? What's in here?"

"Witch supplies?" someone asked.

This was getting ridiculous. "You're so curious? Open it."

Mabel did just that. Her face fell as she pulled out night clothes, the sketchbook, and toiletries. She was clearly disappointed.

Justine took possession of the bag and began folding the clothes, putting them inside.

Harland stepped forward. "You need to quiet yourself, Mabel. Running through town, making wild accusations, telling everyone nonsense . . ."

"She said you were a witch because you disappeared," Mrs. Beemish said. "As in *poof* you were gone."

"Hush now, woman," her husband said. "I should never have let you drag me here to see her reappear—or whyever we're here." He began to leave.

Mabel ran toward them, panicked she was losing her audience. "Someone else saw her disappear."

"Who?" Mr. Beemish asked.

"The caretaker here."

"Caretaker?" Pastor Huggins asked.

Mabel nodded. "Simeon. He was here with us. I spoke to him. He saw what happened. Ask him."

Everyone exchanged confused glances. Then Pastor Huggins said, "There is no caretaker, Mabel. Church volunteers keep the grounds nice and help when there's a burial."

"But . . . but I saw him go into that shack like he lived there."

Mr. Moore walked to the shack and opened the door. "Nothing in here but tools." He pulled out a shovel.

Mabel's face was a mask of panic. She pointed at Justine. "She talked to him too! She was there—"

Suddenly, Goosie stepped around Justine. She pointed to the grave of her father.

Dr. Bevin was the one to get the connection. "Your father, Goosie. His name was Simeon Anders."

"You talked to a dead man?" Rachel Moore asked.

Goosie pointed to the dates.

Justine read them. "He died in the year 1800."

"That's long dead," Mrs. Beemish said.

Mabel pressed her hands to her head. Justine felt bad for her but had to let it play out.

"It was a different Simeon," Mabel said. "My Simeon had red hair and—"

Goosie nodded and pointed to her own hair—which was gray.

Mrs. Huggins stepped into the fray. "Goosie's hair used to be red. Bright red."

Goosie nodded.

"Maybe you should go lie down, Mabel. Rest. You're clearly hallucinating."

"Which proves that your accusations against Justine are also just your imagination," Mr. Beemish said.

"No!" Mabel cried. "Everything I said was true!"

While people argued and cajoled Mabel into leaving, Justine tried to figure out how the unveiling of the Piedmont secret should be revealed. *God, give me the words.*

The townspeople finally let Mabel win the argument about staying. With that accomplished, Justine knew it was time to implement some long-overdue justice.

Her heart beat double time in her chest. Now was the culmination of all her travels. "I am glad you have all gathered here," she said. "For I have some important information that will change the face of Piedmont."

Quinn scoffed. "Sure you do."

"I do." With effort she kept her voice steady. "I have absolute proof that your grandfather was named Samuel Hill."

"His name was Isaac Piedmont."

Justine shook her head. "Samuel Hill *killed* Isaac Piedmont and his family in 1790, just as the town was about to be formed."

"Why would he do that?" Pastor Huggins asked.

Justine began looking around, seeking each person's eyes. "Greed. Samuel came here with the Piedmonts and Simeon Anders when Goosie was a baby, to implement a deed owned by Piedmont." She met Goosie's eyes and gave her a nod. "The three men knew each other from the war. Isaac had bought the land with the intention of parceling it out to sell to other settlers, creating a town—a town called Justice, not Piedmont."

"Sell to others?" Mr. Moore said. "We're supposed to own our property, not lease it?"

"You are."

Quinn began to leave, waving off Justine's words. "Enough of this. I have work to do."

But Harland and Mr. Moore took his arms, stopping him. "You stay until Justine has finished." Harland nodded to her. "Go on."

"Samuel Hill killed the Piedmonts, stole the deed, then took over the identity of Isaac Piedmont."

Quinn balked. "A wild and unfounded accusation. Who here ever met my grandfather, hmm? No one. He died in the early 1800s. You have no proof, and so I am done with—"

Goosie stepped forward and took a deep breath. "I met him. I came to Piedmont when I was ten. My father was going to expose the entire lie."

"He didn't do a very good job of it, did he?" Quinn said. "Because no one *could* believe him. Your father lied."

No one responded to Quinn's statement. They were all staring at Goosie.

"You can talk?" Dr. Bevin said.

"I most certainly can."

The ladies of the quilting club rushed toward her. "You can talk? Why haven't you? Why did you pull away from us?"

Goosie pointed at Quinn. "Because of him. He threatened me, wanting to find out where Mavis lived, wanting to harass her. The only way I could escape his bullying was to pretend I wasn't all *here*."

"We're so glad to have you back," Rachel said.

Goosie nodded but stepped free of her friends, moving beside Justine. "Go on, Jussie. Tell them everything you know."

Justine took her hand and spoke softly. "I need your patchwork blanket."

Goosie looked confused. "Why?"

"You'll see." She motioned Harland over. "Tell Harland where it is, and he can run and get it."

Harland and Goosie talked, then Harland ran toward the house.

"You're cold?" Quinn said. "You need a blanket?"

"Be patient."

While they waited, Mabel sank unto a stone bench, muttering, "He can't be dead. I talked to him . . ." The Moore children—her students—gathered around, trying to comfort her.

You can ease her pain.

Justine balked at the thought. To ease Mabel's pain would mean telling everyone about her gift. Hopefully her quest for justice could be accomplished without that.

Harland came running back, carrying the blanket. He handed it to her. She found the blue square—much faded after eighty-eight years—and felt a slight stiffness inside. *It's still there!*

But would it be readable?

"Do you have a pocketknife?" she asked Harland.

He opened the knife and she slit the threads. Everyone had gathered close to watch. She retrieved the folded page.

"It's a letter!" Mrs. Huggins said.

"From whom?" her husband asked.

"From Simeon Anders. This is his deposition about what happened on the night of October the first, 1790."

Quinn huffed. "This is preposterous."

"Shush, man," Dr. Bevin said. "Read it aloud, Justine."

As an outsider, Justine thought it was best if someone else did the honors. She handed it to Harland.

"Here's what Simeon wrote . . ." He read Simeon's detailed description of the pact between himself, Samuel Hill, and Isaac Piedmont, their past affiliation, and their goal for the town. He gave a description of Isaac, Mary, and Sophie, and mentioned Isaac having a wooden leg.

"Again," Mr. Moore said. "That says we're supposed to own our property, not lease it."

Harland put up a hand, delaying that discussion. "He continues to say that he heard Mr. and Mrs. Piedmont arguing with Hill about the deed. Isaac refused to give it up, saying the land was legally his to develop how he wished. Samuel lunged at him and slashed his throat, right there in front of his wife and daughter. When Mary screamed and went to his side, Hill stabbed her to death, and then killed little Sophie."

There was an outcry of disgust and disbelief.

"They were murdered?" Pastor Huggins asked.

"An entire family?" his wife added.

"That has nothing to do with me," Quinn said. "If it's even true."

Dr. Bevin stepped toward him. "Everything your family has is based on a lie? on murder?"

"You take some random letter as gospel—from someone none of you knew—when my family has given you a place to live and work for 90 years?"

"You've bullied us. Cowed us."

"Arrested us when we couldn't pay," Mr. Moore yelled.

"Burned my barn," Mr. Simmons added.

Everyone talked at once. People yelled. Justine celebrated their release, but wanted the letter read in its entirety. "Quiet everyone. Let's finish this. Go on," she told Harland. "Read the rest."

"Simeon says, 'I hereby attest that Samuel Hill murdered Isaac, Mary, and Sophie Piedmont in order to gain control of the property purchased by Isaac. I have no proof of his actions beyond what I witnessed—for I had to flee for my life and the life of my daughter — but I suspect Hill will find the deed and take ownership of it — in all ways. Logically, it follows that he will assume the identity of Isaac Piedmont to solidify his ownership of the property. This is my true testimony. Signed this first day of October, 1790. Simeon Anders —'"

Harland stopped reading mid-sentence and stared at the letter. Then he looked at Justine.

Oh! My name is there!

"What's it say?" everyone asks. "Read the rest of it."

She'd known there could be repercussions . . . it was best to finish it. Justine took the letter and held it for all to see. "It says, 'Signed this first day of October, 1790. Simeon Anders, witnessed by Justine Tyler Braden.'"

She expected an uproar. Instead she got silence.

Quinn took advantage of the furor. "How can her name be on a document from 1790? It proves everything's a fake. A lie. All of it." He pointed at Justine. "This woman has done nothing but cause trouble since she arrived. Mabel may be hysterical and dramatic, but Justine is the instigator of a conspiracy of lies against my family."

Justine looked at Harland and Goosie — the only two people who knew about her gift. Goosie shook her head no. Harland nodded.

God?

She received an inner nudge. *Truth is proof.*

Justine Tyler Braden spread her arms, quieting the crowd. "The letter is genuine, the events it details are real and true."

"How can the letter be real, when your name is on it, as a witness?" Mr. Moore said.

She took a deep breath, said a quick prayer, and began. "Because I *was* there. I was there with Simeon and baby Goosie in 1790. I was there when he wrote his testimony. We were hiding in a cave, on the run from Samuel Hill."

The crowd was silent a moment, taking it in. Then came calls of "How?" and "That's impossible."

Mabel raised a hand, her face a mask of relief. "See? Like I said, she talked to him too!"

"I did," Justine said. "Mabel and I both talked to Simeon in this very place."

"But he's dead."

"He is." She thought of something to add. "I was with him in 1790 and also in 1800."

"Talking with ghosts..." Mrs. Beemish said. "Maybe you are a witch."

Her words brought more murmurs, spurring Justine to raise a hand to quiet them. "There is something you should know that happened in 1800. Simeon Anders was in Piedmont, staying at my family's house. He confronted Samuel Hill about his deed. Samuel—pretending to be Isaac Piedmont—murdered him. I saw it. He caused Simeon to fall from a ladder, then bashed his head in with—" Justine rushed to retrieve the bloodied rock. "This stone. See the dried blood?"

The people vied for a look.

"That's just lichen," Quinn said. "You can't prove nothing."

Goosie took possession of the rock, cradling it in her hands. She took a shaky breath. "My father was murdered by Samuel Hill pretending to be Isaac Piedmont."

Mr. Moore slapped Quinn on the shoulder. "Some family you have."

"Shut up."

At least you're not denying it.

There was more discussion about the impossibility of it all. Justine had to make them understand the unexplainable. "I know what I say—what I claim I can do—sounds bizarre and even rather frightening."

"Things like that don't happen," Rachel said. "Admit it, Justine. What you're asking us to believe . . ."

"I know how you feel. I didn't believe it either until it happened to me. I—"

"The explanation can wait." Goosie looked out over the townspeople—people she'd known all her life. "Listen to Justine. Quit harping on what you think is possible and listen to what she discovered in the past. *That's* what's important here. *That's* why she's been given this gift." She nodded at Justine. "Tell them what you saw," Goosie said.

Thank you, Goosie. "Simeon came back to Piedmont in 1800 to try to set things right and avenge the death of Isaac

Piedmont and his family. He knew something was amiss when he heard about the town being called Piedmont. He knew that Isaac was going to name it Justice."

"So what?" Quinn said. "They changed their minds."

Justine continued. "Goosie was with him." She nodded at Goosie. "You were about ten, yes?"

"I was. And I wasn't feeling very well. The Hollorans — Winifred Tyler's parents, Justine's great-grandparents — lived in that very house and took us in."

Justine nodded. "Let me tell you it was *very* odd to meet my great-grandparents at a time before Granny was even born."

"This is absurd," Quinn said, waving their words away. "It's a made-up story. She never went back anywhere."

"Sounds like she did," Rachel said. "She knows too many details."

Mr. Moore nudged Quinn. "Shut up, you. Let her finish."

It was invigorating to have a chance to tell her story — and have it be believed, if not by all, by some. "Simeon was helping my great-grandfather build that chimney over there." She pointed across the road to the house. "Simeon was up on the ladder. After Simeon confronted him about his true identity, and threatened to let everyone know what he'd done, Samuel Hill pulled the ladder backwards, so Simeon fell. He did *not* want Simeon exposing him. While Simeon was down and hurt, Hill pounded his head with a stone until he was dead." She pointed to the stone in Goosie's hands "I brought this back with me. This *is* Simeon's blood."

Quinn began to laugh. "A stained stone." He pointed around the cemetery. "Oh! There's another one, and another! They all must be covered with blood." He scoffed. That's not proof. It's a joke."

He was right. It was not proof.

"And so what if it's true?" Quinn said. "My grandfather is long dead. None of this has anything to do with me."

"Except that you're benefitting from his actions," Mr. Beemish said. "You're the mayor and the constable."

"You men voted me in."

"Out of fear," Rachel said.

Mr. Simmons stepped forward. "None of us want you in charge, Quinn Piedmont—or whatever your name is. But we all know what happens if we cross you." He looked to the others and got nods and murmurs of affirmation.

"You put me in jail because I was behind on rent," Mr. Moore said. "How can I make a living when I'm in jail?"

Harland raised a hand. "Which illustrates how your family hasn't used the land as it was originally intended. You took it all for yourself."

The crowd got louder.

"Again, not my problem," Quinn said. "My grandfather set it up. Pa and I have just been following what he put in place."

There were more murmurings against him, but Justine knew he had good points.

Pastor Huggins raised a hand. "Back to you, Justine. You truly are expecting us to believe you travel back in time."

"Yes. I do. Because it's true." She didn't know what else she could say.

Mabel jumped up from the bench, spilling children around her. "I told you she disappeared!"

Amid more yelling, one stood out. "Prove it."

Quinn grinned. "See? No one believes you. All your lies are just a made-up story."

Suddenly, the right words came to her. "Pastor Huggins. I was here in 1800 when the steeple was being built. I saw the workmen."

He cocked his head "That *was* the year it was built."

"I also traveled back to 1860—"

Dr. Bevin interrupted. "Do you have control over what year you visit?"

"I do not. I simply go where time will take me."

The crowd seemed to accept that answer—which was good because she had no other. "As I said, I traveled to 1860 and met Harland's parents, Jesse and Dorthea Jennings. I visited in September when Harland was five." She smiled at Harland. "Actually, he made sure I knew he was five and a half." He winked at her, giving her strength to continue. "He had two sisters. Phoebe—Beebee—was seven, and Ellen—who they called Ellie — was only four months old. During my visit his father fell and cut his head on a hoe. Harland took care of him with skill far beyond his age."

Mabel joined the group. "That doesn't prove anything. Harland could have told you all that."

"But I didn't," Harland said.

"You could have."

"Are you calling me a liar, Mabel Collier?" He leveled her with a look.

Justine extended her hands calming them. Thus far her proof hadn't been very convincing because it involved generalities, or details about times that predated most of the people standing before her.

Then she spotted Dr. Bevin and took a step toward him. "Dr. Bevin. When I was in 1860, the young Harland drew me into your office to help set Arnold Piedmont's right arm."

"Which time?"

People reacted with knowing murmurs.

"The time you asked me to sing to him, to calm him." She began to sing the song she'd sung back then. 'My Jesus, I love Thee, I know Thou art mine. For Thee all the follies of sin I resign . . .'"

Dr. Bevin gasped. "Miss Miller?"

"Susan Miller was the name I used."

"Why didn't you use your real name?" Mabel asked.

"Because I'd also come back here during 1857 — just three years before — and had met many of the people. I felt safe to use Justine Braden then because it was a time before I was born. But when I went back into 1860 in reality I was three years old and had already visited Granny. People in town would have known about 'Justine.'" She shrugged. "So I used the first name that came into my head: Susan Miller."

"Like I told you," Rachel said. "She offers too many details for it *not* to be true."

The doctor shook his head. "I don't know how this is possible, but what she says is accurate. I've never spoken about it to anyone, because Arnold always asked me to keep his injuries from Quinn a secret."

All eyes turned to Quinn. "I never hurt my father."

The crowd scoffed.

"We all know that's a lie," the doctor said. "You've hurt him many times. My largest regret is that I never had the courage to do anything to stop you."

"He's still hurting him," Justine said. "I've seen bruises on Arnold's arms."

"He's a senile old man, sitting around doing nothing but cause me trouble."

Suddenly, a voice sounded from behind the crowd. "I am not senile!"

The crowd parted to let Arnold Piedmont walk through. A younger man walked along side, supporting him.

Suddenly, people gasped and ran toward the man.

"Thomas!"

Thomas Piedmont?

Even without knowing his name, or even the fact she'd met him in the past, Justine recognized the family resemblance. For Thomas shared his father's and brother's black hair, strong chin, and solid build. But physicality was where the connection ended. It was *how* Thomas carried his physical frame that set him apart from Quinn. Thomas had a lightness to his movements, an impression of peace and goodwill, while Quinn exuded brute force, conflict, and cruelty.

Thomas and Arnold made their way through the crowd and were greeted happily. He helped his father sit on the bench.

Arnold beamed and held Thomas's hand. "My boy is back. Do you see? My boy is back!"

Quinn scowled.

Thomas faced his friends. "As Father said, I am very much alive." He nodded toward Quinn. "No thanks to my brother who tried to kill me by pushing me in the river eighteen years ago."

Quinn's face displayed his confusion and — dare Justine hope — fear?

Suddenly Quinn bolted from the crowd, heading toward the river. But he was more brawn than speed and three men caught up with him, pushing him to the ground. They yanked him to his feet, brought him back, and stood him in front of his father and brother.

"It's time to pay the piper, Quinn. The tide's turned," Arnold said. "And I'm enjoying every minute of it."

"As am I," Thomas said.

"You need to stop right now," Quinn hissed, "before you say something you'll regret."

"I will regret nothing," Thomas said. "I've waited eighteen years to bring the truth into the open."

"Why so long?" Dr. Bevin asked.

"Where have you been?" someone else asked.

"Why haven't you shown yourself before now?" asked another.

Thomas raised his hands, quieting them. "First things first. Miss Braden. I seem to remember meeting you, was it in 1857?"

"I believe that *was* the first time. We met at a church dinner on New Year's Day, then again the next day, after my mother had run off to New York City with Quinn. I believe he'd stolen some money from the store." She glared at Quinn. "I don't know what happened between you, but I thank God she found my father to love. *He* was a good man."

"I was always glad to know Mavis found happiness," Thomas said.

"How did you know that?" she asked.

He waved her question away and asked his own. "I met you another time, I believe. In 1860?"

"You are correct."

There were more murmurings. Justine knew that what they were being asked to believe was . . . nearly beyond believing.

Pastor Huggins quieted the crowd. "If Thomas says it happened then I believe it. He is a man of God."

The crowd quieted.

Justine felt a wave of pleasure. Obviously telling them about her gift was the right choice. She addressed them. "Thank you for believing me."

"I believe you, all right," Mabel said. "You are a witch!"

Her accusations were getting tedious. "I am not a witch. I have a gift—a gift from God."

"That's a new word for it."

"Mabel, I'm not going to argue with you, or anyone else in this town. You can believe me or not. My ability comes from God. If you wish to argue with *that* you'll have to take it up with the Almighty."

There was a smattering of nervous laughter.

Pastor Huggins stepped forward. "I'm not arguing with you, Justine. But why would God give you this gift?"

She sighed deeply. "I've asked myself the same question. I think it comes down to what Granny told me when I visited her in 1857. She told me to stand up for what is right, no matter the cost. My goal is to facilitate justice."

"Amen," Goosie said.

"Your name is appropriate to your goal," Mrs. Huggins said. ""

"It's a name Granny chose for me."

"Like she knew," Rachel said.

Others nodded.

"It wasn't just me. My mother had this gift, and my grandmother and all in my line before them, going back to Ireland."

Arnold waved his cane. "I know your grandmother had it. It riled my brother Ned something awful. *He* called *her* a witch." He looked at Mabel. "Wrongly accused then as wrongly accused now."

Mabel looked to the ground, finding a pebble to move around with the toe of her shoe.

Arnold stood with the help of Thomas. "Since this is a time of confession, I have to say that I blamed Winnie for Ned's death and was ready to string her up for it—even though I knew she was innocent." He shook his head forlornly. "Ned was a mean cuss. They argued and she pushed him. His death was an accident."

"He fell and hit his head on the andiron," Justine said.

"How do you know that?"

"I was there. In 1826." She looked for Goosie and drew her forward. "Goosie was there too."

Goosie nodded. "Ned dying was the best thing ever happened to Winnie."

"That's a horrible thing to say," Mrs. Huggins said.

Arnold came to Goosie's defense. "It's a true thing. My brother's anger and plain old cussedness doomed him to death, if not then, later." He looked pointedly at Quinn. "You're lucky someone ain't killed you."

"Shut up, old man!" Quinn lunged toward him, but two men held him back.

Justine felt a deep satisfaction that Quinn was finally being called out for the cruel man he was. But his father's disdain was only the beginning of righting wrongs. "Thomas," she said, "you mentioned that Quinn tried to kill you. Everyone thought you'd drown, and there *were* rumors he *had* killed you."

He helped his father sit again. "My dear brother hit me over the head and shoved me in the river."

"We thought you died," Dr. Bevin said.

"Almost died. Wound up downriver, caught up in some branches. A man found me and took me in. His family saved me."

"Why didn't you come back here?"

"For fear Quinn would try it again."

"Why did he try to kill you?" Mr. Beemish asked.

"I found out some awful truths about our family. Shared them with Quinn." He glared at his brother. "He knew all about them already, and tried to silence me. And did silence me for a while. As I said, I didn't come back because I was afraid, but also because I was ashamed at what my family had done in the past. I wanted nothing to do with them anymore. And so I chose to start over. I moved to New York City."

Justine perked up. "You lived in New York?"

"I did."

"You should have contacted my family. My mother would have loved to see you."

He shrugged and changed the subject. "Would you like to know the details that spurred Quinn to want me dead?"

Of course.

He pulled a yellowed piece of paper from the inner pocket of his coat. "He tried to kill me because of this deed, showing that Isaac Piedmont purchased 100 acres of land where Piedmont stands today." He carefully unfolded the delicate page and held it up for all to see. "Dated June the first, 1790." He turned it over and brought the page close to read it. "On the back Isaac wrote: 'My wish is for the town of Justice to be divided among settlers for a small price. Together we will build a new town and a new life in our new country.'"

Quinn jumped in, "The town of Justice. That's not here. This is Piedmont."

"It was supposed to be named Justice," Thomas said.

"And we're supposed to own our property!" Mr. Moore yelled.

Others joined in at the proof, their pent-up anger toward their evil landlord, spilling out.

"It's just a piece of paper," Quinn yelled. "One that proves our grandfather owned the land."

Harland shook his head. "You can't have it both ways, Quinn, saying that Justice isn't Piedmont, and now saying the deed proves your family owns this place."

Quinn's forehead furrowed.

Thomas held up a finger. "Our grandfather wasn't Isaac Piedmont. His name was Samuel Hill."

Dr. Bevin carefully took the deed and looked at it. Then he said, "So Simeon's letter was correct? Hill murdered the Piedmonts?"

"He did."

"You can't prove a thing," Quinn hissed.

"But I can. Follow me."

Justine had an idea. "Follow *me.*"

Thomas looked at her, curious.

"You showed me the grave in 1860. I know where it is." *And it will prove I was there.*

He smiled. "After you, Miss Braden."

Quinn tried to escape his captors. "Let me go. I didn't kill them."

"Maybe not," Thomas said, "but you tried to kill me."

One man who'd hung back at the cemetery, ran forward with a length of rope. "Found this in the shack." Quinn's hands were tied.

Justine led the entire town out of the cemetery and down the river road toward the apple trees.

**

Harland moved beside Justine. "It's happening. It's finally happening."

She pressed a hand to her chest. "I'll be glad when everything is revealed."

He put an arm around her shoulders. "You did this."

"God did this — *is* doing this."

Justine led the townspeople off the road and into the grove of apple trees. Her stomach clenched. The grave would finally be revealed.

Justine walked to the site and was surprised to see it was partially uncovered, with a shovel sitting nearby.

Thomas explained. "Before I spoke to anyone, before I went to see my father, I wanted to make sure the Piedmonts were still here." He pointed to the uncovered section. "There, ladies and gentlemen, are the bones of Isaac Piedmont. And if we dig more, we will find his wife, Mary, and their daughter, Sophie."

"Just like in Simeon's letter," Pastor Huggins said.

Quinn scoffed. "Could be anyone. People died all the time. Disease. Indians."

"And murder," Justine said.

"My father's deposition proves it," Goosie said.

"Where'd you get the deed?" Dr. Bevin asked Thomas.

He told a story set in 1860, of picking apples and having his ladder sink into the ground. Then finding of a grave containing the remains of a Colonial family. "Their clothes were decomposing, but I saw a wooden leg. And then I spotted something in the hem of the man's tattered coat. A piece of paper folded many times. It was the deed, sewn inside."

"So Samuel never found it," Justine said.

"He buried it."

"No, he didn't," Quinn said. "We have a deed."

"A fake deed," Thomas said. "After finding the grave I confronted you about it and you showed me the other deed, probably falsified by our grandfather. It wasn't witnessed and didn't have the legal boundaries noted. It would — it will — never hold up in court."

"And that faded piece of nothing will?"

Justine saw the truth of it. "The original deed in Thomas's possession was found upon the body of a man in a grave. Simeon's testimony corroborates that the man — and his family — are the Piedmonts. And your assault on your own brother after he brought you the evidence, added to my experiences, including witnessing the murder of Simeon Anders who was killed in order to cover up his secret, completes the story of Samuel Hill's crimes." She walked over to stand directly in front of Quinn. "Hill is long dead, so he can't be held accountable. But you can."

"What about my father?" Quinn said. "He was Samuel's son."

"I knew nothing of any of this," Arnold said. He raised his right hand. "I thought my father *was* Isaac Piedmont. I thought the land was ours — to lease out, just as Father had done." His composure broke. "I'm so sorry. I didn't know."

"Which leaves you," Justine said, glaring at Quinn. "You *did* know. Thomas told you, even showed you?" She turned to Thomas.

"Before I talked to Quinn, I hid the deed for safekeeping, suspecting — rightly — that Quinn would want it destroyed." He held it up again. "While you were all at the cemetery, I recovered it from its hiding place under some floor boards at the store. I showed Quinn the grave in 1860. That's when he tried to kill me."

The people gasped.

Quinn growled — actually growled. "I shoulda made sure you were dead."

"What now?" Rachel asked.

Justine stood beside Thomas. "Thomas and I have given you the evidence. Now it's up to all of you to make sure justice is done."

Mr. Moore pumped an arm in the air. "Take him to jail!"

The people joined in the cry, "Jail! Jail!" Quinn was led toward town, leaving but a handful of people left at the site.

Justine watched them go. "I didn't expect such fervor."

Thomas peered down at the grave. "I did. 'For the arms of the wicked shall be broken: but the Lord upholdeth the righteous.'"

"Tis a good verse," Harland said.

Goosie started to walk away. "If you'll excuse me, I've wanted Quinn Piedmont locked away for so long, I don't want to miss it." She moved to Arnold's side. "Do you want to come with me?"

He shook his head, leaning against a nearby apple tree. "I'm glad for the justice, but sad for the son."

"Understood." When she was gone he said, "I'm mightily sorry for any part I had in all this. There is no excuse for ignorance and . . . ."

"Fear?" Justine asked.

"That too." He moved to pick up the shovel. "Let's return this family to rest."

"I'll do it," Thomas said.

But his father shooed him off. "I may have *been* feeble, but I'm feeling stronger now. Let me at least start it."

He was a bit wobbly as he took the first shovelful of dirt, but he managed to get it in the hole. Justine admired his determination.

Between the three men, the grave was filled and the dirt tamped down. Justine picked some wildflowers and set them on the ground. They all stood in silence a moment. Then Thomas led them in the Lord's prayer. . . "'Forgive us our trespasses as we forgive those who trespass against us. Lead us not into temptation but deliver us from evil . . .'"

Justine was overcome with a wave of emotion and began to cry. Harland came to her. "Are you all right?"

She reassured him. "I am more than right. I am relieved, excited, jubilant, and . . ." She looked at the men around her. "Very, very grateful."

"As are we." Thomas held out his hand for her to shake. "My father and I can't thank you enough for all you've done to bring justice to the Piedmonts."

Arnold piped in, "And being a part of bringing my boy back to me."

But I didn't do anything to bring him back. I didn't even know he was alive.

Yet those details faded as she witnessed the love on Arnold's face when he looked at Thomas.

"I am very glad it turned out the way it did. I thank God for allowing me to be a part of it."

"We should celebrate," Harland said.

A wonderful idea. "Come back to the house and we can celebrate together."

CHAPTER SIXTEEN

Goosie looked surprised when she returned from the jail to find Justine, Harland, Arnold, and Thomas sitting in the parlor.

"Oh dear," she said. "I didn't know we were having dinner guests. Let me see what I can make for—"

Justine stopped her from going to the kitchen. "Don't worry yourself about dinner. I've put the kettle on. I want you to sit with us. You are an integral part of everything that has happened."

Goosie tucked some stray hairs behind her ears and perched on a chair near the foyer.

"You are the *only* one who's been through it all," Harland told her. "You were there through the death of the Piedmonts, the fake Isaac Piedmont, your father's tragedy, Ned's death, the accusations against Winifred . . ."

Justine took over the list. "My mother running away to New York with Quinn."

"My so-called death," Thomas said.

"Granny's passing and then my mother's."

Goosie nodded forlornly. "And the passing of the Hollorans and so many others." She looked up, tears in her eyes. "It's hard outliving those I love."

"Oh, Goosie," Justine went to her side, knelt before her, and took her hand. "I'm still here. I won't leave you. Ever."

Goosie touched Justine's cheek. "You're a good one, Jussie. God sent you to me, I know it."

"I'm not one to talk about God much," Arnold said, "but I's a-thinking He sent you to me too." He looked at his son. "Thomas, you need to know that of all the people in this town, Miss Braden here was the one who reached out to me. She came to talk to me when most had written me off as the dumb nothing Quinn made me." He smiled at Justine. "She also brought me a rhubarb pie."

Thomas laughed. "You discovered the key to my father's heart."

With a pat to Goosie's knee she said, "Goosie made it. I delivered it." She welcomed the levity and returned to her seat on the settee beside Harland.

Thomas looked around the room. "I remember being in this room before. With you and your grandparents."

"Right after Mother ran away with Quinn."

"And stole from me," Arnold added.

Thomas shook his head, as though passing over the latter sin. "Tell me about your life in New York."

Justine was taken aback. Her thoughts were focused on Piedmont, in the here and now, not in New York and her past. "I was happy. I had a good life."

"A life of privilege?"

What? The way he said it made her feel oddly ashamed. "Father was a successful banker. We lived well."

"You were active in society?"

"We were. Mother thrived on the parties, the dinners, the opera . . ."

Thomas seemed pensive. "Did you?"

"I did." She glanced at Harland. "Until I came to Piedmont, socializing was the most important thing in my life."

"Was?"

She looked around the tiny parlor that would have fit into the foyer of their New York mansion. "I find Piedmont quite enough for me. And far more fulfilling."

Thomas smiled. "By the looks you and Harland are exchanging, I don't need to ask the reason for your change of attitude."

Justine felt herself blush, and Harland cleared his throat before saying, "We are very happy to know one another."

Everyone laughed. Even Arnold. Was their attraction so obvious?

Enough about her. Justine had her own questions. "What happened with my mother and Quinn? You went after them, correct?"

"I did. The next day. Actually, I met Quinn in the train station in New York. He was coming home because Mavis had kicked him out. He made light of it, implying that he'd . . . gotten what he wanted, and was done with her."

"Oh dear."

"I was furious with him, yelled at him for being so crass and offensive toward a good woman. But he laughed at me and called me . . . well, called me names I won't repeat."

"I'd like to call *him* a few names myself, "Arnold said.

With a nod to his father, Thomas continued his story. "Quinn told me where to find Mavis—at the hotel where he and I stayed when we went to New York on business. It was *not* a fancy place and once I got there, Mavis made it clear the entire situation was *not* what she had expected when she ran away."

Justine could easily imagine her mother's complaints about Quinn, and about any lack of comfort, cleanliness, and class. "Was she all right?"

"Mostly. As I expected, Quinn had over-stated. They had not . . . nothing happened like that. She saw his true colors even before they reached the city."

"Whatever did she see in him in the first place?" Harland asked.

Justine remembered the conversation she'd had with her mother back in 1857 regarding Quinn. *I want someone with fire in him. I don't want a bookworm like Thomas. He'd smother me with politeness, fawning over me until I'd want to scream.*

Justine didn't share that memory but chose another. "She wanted to get away from Piedmont and longed for the excitement of the city." She looked at Thomas. "I have no way of truly knowing, but I think she was using Quinn as a means to leave."

He nodded once. "Your mother was headstrong. What Mavis wanted—"

"Mavis got," they said together.

Thomas moved to the fireplace, touching the clock on the mantel. "She was upset when I found her, for even if my brother was unsuccessful in his overtures, he *had* pressed the situation. Mavis was offended and rather shocked by all of it."

Arnold mumbled under his breath. "The cad."

"I tried to convince her to go home, but she refused. She was determined to stay in New York."

"How?"

"The first night there, at dinner, she and Quinn had met a man called Macy, who was talking about opening a dry goods store in the city. Mavis hoped to get a job as a clerk there."

"Mother? Work?"

"She would do whatever it took to achieve her goal. She was quite stubborn."

"Yes, she was," Justine said.

Thomas sighed. "To get her mind off Quinn's offenses, she and I went out to dinner and walked in Central Park. Since she didn't have a way to sustain herself yet, I stayed and got my own room in the hotel. I wish I could have moved her to a better one, but I didn't have the money." His hand fell to his side and he stared at the fire. "We had three wonderful days together, exploring New York. She seemed to forget about Quinn. She seemed happy."

"She had the attention of a wonderful man," Justine said.

Suddenly he turned around, his expression strained. He raked a hand through his graying hair. "We didn't mean for it to happen."

What? Justine's stomach flipped.

Harland voiced the obvious question. "Didn't mean for what to happen?"

He looked right at Justine. "On the last night . . . your mother and I were . . . intimate."

She gasped.

"It was just the one time. Mavis needed to feel loved. And I . . ." He sighed. "I loved her. I'd loved Mavis for years, but she only had eyes for Quinn."

Justine collected herself. "I believe you. That's what I saw in 1857. She flirted shamelessly with Quinn."

"Because he could get her out of Piedmont?" Harland asked.

Thomas nodded. "After . . . I asked her to marry me."

"You did?"

"But she said no. She told me to go back to Piedmont."

"Did you?"

"I left but I didn't go home. I stayed in New York for nearly six weeks, moving to a different hotel, giving her space even as I hoped she would change her mind. I tried repeatedly to speak to her, but she wouldn't see me. I followed her when I could and cherished every sighting I had of her. I was so smitten. She wasn't idle but seemed to be implementing a plan. Then one morning when I caught her leaving the hotel, she finally agreed to a walk in the park. We walked. We talked. And I poured out my love for her. But then she felt sick and . . . and she vomited in some bushes. She was very embarrassed. When I voiced my concern, she grew angry at me. She snapped at me."

"Why?"

He left the fireplace and faced her. "I am your father."

The whole of Justine's life flashed through her mind. Her father — Noel Braden — holding her hand, helping her cross a busy New York street. Sitting on his lap, playing with his beard. His mellow baritone singing hymns beside her in the family pew. Visiting his office at the bank where he proudly showed her off to his colleagues. And his pale, weakened face as he lay dying from a heart attack.

Suddenly, his final words called out from her memories. *"I did my best for you, Justine. I loved you, I love you."* She gasped at the implication, the words unsaid: *I wasn't your birth father, but I raised you as my own. I loved you.*

She waved her hands in front of her face, fending off this alternate history — *her* alternate history. "I was born on November 2, 1857. My parents were married March the fifteenth. I am my father's —"

Thomas shook his head. "During the six weeks I waited for her, tried to see her, Mavis met your father at his bank. I never knew the details, but I suspect she went to the bank, needing a loan, and used her considerable charms to gain his sympathy for being a single woman alone in New York. She stole his heart as she'd stolen mine."

"You make her sound so callous."

"Driven is a better word."

It was a word Justine herself had used to describe her mother. *What Mavis wanted . . .*

"When she finally told me she was with child, I proposed again. She declined, repeating what she'd told me before, that life with me in Piedmont was *not* the life she wanted — nor was being the wife of a pastor. Then she told me she was already betrothed to Noel Braden, a banker. *The* banker. They were going to be married in two weeks, on March the fifteenth." He hung his head. "That's when I knew I was beaten. Mavis had everything she wanted: a wealthy husband, a place in the big city, and soon after, a child. You. Beaten, I went back to Piedmont. I heard about the wedding from your grandmother — who was very upset for the quickness of it, but mostly, for not being invited."

In spite of wanting to discount everything Thomas said, Justine believed him. "Mother said I was born early."

Thomas merely shook his head. "When the time grew near, I returned to New York and found out from some servants I befriended in the Braden household that your mother was in labor. I stood outside and watched the window of your mother's room, saw movement in the lamp light, saw the doctor's arrival, and even heard your first cry." His expression crumpled to one of deep emotion. "My child had been born and I couldn't even see her! See you." He pressed a hand to his heart. "I loved you before I even saw you."

Arnold held up his cane. "So you're my granddaughter?"

Oh my.

Justine bolted from her chair and brushed past Thomas, needing to stand alone. "Everyone, stop. You've upended everything I knew to be true."

Thomas nodded and returned to his chair, giving her a moment to think. Then he said, "I know how shocking this is. And I only tell you now because your parents are gone. You are the main reason I risked coming back to Piedmont. I knew of your mother's death and heard that she was to be buried here. That meant you would travel to Piedmont to take care of the arrangements and this house. Finding you involved in my family's secret and being able to help the truth be revealed was a happy bonus."

"I filled him in with the doings of the town," Arnold said. "He showed up at the store, and I told him about that silly

Mabel-girl's accusations, and that everyone was at the cemetery."

Justine's mind re-prioritized her day. The secret revealed and the justice done faded to a lesser place of importance. A love of a father for his child stepped forward in front of all other issues. "You came back for me?"

He nodded. "I'd been tempted to approach you in New York so many times. But I knew that would be unfair, for your parents loved you, and you seemed happy."

"You knew I was happy?"

"I watched you through the years. One of the servants in your household remained my friend and kept me informed as to the events and happenings in your family's life."

"What was the servant's name?"

"Burt Owens. He moved up from second footman to footman, I believe."

She knew Owens well. He always had a ready smile for her. Yet knowing he had given her real father information about her life was a bit disconcerting.

"I also visited a few times, watching you from afar."

Harland raised a point. "But you 'died' when she was three."

He nodded. "Earlier I was asked why I stayed away after Quinn tried to kill me. Guilt is the reason."

"Guilt?" Harland said. "He tried to kill you."

"I felt guilty for being intimate with Mavis when she clearly didn't love me, as well as feeling guilty for my family's sins. So when Quinn tried to kill me, I took it as my punishment. I stayed away and ended up working with the poor in New York, finding a church that needed me to pastor them. Penance, if you will. It was nice being close to you but excruciating to not be able to approach you. Or Mavis."

Justine took a deep breath, letting this new reality settle. She found it unsettling, yet . . . pleasing. "The fact you thought of us before yourself proves what a good man you are."

"A work in progress. But when I heard about Mavis' death and her being buried in Piedmont, I took that as direction from God to go home. It was time."

"Did you continue to love my mother?" Justine asked.

"Ever and always. I know it didn't make sense, for she never reciprocated the feelings, but . . ." He shrugged. "Love is rarely logical."

"But always eternal," Goosie said.

"Amen to that," Thomas said.

Justine thought of her father, of Noel. "Did he know about you?"

"I'm not sure. I doubt Mavis would tell him, yet the fact she wanted such a quick wedding might have made him suspicious." His face softened. "Was he a good father?"

Her memories were poignant. "He was a wonderful father." Justine wasn't sure whether she hoped her father *had* known or not. Either way, she adored him for loving her so well.

"I'm glad of that."

Justine had a sudden thought. "No wonder I couldn't travel back into your life. You were alive! I traced my fingers along your headstone but nothing happened."

"That's how you do it?"

"It is."

"I have a headstone?" Thomas asked.

His father answered. "I gave you a very nice funeral, Thomas."

"But there obviously was no body."

"We had a funeral, just the same. Do you want to see?"

He laughed. "I have no need."

There was a knock on the door. Goosie opened it to Pastor Huggins. He looked at those in the parlor. "I'd hoped I would find you all here."

"I'll bring us some tea," Goosie said, leaving the room.

Justine offered him a chair. He looked at each in turn, returning his gaze to Thomas. "Although I wasn't here when you were . . . killed, I am glad to see you are very much alive."

"As am I."

"Truth is, I . . . I was hired to take your place."

There was a moment of awkward silence. Then Pastor Huggins smiled at Arnold. "And you, I rejoice with you for your son's return."

273

Arnold nodded. "I thank God for his return." His face turned sad. "But I grieve the virtual demise of my other son. I also grieve because I stood by while his baser nature took hold of him." He shook his head forlornly. "Many suffered because of Quinn."

"As did you," Justine said.

"But now you are free of him," Harland added.

But was he? "Pastor, how is Quinn?" Justine asked.

"He's a growly bear in a cage. And . . ." He looked embarrassed. "We have learned many new epithets."

"What will happen to him?"

Arnold piped up, looking nervous, "He's not getting out, is he?"

"We have sent to Haverhill for the sheriff. It will be in his hands."

Thomas looked worried. "But since he didn't kill me will he be let loose?"

"He tried to kill you. And he hurt your father many times."

Harland added more offenses to the list. "He falsely jailed tenants, burned a barn, cheated people, caused unexplained accidents, and was a bully to all. Surely there will be dozens of citizens to testify against him."

"I hope so," Arnold said. "I have my Thomas back. Tis a chance to start over and create a family without the cancer of Quinn poisoning us."

Justine had a different question. "What will happen to the town of Piedmont now? Quinn had all the power. With him gone . . ."

"There are many good men here," Pastor Huggins said. "Men who have cowered under Quinn's threats. But now they will step up and do what needs to be done."

"Will they?"

"I will make sure of it. Don't worry about us, Miss Braden. You have opened our eyes to truth. The rest is up to us."

Thomas seemed preoccupied. "My brother . . ." he said. "We need to forgive him."

He received the stares of all—even Pastor Huggins. But the pastor was the first to speak. "Your attitude is commendable."

Thomas sighed. "We must forgive others as we ask for forgiveness."

"As God forgives us," Justine added. "You said that before."

He smiled. "I did?"

Justine thought about the Ledger. "You did." She stood. "Pardon me a moment. I have something I need to show all of you." She hurried upstairs and retrieved the Ledger from her desk. She returned and showed it to Thomas.

He leafed through it. "What is this?"

"Granny called it the Ledger. In it, she and all the time-traveling women of my family wrote down the wisdom they learned during their visits to the past. I call them life lines, enduring truths that connect the past to the present."

"That can inspire the future," Harland said.

"These wise words were said by ordinary people, not people of power or status. They are eternal and timeless."

"Timeless," Arnold said. He cocked his head. "Is that the book my brother wanted to find?"

"I believe it is."

"It was," Goosie said. "He'd seen Winnie writing in it, and thought she was writing down the awful things he'd done."

"But it's not a diary," Justine said.

Thomas pointed to a page. "This goes back to 1530, but here's a good one from 1627, a life line written by Fanny Lees."

"A distant relative," Justine said. "Read what she wrote."

"'Marry only for love.'"

"There's truth in that," Arnold said wistfully. "How I loved my Sally. Even though she's been gone over forty years, I miss her every day."

Justine never would have thought Arnold was a man who could love so deeply.

Thomas skimmed through the pages. "Notations from 1530, 1700 and other dates. But then nothing for years between the 1800 and 1826, with a notation then from Winifred Tyler."

"Granny."

"It's attributed to Joshua Holloran in 1801: 'Look beyond what you see.'"

"That's Granny's father," Justine said.

Pastor Huggins spoke up. "It makes you wonder if he knew Isaac Piedmont wasn't Isaac Piedmont."

Thomas was reading another page in the Ledger. Then he looked up. "You've written in here, Justine."

"I have. You can read them if you'd like."

Thomas read the first two aloud. Then . . . "Here's my quotation about forgiveness, from 1860."

"You said the same words just now, but I knew you'd said them before. That's why I wanted you to see the Ledger. Your words will carry on."

He stared at the page. "Eighteen-sixty . . . I'd just found the grave of the Piedmonts and had seen the deed. I knew my family were imposters." He pressed a hand to his chest. "I was so full of anger."

"Go on, Thomas," Arnold said. "Read the rest of Justine's entries."

Thomas hesitated a moment, then handed the Ledger to Harland and pointed at his place. Justine knew which quote he'd seen.

Harland read it. "The next one is from my father, also in 1860. 'Take time.'" He sighed. Twice. "Pa didn't always take time with me, and was usually impatient because I wasn't interested in farming but in helping Dr. Bevin. But then . . . then he grew more patient. He *did* take time and was less judgmental. I'm glad we had good times together as father and son then, because soon after that he went to war. And died."

Harland read the last three quotations, two from Simeon and three from Abigail Holloran. Then he hesitated.

"There's one more," Justine said.

"It's from me. You wrote down something I said?"

"It's very profound. It deserves its place in the Ledger. Read it."

"'The person you were has led you to become the person you are.'"

"That *is* profound, Harland."

He squeezed Justine's hand and whispered, "Thank you."

"I praise all the wisdom in the Ledger," Pastor Huggins said. "But why the long lag in entries between 1800 and 1826, and then between your grandmother and you?"

"Though every female in my family receives the gift at age twenty, they are not required to use it. My great-grandmother, Abigail Holloran has no entries. When I visited her in 1800 she had only just turned twenty, and had recently arrived from Ireland. There was only one headstone in the cemetery here—that of her baby, Nathan. I don't know if she knew about the gift, but even if she did know, she did *not* have the means to use it."

"By touching the name on the headstone," Arnold said.

Justine nodded. "And Granny told me that she only went back a few times. After her first husband died, her second husband, Ross Tyler—my grandfather—forbid it. My mother only went once. She wanted nothing to do with it."

"But you have embraced the gift. Why?"

"I feel a responsibility to do so."

"You brought justice to Piedmont," Harland said.

She appreciated his support and encouragement. "Perhaps. But I am very glad it is over."

Pastor Huggins took a look through the Ledger. "These are wonderful, insightful quotations, Justine. It seems a shame that they've been hidden so long."

Goosie brought a tray of tea and all were served. The simple act seemed to calm the room like a balm.

Arnold suddenly decided to stand, and did so with Harland's help. "I want to make a proclamation."

"The floor is yours, Mr. Piedmont," Justine said.

"Hill," Arnold said. "The name is Arnold Hill. But you, my dear granddaughter, can call me anything you'd like."

"I have no other grandparents. I would be honored to call you Grandfather."

His eyes misted. "I'd like that very much . . . Justine."

She went to him and kissed his cheek, then returned to her chair. "You have the floor, Grandfather."

He cleared his throat. "Although not all is resolved, I am encouraged for the future. And so I think it would be appropriate for the town of Piedmont to start over, to start fresh." He bobbled slightly on his cane but remained standing. "As stated, I would like to be known as Arnold Hill from this point forward."

"I agree," Thomas said. "I am now Thomas Hill."

"And," Arnold raised a finger. "I'd like everyone to consider renaming the town, back to its intended name, Justice."

With that, it was agreed. Justice was born. In so many ways.

**

After everyone but Harland had left, Justine helped Goosie bring the teacups to the kitchen.

"Don't mind these. I'll get them washed," Goosie said. "Go back to Harland now."

But Justine didn't want to go just yet. She retrieved the sketchbook from her carpet bag and turned to its newest page. "This is for you."

Goosie wiped her hands on her apron and took it. She studied it a minute. "That looks like Pa."

"It is. And that baby lying beside him is you."

Goosie put a hand to her throat. "Me?"

"We three were hiding from Samuel Hill in a cave. Your father was writing the deposition I shared with the town. You were sleeping beside him."

Goosie's voice was tight. "You captured his features well." She touched the page tenderly then looked up. "You realize I haven't seen him since I was ten."

Justine's own throat tightened. To not see her father for 78 years . . . "You've been alone a long time."

"Alone but not alone. God's been with me. And your family has always been there for me."

"And you for them."

She nodded. "Me for them." She gave the sketch an odd look, then pointed. "I'm wrapped in my blanket, the one with the note in it."

"The note wasn't in there yet, but would be very soon, right after he was finished."

"When I was five or so, Pa told me he'd written a letter and hid it in my blanket."

"Did you ever open up the blanket and read it?"

Goosie shook her head. "He told me not to. And anyways, I can't read. Pa said it was safer for me that way. 'Keep the blanket safe' he said. 'Someday the truth will come out.'" She looked at Justine. "Like it did today."

"After eighty-eight years."

Goosie gazed at the sketch. "You captured a slice of my life here, Jussie. May I keep this?"

"Of course."

Goosie drew Justine into a long embrace, bound by the time—the times—they shared.

**

Finally, Justine was alone with Harland, which all in all was better than being fully alone.

They sat on the front porch. She shivered.

"Would you like me to get your shawl?"

Granny's shawl. "No, thank you. I like the crispness of the spring evening. For the first time she noticed she was still wearing the old and wrinkly clothes she'd worn into 1790. She lifted the skirt that lay across her legs and chuckled.

"What's funny?"

"In my old life I would have called what I'm wearing 'rags'. I did not leave the house—nay, my bedroom—without being fully dressed with five layers of couture-designed clothing."

"Five layers?"

Camisole and pantaloons, corset, bustle, petticoat, and dress. "I am *not* going to speak of underthings to a man, even to you, Harland."

One of her mother's oft-repeated snippets came to mind and she shared it, trying to mimic her tone. "'A woman's appearance speaks for her, even before she speaks.'"

"Should you add that to the Ledger?"

She shook her head. "The world will carry on without that particular nugget." She smoothed the fabric of the skirt. "But I find it incredible that I thought nothing of my attire the entire day."

"There *were* other things going on. It's been quite a day for you — for everyone."

"Is it finally over?"

"If by 'it' you refer to your mission for justice in Piedmont, I'd say yes. Or at least your part in it is over."

"Justice, yes. But more so I discovered my real father. My other father."

"Are you happy about that?"

"It's a complicated question but boils down to this: Thomas is a good man who loved my mother very much. And Noel Braden was a good father who loved *me* very much. I am very blessed."

"So Justine the daughter and Justine the purveyor of justice are satisfied, and questions are answered. But . . ."

"But what?"

"But what about another question that looms? The question of your place in Piedmont, as Justine Braden, the woman . . . the incredible, beautiful, amazing woman whom I love."

She did a double-take. "Love?"

He stood and drew her to standing. "I love you, Justine."

She let his words sink in. They settled easily and made her feel warm inside.

Her hesitation caused his expression to change from care to concern. "Did I misspeak? If so, I apologize for being presumptuous, but I — "

She put her hand on his cheek and looked into his brilliant blue eyes. "Your words are not presumptuous, but proper and very welcome, because they are reciprocated."

"They are?"

She nodded, the tightness in her chest preventing more.

"So Thomas was right? Did you stay because of me?"

Her honest answer of "partly" would dilute the moment. Instead she said, "I *will* stay because of you."

He gently lifted her chin and kissed her.

**

Justine wrote and wrote and wrote. She barely looked up. Only when the sun shown in the window did she realize she'd worked through the night.

Only one to go.

She copied the newest entry in the Ledger: Simeon Anders 1800: "Life is short. Love now."

She blotted the ink, then set down her pen. "It is finished." Or almost.

She stacked the pages and took the blue ribbon out of her hair. She tied it around the papers. Then she wrote a note to slip under the ribbon:

> *Pastor Huggins,*
> *You said it was a shame the Ledger had been hidden so long. I agree. Accept this copy of the Ledger for the people of Piedmont. Use these truths of the ages to enrich their lives. Add new wisdom for those who come after.*
> *With God's blessings,*
> *Justine Tyler Braden*

She sat back and let herself breathe. She pulled Granny's shawl closer, then caught a whiff of honeysuckle. "I knew you'd approve."

Then, even though it was too early for most of Piedmont to be awake, she walked across the street and carried the new Ledger to the front of the church where she laid it on the altar as an offering.

"It is Yours, Lord. I am Yours."

Then Justine Tyler Braden went home.

THE END

**

"Then you will know the truth,
and the truth will set you free."
John 8: 32

Dear Reader,

Piedmont, New Hampshire was inspired by a town in my family's history.

It all started in 2007 when my husband and I went to New England. Yes, we were "leaf peepers", going to see the fall foliage—which truly is astounding. I decided to take advantage of the trip to see a place that is key in my family's history: *Piermont,* New Hampshire.

Let me back up a bit . . .

Back in the 1970s, my mother researched our family history (on both the Swenson and Young sides). This was before the Internet, so it was a painstaking process. I remember being excited that we had an ancestor, Job Tyler, who had traveled from England to America in 1638, landing it what *would* become Newport, Rhode Island seven years later. In 1639 he became one of the first settlers in Andover, Massachusetts.

Apparently he was not a very easy man to get along with. William Irving Tyler Brigham wrote a genealogy of the Tyler Family (one of whose branches produced President Tyler!) Brigham said Job was described as "a rude, self-asserting, striking personality. Not to be left out of account in the forces which were to possess the land." Ordered to publicly post a confession as punishment for slandering a man, Job did so— but repeated all the slander in his confession!

What touched me was when Brigham said this about Job: "Yet, when you shall read hereafter what manner of men his sons and grandsons were and what they stood for in all the places where they lived; as you come down through the years, generation by generation, and see what thousands of his descendants have stood for in their homes and before the public, in peace and in war, as pioneers and as dwellers in the cities, you will realize that there must have been good stock in the old man; and he trained a family to be useful and honored in the communities where they dwelt. Superstitious, wilful (sic), hot-tempered, independent and self-reliant Job Tyler lives and breathes in this record nearly three centuries after his time. He did not have saints to live with; were all the truth known, it would be seen that he was on a par with a large proportion of his neighbors. The Puritan iron rule, which made no allowances for any man, met a sturdy opposition in this possible descendant of Wat Tyler of England, and it is now too late to determine whether he was always justified. From this old canvas there gazes steadily out, not an ideal but a very real personage, an out and out Yankee type."

I am here because of him—and perhaps because of his tenacious, exasperating nature.

Through his son, Moses, then Ebenezer, then David and his son, Jonathan, the Young side of my family arrived in Piermont, New Hampshire. They were some of the first settlers there in 1768. This made me think of creating a character (Isaac Piedmont) who had my family's gumption and took risks to brave a new frontier. It's not coincidental that I named his descendants "Tyler" after mine.

Piermont (and Piedmont in my book) started as a settlement on the banks of the Connecticut River at what would become the New Hampshire-Vermont border. These pioneers created a life for themselves out of nothing. They fought for their lives—some literally.

In 1777, Jonathan Tyler (a great-great grandson of Job) fought in the Battle of Ticonderoga in the Revolutionary War. It wasn't much of a battle. The Continental Army of 2500 was celebrating the one-year anniversary of the Declaration of Independence in the fort. They didn't realize that England's General Burgoyne (with about 10,000 troops and followers) had surrounded them. The next day, when they found out, the American general surrendered, and the troops withdrew from the fort.

At some point Jonathan Tyler was captured by Burgoyne's army. While prisoner, he and two others volunteered to build a block house on the east side of Lake George. But when they went down to a stream to sharpen their axes they realized they were alone. I can imagine their shock! They took "French leave" and ran into the wilderness. Without food or guns, they ate leaves, twigs, and roots, and traveled the *very* long way home, east across Vermont. At least it wasn't winter!

While in Piermont (which has three cemeteries!) my husband and I finally found Jonathan's grave next to his wife's. He died at age 96 — longevity still runs in my family. We also found the graves of other Tylers — many who were children. We walked through the old cemetery by the river, and shouted happily each time we found someone, as though they were right there with us.

Grave of Jonathan's wife, Sarah. The poem is lovely: "While you stand gazing on this, drop a pensive tear. A tender mother, wife and friend, lies rapt in silence here."

Me, at the grave of Jonathan Tyler and his wife, Sarah McConnell (who he married when she was 12 ½!)

I left Piermont with a deep sense of family, of roots. We live in Kansas now, where our history began in the very modern 1991. To discover the family

This is the grave of Aaron Tyler who died in 1777 at age three. So many children... I love the face at the top.

who started it all makes me feel as if I truly belong to something larger. As I said in this book's dedication, I am grateful to all the Tylers who were brave enough to birth my American story.

A couple other points of history I'd like to share:

- Granny's rocker in Chapter 3: I mention it had one arm worn down from Granny pushing down on it to get up . . . My Grandma Swenson had such a rocker. *My* grandma spurred a detail for another granny.

- In Chapter 18, the Mr. Macy who Mavis and Quinn meet in 1857 was R.H. Macy, who opened his first dry goods store in New York City in 1858. The first day's total sales were $11.06. His store evolved into the Macy's we still shop at today. If you want to read more about the history of Macy's, read my book, *The Pattern Artist.* One of my characters works there in 1911.

Stay tuned for two more books in the Past Times series: *Where Life Will Lead Me* (taking Justine to Kansas City where Harland's family lives), and *Where Hope will Find Me* (taking Justine to Ireland, to her family's roots.) I'd like to tell you more about the books, but I can't because I have no idea what they'll be about except family, history, and justice. As Justine discovers the story, so will I.

In closing, I want to encourage all of you to write down your own family's Life Lines, those things they always say or said, or jewels of family wisdom that should be chronicled. Start your own Ledger. It will be a legacy that can be passed down through the generations. What could be better than that?

Here's to families!

Nancy Moser

THE FASHION IN
WHERE TIME WILL TAKE ME

Justine going to the opera:

Chapter 1: "Mother retrieved a citron yellow dress which was heavy with ruffles made of accordion pleats. It had bows on its backside, and was embellished with lace and fringe wherever there could be lace and fringe. It was the antithesis of comfort."

Godey's Ladies Book: August 1878
Justine's dress is the second dress from the left.

Chapter 5: Mrs. Beemish reached over and touched the pleats that formed a ruffle on the three-quarter sleeves, then fingered the lace ruffle beneath it. "So fine."

"The lace matches the lace at your neckline," Mabel said. What could she say? "Yes, it does."

"I appreciate the covered buttons," Rachel said. "That's a lot of work."

www.antique-royals.tumblr.com/post/111707676018/1870s

Chapter 11: She opened a trunk and picked out a sage-green skirt that Goosie deemed Mavis's favorite, and a matching buttoned bodice with long sleeves cuffed at the wrist.

https://www.aliexpress.com/store/product/CUSTOM-MADE-1860s-Civil-War-Era-Arm-Green-Victorian-Day-dress

Chapter 12: The dress had a low scooped neckline. "I need a scarf of some kind. I feel too exposed."

"A fichu," Goosie said. She pulled a sheer scarf with a collar attached out of the trunk and wrapped it around the neckline. "You can wear it out, tied in a knot, or overlap it and tuck it into the bodice."

Justine tried it both ways and preferred the tuck. "I 'll use the same shawl, capelet, and bonnet I've used before."

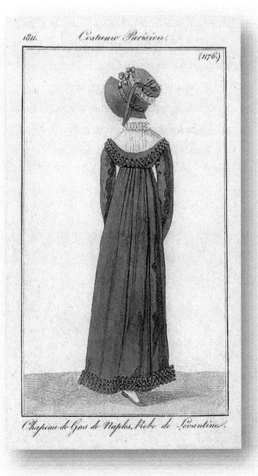

Life Lines

"Stand up for what is right, no matter the cost."

"Don't let the past dictate the present."

"We must forgive others as we ask for forgiveness."

"Take time."

"You don't reach your destination by standing at the river.
You have to wade through it, one step at a time."

"Truth is proof."

"There is no uncertainty in God, only confidence."

"God's ways are not our ways."

"Stranger helping stranger makes us strangers no more."

"Abide by the wisdom of the past."

"Family ties bind beyond death."

"Marry only for love."

"Bitterness kills."

"God provides."

"Avoid foolishness."

"Embrace the work."

"Trust and obey."

"Love Jesus."

"Look beyond what you see."

"Life is short. Love now."

"God's gifts can't be returned."

My Challenge to You:
Write down Life Lines
from those you meet and love.

DISCUSSION QUESTIONS
Where Time Will Take Me

1. In Chapter 1, Justine's friends say they aren't interested in anything that came before. Justine says, "If we ignore history we remain ignorant of its lessons." Is she right?

2. In Chapter 2, the Braden family lawyer says, "I am a man of facts and paperwork. If only family members would be concise and plain in letters they leave to those left behind. One more sentence here and there would shed much-needed light on the questions such a letter raises." Have you ever experienced a mystery left behind by a loved one?

3. In Chapter 4 Harland describes Piedmont: "It is home — a distinction that increases each attribute and overshadows all insufficiencies." What are the attributes of your "home" place?

4. In Chapter 7, Justine and Harland talk about the kind of people they are… He believes that God put him where he is for a reason — it's not a coincidence. Do you agree with his view? Why or why not?

5. In Chapter 13 while looking at clouds, Justine notices how they change constantly. She applies it to her life. How has Justine changed since her life in New York? What circumstances caused her to change?

6. In her discussion about change Justine mentions, "Mother's death started it all. I hate to say that something so awful could amount to good, but there's no denying it." How did a tragic event in your life lead to something good?

7. In Chapter 13, Harland tells Justine: "The woman you were has led you to become the woman you are." Think back a few years. How has the person you were led you to become the person you are?

8. Chapter 13: Abigail Addington tells the story of how they ended up in Piedmont. She mentions praying for direction and having a dream leading her to New Hampshire. Once she got to Piedmont, she had a feeling — "a knowing" that this was the place to settle. God didn't tell her the full answer to her question, but gave her stepping stones. When has God led you to a goal bit by bit?

9. Justine sees how God has made good come out of the bad regarding her mother's death. What good came from bad in your life?

10. In Chapter 13 Harland says he totally believes the Bible. "I don't think the Bible should be read with the attitude of pick and choose." What do you think about this?

11. In Chapter 16, Justine remembers something her mother used to say in regard to looking nice: "'A woman's appearance speaks for her, even before she speaks.'" Harland asks if she's going to write that in the Ledger and she says no. And yet . . . do you think her mother was speaking a truth that *should* have been included in the Ledger? Why or why not?

12. Three times Granny repeats Luke 11: 48: "For unto whomsoever much is given, of him shall be much required: and to whom men have committed much, of him they will ask the more." How has this verse played out in your life, or the lives of those you love?

WHERE LIFE WILL LEAD ME

Book 2 of the Past Times Series

Coming in 2020

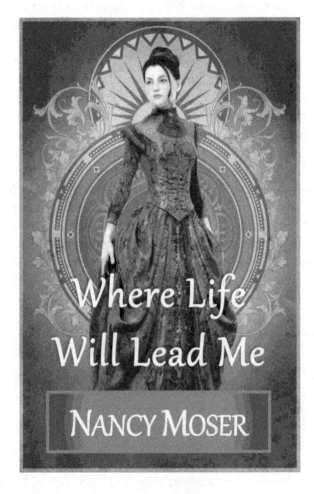

Justine Braden's work in Piedmont, New Hampshire is complete. And so she heads west to Missouri.

Will her gift of being able to travel through time work beyond Piedmont?

If it won't . . . will she be disappointed?

If it does . . . what adventure of justice awaits her?

ABOUT THE AUTHOR

NANCY MOSER is the best-selling author of thirty-four novels, novellas, and children's books, including Christy Award winner *Time Lottery* and Christy finalist *Washington's Lady*. She's written sixteen historical novels including *Love of the Summerfields, Masquerade, The Journey of Josephine Cain* and *Just Jane*. *An Unlikely Suitor* was named to Booklist's "Top 100 Romance Novels of the Decade." *The Pattern Artist* was a finalist in the Romantic Times Reviewers Choice award. Some of her contemporary novels are: *The Invitation, Solemnly Swear, The Good Nearby, John 3:16, Crossroads, The Seat Beside Me*, and the Sister Circle series. Nancy has been married for over forty years—to the same man. She and her husband have three grown children, seven grandchildren, and live in the Midwest. She's been blessed with a varied life. She's earned a degree in architecture, run a business with her husband, traveled extensively in Europe, and has performed in various theaters, symphonies, and choirs. She knits voraciously, kills all her houseplants, and can wire an electrical fixture without getting shocked. She is a fan of anything antique—humans included.

Website: www.nancymoser.com
Blogs: Author blog: www.authornancymoser.blogspot.com, History blog: www.footnotesfromhistory.blogspot.com/
Pinterest: www.pinterest.com/nancymoser1
Facebook and Twitter:
www.facebook.com/nancymoser.author, and www.twitter.com/MoserNancy
Goodreads:
www.goodreads.com/author/show/117288.Nancy_Moser